Alexander Balloch Grosart, Sir John Beaumont

The Poems of Sir John Beaumont

Alexander Balloch Grosart, Sir John Beaumont

The Poems of Sir John Beaumont

ISBN/EAN: 9783337407827

Printed in Europe, USA, Canada, Australia, Japan

Cover: Foto ©Andreas Hilbeck / pixelio.de

More available books at **www.hansebooks.com**

The Fuller Worthies' Library.

THE

POEMS

OF

SIR JOHN BEAUMONT, BART.

FOR THE FIRST TIME COLLECTED AND EDITED:

WITH

Memorial-Introduction and Notes

BY THE

REV. ALEXANDER B. GROSART,

ST. GEORGE'S, BLACKBURN, LANCASHIRE.

PRINTED FOR PRIVATE CIRCULATION.

1369.

156 copies only.

To
Joseph Lemuel Chester, Esq.

MY DEAR SIR,

Allow me the pleasure of associating your name with this Worthy and my labours on his too little known Poetry. I like you for your English Puritan name and for your English face—that of 'a brave gentleman' all of the olden time; I like you for your right and good service in writing for the first time adequately, the Life—a supremely noble and beautiful one—of 'John Rogers' Proto-martyr of England, under Mary; I like you as an American proud of your ancient lineage and unmixed English descent; and I like you for your catholic literary sympathies and brother-hood. Moreover, with 'Sunny Memories' of my pilgrim-visits to shrines of the New World—human and of Nature—from the graves of my fellow-Scots, Alexander Wilson the Ornithologist and Poet and leonine Dr. John Witherspoon, and the Homes and Haunts of David Brainerd and Jonathan Edwards, and Franklin and Washington, and of the illustrious Living, to the palace of Thunder of Niagara and scenes in fair Virginia all transfigured with the glory of RALEIGH and other of the Elizabethan heroes—I must ever have a warm hand-clasp and heart-clasp for your mighty Country's masterful and most lavishly-kind countrymen. By-and-bye these Worthies will find their widest realm over the Atlantic.   You will agree with me that it is well to get away o'times from the inevitable strivings and vulgarisms of the Present into the calm of — thank God—the changeless Past.

Yours very cordially,

ALEXANDER B. GROSART.

Prefatory Note.

THE present Volume for the first time brings together the hitherto somewhat scattered and carelessly-kept Poems of SIR JOHN BEAUMONT. BART. It contains the whole of the volume of 1629, edited by his son; and also a number of additions gathered from various sources, as told in the relative foot-notes. I have also reprinted the 'Metamorphosis of Tabacco', from the solitary surviving copy preserved in the British Museum Library. These additions are marked with an asterisk [*] in the Contents.

I indulge a hope that from some unexpected quarter—perchance an old Library of Leicestershire—the certainly printed, if not published 'Crowne of Thornes', will turn up. For more on it see our Memorial-Introduction: where will also be found curious details of a cancelled leaf in the volume of 1629. As an Appendix I give two poems by our Worthy's son and heir, Sir John Beaumont, Bart.

The same principle has been acted on throughout this addition to our Library, as in the others : the text is reproduced in integrity, all original notes are faithfully given, under the initial B., with biographic and elucidatory additions, under my own initial, G., and noticeable words marked, and the like. The edition of 1629 was not very well overseen in printing, and still worse in its pointing. The more important misprints are noted in their places, others self-evident are corrected silently. The original arrangement is slightly departed from, by placing the poems on more or less sacred subjects as one class, and all the translations as another. I owe thanks to the present Sir George H. Beaumont, Bart., of Cole-orton Hall, Leicestershire, James Delano, Esq., London, W. Aldis Wright, Esq, M.A., Trinity College, Cambridge, J. Payne Collier, Esq., Maidenhead, J. L. Chester, Esq., of U.S.A., and S. Christie-Miller, Esq., of Britwell, for aid very pleasantly rendered. By the kindness of the Proprietors (Messrs. Routledge) I am enabled to furnish (in large paper) Finden's exquisite steel-engraving of the Beaumont-home, Grace-dieu.

A. B. G.

Contents.

---

* Lady, dropped out in heading, inadvertently. G.

---

* No 15—17 are not 'Elegiac', but naturally take their place
among 'Memorials'. G.

Memorial-Introduction.

YOU have opposite our title-page,[1] a daintily-rendered view of the ruins—Bancroft's " grand relic ",[2] and Nichols's " noble fragment "[3]—of Grace-Dieu : and what the rage of man and the teeth of Time have done on the originally grand and indeed magnificent religious House, has been done, even more sorrowfully and irrevocably in the family papers. So that with ' gentle' as with ' simple ' it is found hard to recover memorials of our Worthy—as DARLEY[4] and DYCE[5] and others had to lament in trying to keep in remembrance the greater name and fame of his younger brother, FRANCIS BEAUMONT,

---

1 In large paper copies only.
2 See lines onward a little.
3 Nichols's Leicestershire, iii., 651.
4 Memoir prefixed to his Beaumont and Fletcher.
5 Memoir prefixed to his Beaumont and Fletcher :

Vol. i.

the Dramatist—to whose memory our Sir John
dedicated some of his most pathetic verses.

Grace-dieu is beautifully situated—lying low
in a valley, upon a little brook,—in what was
formerly one of the most recluse spots in the centre of Charnwood Forest—within a little distance
of the turn-pike road that leads from Ashby-de-la-
zouch to Loughborough. It stands within the
parish of Belton, but ecclesiastically in the deanery
of Akeley.

Its name, Grace Dieu,—in Latin *de Gratiâ Dei*
—recals the pre-Reformation times, and its present re-possession by a Roman Catholic Family
(Phillips), curiously confirms the old creed of
indelibility or indefeasibility. The Foundress of
the 'Nunnery' and the giver of the name, was
one Roesia de-Verdun, daughter and co-heir of
Nicholas, Lord Verdon—reaching away back to
1236 and 1247. Wide-brained and saintly Bishop
Grosseteste and the earlier Henries, come up in
connection with the Foundation. I must refer all
antiquarianly-disposed to Nichols' *Leicestershire*,
where will be found abundant details, from Agnes
de Gresley first prioress and Mary de Stretton, to
John Comin, Earl of Buchan.[1]

---

1 As before, Vol. iii., 655—661* *et alibi*. Where other
reference is not given, Nichols is my authority.

THOMAS BANCROFT, the Epigrammatist, thus sketches Grace-dieu as associated with the Beaumonts :[1]

" Grace-dieu, that under Charnwood stand'st alone,
As a grand Relicke of Religion,
I reverence thine old, but fruitfull, worth,
That lately brought such noble Beaumonts forth :
Whose brave Heroick Muses might aspire
To match the Anthems of the Heavenly Quire :
The mountaines crown'd with rockey fortresses,
And sheltering woods, secure thy happinesse,
That highly favour'd art—though lowly plac'd—
Of Heaven, and with free Nature's bounty grac'd :
Herein grow happier ; and that blisse of thine
Nor Pride ore-top, nor Envy undermine !"

John Beaumont, Esq., of not distant Thringston, was the first Beaumont-owner of the venerable Priory. He obtained a grant of the site. He had been appointed by the king's writ—January 30th, 1534-35—to " take the ecclesiastial survey of the county of Leicestershire :"[2] and in association with Drs. Leigh and Layton, he 'reports '— as told in the ' Compendium Compertorum'—charges of ' incontinentia ' (alas !) and ' superstitio '

---

1 Two Bookes of Epigrammes and Epitaphs, &c. (1639) B i. Ep. 81.

2 Nichols, as before.

against Elizabeth Hall and Catharina Ekesildena, 'nuns'—the latter because of veneration paid to the girdle and part of the tunic of St. Francis. The great strong wall, with which the Priory was 'compassed' and the garden in resemblance of Gethsemane, failed—I fear—to keep out the three enemies, " the world, the devil, the flesh ". Be this as it may, Grace-dieu was included in the Suppression of 1536. Agnes Litherland was the last Prioress. There were delays in consummating the Suppression: but it was finally surrendered on October 27th, 1539. In that year it was granted to Sir Humphrey Foster, Knight, who thereupon conveyed it to John Beaumont, gent— oddly mispelled Bewman. Mr. Beaumont seems to have been interrupted in the possession of his newly-acquired property by a claim on the part of the Earl of Huntingdon. A vigorous remonstrative Letter to Lord Cromwell remains, reminding of the transition period. He is very earnest, indeed vehement: "for I do feyre " he says, "the scyd erle and his sonns do seke my lyfe, and all for the truthe sake."[1]　In 1541 this John Beaumont was cited to shew by what title he held the

---

[1] Wright's Letters relating to the Suppression of Monasteries, p. 251.

Priory of Grace-dieu. Disputes went on for a number of years, and only closed apparently, by intermarriages of the Families concerned. In 1550, JOHN BEAUMONT, Esquire, was elected Recorder of Leicester, and in the same year (Dec. 3) Master of the Rolls. In 1551 a fine, with proclamation, was levied on the lordship, by the Master of the Rolls, to the use of King Edward VI. and his successors: and perplexingly, the Earl of Huntingdon in 1552 " did get a fee-farm of the manor-house of Grace-dieu and the whole manor and grange, called Myral Grange." On the accession of Mary " the Bloody "—pity so sacred and softly-sweet a name should have epithet so dark !—the ' Recorder ' and ' Master ' lost his offices—to him a favorably significant fact.[1] John Beaumont was married twice. First to Isabel, daughter of Lawrence Dutton, Esq., of Dutton, co. Chester, by whom he had two daughters, Dorothy and Anne. Secondly, to Elizabeth, eldest daughter and coheir of Sir William Hastings, younger brother to George, Earl of Huntingdon, by whom he had issue, viz,, Elizabeth, who was married to William, Lord Vaux of Harrowden—Jane—Fran-

---

1 Nichols's *Leicestershire*, as before, Vol. III., Pt. II., pp 651—*664.

cis, his successor, and Henry, who died unmarried. and was buried at Temple Church, London. Within five years of the death of her husband, Elizabeth Beaumont claimed and obtained posession of Grace-dieu : and in 1574 Henry, Earl of Huntingdon, reciting the conveyance of Sir Humphrey Foster to John Beaumont and Elizabeth Beaumont and their heirs, confirmed and ratified it all—and so ended protracted disputes and counter-rights.

The family by direct lineage and marriage was ancient and honourable and ' generosus.' Darley has pointed out that the name, in common with Fletcher, is French [*Beau-Mont* and *Flechier*]—indicating a foreign extraction.[1] The extraction is historical, not mythic-heraldic, being directly traceable to the earl of Meulan or Mellent, of BEAUMONT in Normandy, who as a reward for valour displayed at the battle of Hastings, was given many ' lordships ' by the Conqueror, and subsequently created earl of Leicester by Henry the Ist — no fewer than sixteen of his ' lordships ' lying within the county. Robert de Beaumont, earl of Leicester, fills a large space in the county, if indeed it might not be said, the

---

1 As before.

national history of his age : and so onward in
Robert Bossu, i.e. the Hunchback, *the* friend of
Thomas à Becket, and Robert Blanchmains i. e.
Robert with the White Hands, son and grandson
respectively, and all through gentle and noble
marriages—not without tragic and pathetic alter-
nations, as in Hugh, surnamed *Pauper*, the
youngest son of Robert de Beaumont, earl of
Leicester, who fell from the rank of Earl of Bedford to that of knight, and finally became (literally)
a beggar.   On the other hand there were exalt-
ations, as besides above Robert, Waloran became
earl of Mellent, and of the (five) daughters, one
married Strongbow, earl of Pembroke, and two
to members of the house of Simon de Montfort.
Beaumont is thus unquestionably an ancient and
illustrious Norman name—its other form, Bello-
mont, being only a corruption or abbreviation of
the Latin (De Bellomonte) employed by the monk-
ish-historians, and used by Philip King in his
Latin-verses in memory of our Worthy.   Wace
and William of Poitiers, Benoit de Saint More
and Hollinshed, and Thierry in his 'History of
the Conquest of England by the Normans,' have
burnished the names of many Beaumonts.   Of
the first connected with England, viz., above,
Robert de Beaumont, Henry of Huntingdon says,

"he was in worldly affairs the wisest of all men
betwixt England and Jerusalem; eminent for
knowledge, plausible of speech, keen and crafty,
a subtle genius, of great foresight and prudence,
not easily over-reached, profound in council, and
of great wisdom." It is much to be wished that
living Beaumonts would do for their family-history
what has been done so admirably for the Lindsays
by Lord Lindsay and for the Manchesters by the
Duke of Manchester. Born and resident in Leicestershire and within the territories of the original
Beaumonts, there can be no doubt that our Poet's
family belonged to them in one or other of their
manifold branches.[1]

Francis, the first-born son of John Beaumont,
succeeded his father. He was brought up
to the Law.[2] He was appointed one of the Justices
of the Common Pleas, 25th January, 1592-93, and
subsequently he received the dignity of knighthood.[3] Burton terms him "that grave, learned,
and reverend judge".[4] He married Anne,

---

1 See for these details and references, Thompson's
"History of Leicester" [1849] pp 27—61 et alibi.

2 Nichols, as before : and Dyce's Memoir of Beaumont,
as before.

3 As in 2.

4 Quoted in Nichols, as before.

daughter to Sir George Pierrepoint, of Holme-Pierrepoint, co. Notts., knight, and relict of Thomas Thorold, of Marston, co. Lincoln, esq.,— the name of PIERREPOINT recalling that from the same stock sprang in England, Lady Mary Wortley Montagu, and over the Atlantic, the mother of America's greatest Thinker, JONATHAN EDWARDS. His family by her, consisted of Elizabeth, who ultimately married Thomas Seyliard, of Kent:[1] and by the way, Francis Beaumont, it will be remembered also went to Kent for his wife,— fetching his Ursula from Sundridge,—and three sons, Henry, John, and Francis. John is our Worthy. His father died at Grace-dieu, April 22nd, 1598. His Will—wherein he specially remembered troops of lowly friends, his servants, —was made only the day before, and the inquisition, taken June 8th following, recounts that he was "seised of the house and site of Grace-dieu aforesaid, of divers lands in the parish of Belton, Grace-dieu, Meriel, Shepeshed, Osgathorpe, Thringston, and Swannington."[2]

---

1 MS. Visitation of Kent, 1619, College of Arms, as cited by Dyce, as before, p xxi. He corrects Nichols' blunder of "Hilyard" for "Seyliard."

2 The Will is given *in extenso* in Dyce, as before, Vol. I. pp lxxxix-xc.

Henry Fletcher, the eldest son of Judge Fletcher enjoyed his inheritance only a brief period. He died in 1605 aged 24—having been knighted in 1603.[1] John, our Poet, in turn, succeeded him. He was born—no doubt at the family-seat of Grace-dieu—in 1582 or 1583. There are no entries of the baptisms of the Beaumonts—neither of our Worthy nor of Francis—the explanation being that the rite would most naturally be celebrated in the Metropolis, where the Judge must have had a residence. But the birth-year is approximately found from the Funeral-Certificates in the College of Arms, whereby we learn that John Beaumont, "second sonne" was "at the tyme of the death of his father [22nd April, 1598] of the age of foureteen yeares or *thereaboutes*." This takes us back by the Old Style to 1582-3. Of his School and home-training nothing has come down. Probably along with his elder brother Henry, and his younger Francis, and only sister Elizabeth, his education was private. Whether or no, the three brothers in 1596 proceeded to Oxford and entered as "gentlemen

---

1 "Sir Henry Beaumont, knight, buried 13th day of Julio, anno domini, 1605. Belton Church Register, in Dyce, as before, p. **xxi**.

·commoners" in Broadgate's Hall "in the beginning of Lent-term": (4th February, 1596-7.)
ANTHONY A-WOOD designates John as then "aged
14", which agrees with the other authority above.[1]
Broadgates-Hall—on the site of which Pembroke
College now stands—was the principal nursery in
Oxford for students of the civil and common Law.
None of the brothers appears to have resided long
in Oxford: and all quitted the University without
taking any degree. Francis, the Dramatist, was
entered a member of the Inner Temple, 3rd November, 1600: and our Poet is also usually stated to
have entered "one of the Inns of Court."[2] I have
failed to trace him there. If ever he took up
residence, he soon quitted it: in all liklihood on
succeeding to the family-estates on the death of
Sir Henry, his elder brother, in 1605.

During his College residence, and in London,
he must have begun his poetic studies. "In his
youth" says Wood and the Biographia Britannica
and other authorities " he applied himself to 'the
Muses, with good success".[3] When in his 20th
year (1602) he published anonymously, his 'Meta-

---

1 Athen. Oxon. (by Bliss) II. 437: (See also pp.
434-435.)

2 Dyce, as before, p. xxii.

3 Biog. Brit. (1747), Vol. I., *s. n.*, p. 621.

morphosis of Tabacco'—a mock heroic-poem : and
prefixed to it, among others, were dedicatory lines
to MICHAEL DRAYTON, and the first published
Verses of his brother Francis, the illustrious
associate of FLETCHER. Both are very noticeable
and therefore must be adduced here :

I. FRANCIS BEAUMONT, TO HIS BROTHER.

" My new-borne Muse assaies her tender wing,
And where she should crie is enforst to sing :
Her children prophesie thy pleasing rime
Shall neuer be a dish for hungrie Time :
Yet be regardlesse what those verses say,
Whose infant mother was but borne to day."

II. DEDICATION TO " METAMORPHOSIS."

Ad mare riuuli
TO MY LOVING
FRIEND, MASTER
MICHAEL DRAYTON.

The tender labour of my wearie pen,
And doubtfull triall of my first-borne rimes,
Loaths to adorne the triumphs of those men,
Which hold the raines of fortunes, and the times :
Only to thee, which art with ioy possest
Of the faire hill, where troupes of Poets stand,

---

1 See our Volume, p. 272.

Where thou enthron'd with laurell garlands blest,
Maist lift me vp with thy propitious hand ;
    I send this poëme, which for nought doth care,
    But words for words, and loue for loue to share.[1]

From these and after-Verses commendatory, to the (posthumous) volume of 1629, our Poet must early have passed within the 'charmed circle' of the Mermaid, and won the friendship—transmitted to his son,[2] of BEN JONSON and other of the immortals. To vivify our realisation of the glorious company, I will here set down Francis Beaumont's description of their Wit-combats:

    " What things have we seen
Done at the Mermaid ! heard words that have been
So nimble, and so full of subtle flame,
As if that every one from whom they came
Had meant to put his whole wit in a jest,
And had resolv'd to live a fool the rest
Of his dull life ; then when there hath been thrown
Wit able enough to justify the town
For three days past ; wit that might warrant be
For the whole city to talk foolishly,

---

1 *Ibid*, p. 226.

2 See Appendix to our Volume for our Poet's son's strong-thoughted Verses to the memory of Jonson, pp. 325—328. The wonder is that Shakespeare should be unnamed. G.

Till that were cancell'd ; and when that was gone
We left an air behind us, which alone
Was able to make the two next companies
(Right witty, though but downright fools) mere wise."[1]

Let the Reader turn now to JONSON'S somewhat laboured but thought-packed 'Lines', and
ponder the tribute, from the splendid honour of
its first words "This book shall live" to the
close.[2]   It is the more interesting—if that be not
too poor a word—to take note of this friendship,
because if I am not much mistaken, Jonson was
indebted to our Poet for probably the most memor-
able couplet in his ever-memorable Verses on the
Portrait of Shakespeare, prefixed to the folio of
1623.   We may read them and dwell on the
italicized lines :

"To the Reader.
This Figure, that thou here seest put,
It was for gentle Shakespeare cut ;
Wherein the Grauer had a strife

---

1 Works of Beaumont and Fletcher by Dyce, as
before, Vol. XI. pp. 501-502 : Darley, as before, in line
seventh reads 'known' for 'thrown' and in last line
'mere' wise. Probably the latter is the true reading and
meaning as adopted by Seward and in text.
2 See our Volume, pp. 15-16.

With Nature, to out-doo the life :
 O, could he but haue drawne his wit
  As well in brasse, as he hath hit
 His face ; the Print would then surpasse
  All, that was euer writ in brasse.
 But, since he cannot, Reader, looke
  Not on his Picture, but his Booke."

Surely the italicized lines from Sir John Beaumont's Elegy "to the immortall memory of the fairest and most vertuous Lady Clifton" in 1613, —or ten good years before the Shakespeare inscription—must have been read or heard, and lingered in Ben's capacious memory, consciously or unconsciously ?

 " Ah why neglected I to write her prayse,
And paint her vertues in those happy dayes !
Then my now trembling hand and dazled eye,
Had seldome fail'd, hauing the patterne by :
Or had it err'd, or made some strokes amisse,
— For who can portray Vertue as it is ?—
Art might with Nature haue maintain'd her strife,
By curious lines to imitate true life."[1]

I am not aware that this *bit* of Shakesperiana has before been noticed. My ear can't get quit of an echo in the mightier lines from the earlier.

---

[1] See the entire poem in our Volume, pp 193—197.

I have stated that our Poet published the 'Metamorphosis of Tabacco' in 1602. There can be but little doubt of the authorship. The late George Chalmers possessed a copy of the poem, on the title-page of which was written in a contemporary hand "By John Beaumont."[1] In accord with this, is the dedication of it to Drayton, and the initials of the various commendatory verses prefixed. Those by F. B. unquestionably belong to his brother the Dramatist.[2] Besides, the 'Metamorphosis' is the main poem that answers to Sir Thomas Hawkins' happy characterisation of his various-sided genius, as 'sportive' as well as 'serious' *e.g.*

" Nor lesse delight—things serious set apart—
Thy sportive poems yeeld, with heedfull art
Composèd so, to minister content,
That though we there thinke onely wit is meant,
We quickly by a happy error, find
In cloudy words, cleare lampes to light the mind."[3]

In the same year—1602—with the publication of the 'Metamorphosis of Tabacco', appeared—also

1 Dyce, as before, p. xxiii.
2 See our Volume p 272.
3 See the whole poem in our Volume, pp 6—9.

anonymously — the somewhat famous volume called "Salmacis and Hermaphroditus". I think few will disagree with Mr. Dyce in opposition to Mr. Collier, in pronouncing this the genuine production of Francis Beaumont. Among the commendatory verses prefixed to " Salmacis and Hermaphroditus " is a copy signed I. B. which seems plainly to belong to the elder brother, our Poet.[1]

Briefly resident in one of the Inns of Court—if indeed it was so—he retired to his family-seat of Grace-Dieu.[2] When he did so, and for years subsequent, he lacked one element of the Poet's inspiration—a 'lady-love'. This comes out in his lines " Against abused Loue." Thus :

> " How can I write of Loue, who neuer felt
> His dreadful arrow ; nor did euer melt
> My heart away before a female flame,
> Like waxen statues, which the witches frame."[3]

---

1 Dyce, as before, pp xxiii-iv., and see Mr. Collier's Life of Shakespeare and Bibl. Account, s. n.

2 In the Will of Sir Henry Beaumont, which was proved 3rd February, 1605-6, the 'surplusage' of his property not otherwise assigned, was " to be devided into twoe partes," whereof " one parte " went to his ' sister ' and the other was " to be equallie devided " between the two brothers " John and Francis." Dyce, as before, p xxvii.

3 See our Volume pp 101-102.

But he escaped not the inevitable and delicious woe of woman. For he married a 'faire ladye' of the family of Fortescue—her brother GEORGE FORTESCUE, Esq., adding a grateful and graceful commendatory to the others in the volume of 1629.[1] By her he had four sons—John, Francis, Gervase, and Thomas. The first,—who succeeded his father,—was a man of extraordinary strength, a kind of English Grettir the Strong: it being reported by old men who knew him that " he did leap sixteen feet at one leap, and would commonly, at a stand-leap, jump over a high long table in the hall, light on a settle beyond the table, and raise himself straight up."[2] He was not without a vein of the true poetic faculty, if deficient in the music of utterance. To him we are indebted for the precious volume of 1629, and among other things, for a well-put tribute to his " deare father." He fell at the siege of Gloucester, in the service of the king, in 1644.[3] Francis—sometimes confounded with his uncle, as he in turn, by Anthony a-WOOD and others, has been confounded with another Francis Beaumont—of the family of the

---

1 See our Volume pp 10-12.

2 Nichols, as before : iii, Pt. 2nd, p 659.

3 *Ibid* and Dyce, as before.

Beaumonts of Cole-orton and who died Master of the Charter-House in 1624—became a Jesuit.[1] It is much to be wished that more were known of him. His Verses in honour of his father are delicately affectionate. A portrait is assigned to him in Nichols' Leicestershire.[2] The authenticity of this assignation requires confirmation. The whole look of it disposes me to think the portrait rather represents our Sir John Beaumont. Gervase died in his seventh year: and infinitely pathetic, soft and also strong as tears, is his father's poem to his memory. The Archbishop of Dublin, (Trench) has selected it as one of the jewels of that Casket of Jewels, his "Household Book of English Poetry" (1868). It is a curious coinci-

---

1 Wood's Athenæ Oxon. by Bliss II. 434-5.

2 As before. p *662. The present Sir George H. Beaumont, Bart., of Coleorton Hall, informs me that he has "a picture of a boy, holding a bow, with a ruff round his neck—apparently of the time of Elizabeth," and that this picture is called in his Catalogue "Viscount Beaumont, killed at the battle of Towton." On this Sir George remarks "I think this must be a mistake, as the arms are in the corner with an Esquire's helmet." He seems disposed to consider it a portrait of our Sir John Beaumont: but as a 'boy,' the after-Viscount might only be represented as an Esquire.

dence, and one that would bind the two friends all
the closer, that Ben Jonson's first-born also died
at seven years (in 1603) :

"Seven years thou were lent to me."[1]

Thomas ultimately came into possession of the
title and family-property.

It is usually stated—even by Dyce—that our
Worthy's poetry was produced in his earlier
years. The dates of various of his Elegies and
other Verses, disprove this. He seems to have
gone on singing to the close. It was self-evident-
ly his ambition and resolute purpose to win a
name as a Poet. There is the ring of Milton's
lofty ideal in incidental revelations of his yearning
after a true Poet's renown, as in this great line,

"No earthly gift lasts after death, but Fame."[2]

It is here I find the solution of the imagined-
obscure if not enigmatical and mysterious allusion,
of Michael Drayton. That then aged Poet in the
Verses referred to, utters a kind of quiet 'Vanitas
Vanitatum' over his own 'with'ring bayes'

---

1 Works by GIFFORD viii. 175
2 See our Volume p 94,

specifically, and on the thirst after celebrity generally. Hence his plaintive memorial-words of our Poet, must be interpreted as bearing the same burden. The Reader will do well to study the Verses as a whole.[1] This couplet may suffice here :

> "Thy care for that which was not worth thy breath,
> Brought on too soon thy much lamented death."

Over-studiousness and ' o'er-informing of the clay' through an over-hunger after Fame, gives *the* meaning of this cynic-touched lament. Bishop Corbet indeed, had put the thing more directly, of our Poet's brother Francis, on his premature death—being within 30—in the celebrated line

> " Wit's a disease consumes men in few years."[2]

DRAYTON is an authority : for he was a bosom-friend of both the Beaumonts, as witness in one of his well-known Epistles, viz., to REYNOLDS, ' Of Poets and Poetry ' of them and the author of ' Britannia's Pastorals ' :[3]

---

1 *Ibid* pp 17-18.

2 Poems (1672) p 68.

3 The Works of William Browne have at last been worthily reproduced by Mr. W. C. Hazlitt in his Rox-burghe Library : (2 vols.) As Browne's biography is

"Then the two Beaumonts, and my Browne arose,
My dear companions, whom I freely chose
My bosom-friends ; and in their several ways
Rightly born poets, and in these last days
Men of much note, and no less nobler parts ;
Such as have freely told to me their hearts
As I have mine to them."

Very touching, and in the same groove of thought, is our Poet's own ' Epitaph on his deare brother Francis Beaumont,' as here :

"Thou shouldst haue followed me, but Death to blame,
Miscounted yeeres, and measur'd age by fame.
So dearely hast thou bought thy precious lines,
Their praise grew swiftly : so thy life declines." [1]

Our Singer indubitably put forth his whole strength in his " Crowne of Thornes," a " poem in eight books ". If only we were fortunate enough to recover it, the Poem would prove, I feel assured, a profound-thoughted and tender-feelinged and musically-worded addition to our scant sacred Poetry. It is tantalizing to read his

---

meagre, I record here that in Samuel Austin's " Vrania" (1629) is a striking appeal to him, as to Drayton, to turn his mind to sacred poetry. Mr. Hazlitt has overlooked this.

1 See our Volume p 182.

own allusions to it : and scarcely less so those of
Sir Thomas Hawkins. I give them here. First
the Poet's own, in his admirable Elegy on Shakespeare's Earl of Southampton :

> "I keep that glory last, which is the best:
> The loue of learning, which he oft exprest
> By conuersation, and respect to those
> Who had a name in artes, in verse or prose:
> Shall euer I forget with what delight
> He on my simple lines would cast his sight ?
> *His onely mem'ry my poore worke adornes*
> *He is a father to my crowne of thornes :*
> *Now since his death how can I euer looke,*
> *Without some teares vpon that orphan booke ?*
> Ye sacred Muses, if ye will admit
> My name into the roll, which ye haue writ
> Of all your seruants, to my thoughts display
> Some rich receipt, some vnfrequented way,
> Which may hereafter to the world commend
> A picture fit for this my noble friend :
> For this is nothing, all these rimes I scorne ;
> Let pens be broken, and the paper torne :
> And with his last breath let my musick cease,
> *Vnlesse my lowly poem could increase*
> *In true description of immortall things,*
> *And rays'd aboue the earth with nimble wings,*
> *Fly like an eagle from his fun'rall fire,*
> *Admir'd by all, as all did him admire.*"

Mark the close. It seems to intimate that the

book was just printed and ready for issue, dedication and all :[1]

Next, SIR THOMAS HAWKINS:

"Like to the bee, thou didd'st those flow'rs select,
That most the tastefull palate might affect,
With pious relishes of things diuine,
And discomposèd sence with peace combine,
Which—in thy Crowne of Thornes—we may discerne,
Fram'd as a modell for the best to learne
That verse may Vertue teach as well as prose,
And minds with natiue force to good dispose,
Deuotion stirre, and quicken cold desires,
To entertaine the warmth of holy fires.
There may we see thy soule exspaciate,
And with true feruour sweetly meditate,
Vpon our Sauiour's sufferings; that while
Thou seek'st His painefull torments to beguile,
With well-tun'd accents of thy zealous song
Breath'd from a soule transfix'd, a passion strong,
We better knowledge of His woes attaine,
Fall into teares with thee, and then againe,
Rise with thy verse to celebrate the flood
Of those eternall torrents of His blood."[2]

Read in the light of his extant sacred Poems—
so thought-full, rich, solemn, vivid, and of the
cunningest workmanship—our sense of loss in the

---

1 See the whole Poem in this Volume, pp 198—201.
2 See this Volume for the whole poem pp 6—9.

"Crowne of Thornes" is keen-edged and passionate I understand the Poet's own references and
Hawkins's, as declaring PUBLICATION of the Poem
or at least as designating a privately-printed impression, accessible to more or fewer. This being
so, especially in the knowledge of (literally) scores
of others, earlier and contemporary and later, that
survive in single exemplars only,—I shall
cherish the 'Pleasures of Hope' of the Poem
emerging from some hiding-place. May they not
prove the 'Pleasures of Imagination!'[1]

Of literary habits and tastes—as probably of a
shy and retiring disposition—our Worthy seems
to have dedicated daily selected and sequestered
hours, to their satisfaction. We get a glimpse of
him at these studies in a hitherto overlooked
Letter. prefixed to the "Elements of Armories"
(1601) by EDMUND BOLTON. The book is now
rare. It consists of a Dialogue between two

---

1 I regard books like Mr. Collier's 'Bibliographical
Account" (2 vols. 8vo. 1865) and Mr. Hazlitt's "Hand-
Book", as about the most humiliating in the language.
Scarcely a page but tells of some treasure overlooked,
gone out of sight, yet of as real intellectual bullion as
ever lost and recovered coin of the Henries. I hold
myself, precious books of which no other copy is known.

3

Knights, Sir Eustace and Sir Amias.   The Letter follows, *verbatim* : with best thanks to Mr. W. Aldis Wright of Cambridge for calling my attention to it :

> " A Letter to the Author, from the learned young gentleman, I. B. of Grace-dieu in the County of Leicester, Esquier.

Syr, I haue here with many thanks returned to you, your profound discourse of the ELEMENTS of ARMORIES, which I haue read ouer with great profit and delight : for I confesse, that till now, I neuer saw any thing in this kind worthy the entertainment of a studious mind, wherin you haue most commendably shewed your skill, finding out rare and vnknowne beauties in an Art, whose highest perfection, the meanest wits, if they could blazon, and repeat pedigrees, durst heretofore (but shall not now) challenge. Our sight (which of all senses wee hold ye dearest) you haue made more precious vnto vs, by teaching vs the excellent proportions of our visible obiects. In performance wherof, as you haue followed none, so haue you left it at a rash, and desperate aduenture, for any to follow you.   For he that only considers your choice copie of matter, without forcing, will find it an hard task to equall your inuention, not to speake of your iudiciall method, wherin you haue made your workmanship excell your subiect, though it bee most worthy of all ingenuous industry. Beleeue me, Syr, in a word, I cannot but highly admire your attempt so wel performed, and among many others will be an earnest furtherer of that benefit, which this dull age of ours (in this our countrey, carelesse of al but gainful Arts) claimeth at your hands.   In which hope I rest.

> Your most louing friend,
>> Iohn Beavmont."

26. Nouemb. 1609.

Turning elsewhere, our Poet incidentally informs us that it was the Duke of Buckingham who first drew him into publicity.   Thus in his " True greatnesse : to my lord Marquesse of Buckingham," he addresses him :

> "Sir, you are truely great, and euery eye
> Not dimme with enuy, ioyes to see you high :
> But chiefely mine, *which buried in the night,*
> *Are by your beames rais'd and restor'd to light.*
> *You, onely you, haue pow'r to make me dwell*
> *In sight of men, drawne from my silent cell.*"[1]

Again, in his lines " to the Duke of Buckingham at his returne from Spaine " we have the same sentiments : and an intimation that by him the King (James), had been led to read his ' lines ' :

> " My Muse, *which tooke from you her life and light*
> Sate like a weary wretch, whom suddaine night
> Had ouer-spred ; your absence casting downe
> The flow'rs and Sirens' feathers from her crowne :

---

1 See pp 158—161.

Your fauor first th' anointed head inclines
To heare my rurall songs and reade my lines :
Your voyce, my reede with lofty musick reares,
To offer trembling songs to princely eares."[1]

We have already seen that the Earl of Southampton was another of his patrons and friends.
His Elegies—of varying worth, but none without
some choice thought or felicitous epithet—reveal
the society in which he moved.   I do not care to
be critical on his homage, even to prostration
before kings James and Charles.   His was a
gallant, chivalrous loyalty to the throne, irre-
spective of its occupant—that self-forgetting and
beautiful devotion, which transfigured the meanest
and turned the crown into an aureole.   Probably
he uttered his own as well as Surrey's sentiment
in his ' Bosworth Field ' :

" Set England's royall wreath upon a stake
There will I fight, and not the place forsake."[2]

Personal ties to Buckingham and others, explain
if they do not altogether vindicate his verse-beati-
fication of men and women concerning whom
History has little of great or good to tell.   That
our Poet,—Cavalier and Royalist though he was,

---

1 See pp 163—164.   2 See p. 51.

—had touches of the Puritan : or to put it in another shape, was centrally and controllingly a Christian man, through tragic conflict and agony of penitence, and Luther or Bunyan-like fighting "the fight of Faith" as against "the world, the flesh and the devil", is everywhere evidenced. Turn, Reader, to his "In Desolation" and "of the miserable state of man" and "of sinne." Brood over these, if with wet eyes so much the better. Twice over concerning the former, Dr. George Macdonald in 'Antiphon', thus writes : "The following contains an utterance of personal experience, the truth of which will be recognized by all to whom heavenly aspiration and needful disappointment are not unknown :" and "Surely this is as genuine an utterance, whatever its merits as a poem—and those I judge not small—as ever flowed from Christian heart."[1] His "Act of Contrition" is as purged and strong and touching.[2] Of rare beauty, and of exquisite tenderness of feeling, are all his allusions to The Saviour. You have a sense in reading, of a hush on his spirit, a tremble in his tones, a devoutness, soft as light and nevertheless penetrating as the lightning, in His presence, How finely-put is this "of the Epiphany" as one out of many examples ! It

---

1 Pages 143, 145.   2 See pp. 80—82.

would be desecration to mutilate in any way, this
lovely poem : and therefore I give it in full :

" Faire Easterne starre, that art ordain'd to runne
Before the sages, to the rising Sunne,
Heare cease thy course, and wonder that the cloud
Of this poore stable can thy Maker shroud :
Ye heauenly bodies, glory to be bright,
And are esteem'd, as ye are rich in light :
But here on Earth is taught a diff'rent way,
Since vnder this low roofe the Highest lay ;
Ierusalem erects her stately towres,
Displayes her windowes, and adornes her bowres ;
Yet there thou must not cast a trembling sparke :
Let Herod's palace still continue darke :
Each schoole and synagogue thy force repels,
There Pride enthron'd in misty errours, dwels.
The temple, where the priests maintaine their quire,
Shall taste no beame of thy celestiall fire ;
While this weake cottage all thy splendour takes,
A joyfull gate of eu'ry chinke it makes.
Here shines no golden roofe, no iu'ry staire,
No king exalted in a stately chaire,
Girt with attendants, or by heralds styl'd.
But straw and hay inwrap a speechlesse child ;
Yet Sabac's lords before this Babe vnfold
Their treasures, off'ring incense, myrrh and gold.
The cribbe becomes an altar ; therefore dies
No oxe nor sheepe ; for in their fodder lies
The Prince of Peace, who thankfull for His bed,
Destroyes those rites, in which their blood was shed :

The quintessence of earth He takes and fees,
And precious gummes distill'd from weeping trees ;
Rich metals and sweet odours now declare
The glorious blessings, which His lawes prepare
To cleare vs from the base and lothsome flood
Of sense, and make vs fit for angels' food,
Who lift to God for vs the holy smoke
Of feruent pray'rs, with which we Him inuoke,
And trie our actions in that searching fire,
By which the seraphims our lips inspire :
No muddy dross pure min'ralls shall infect,
We shall exale our vapours vp direct :
No stormes shall crosse, nor glitt'ring lights deface
Perpetuall sighes, which seeke a happy place."

On this, Dr. Macdonald remarks " The creatures no longer offered on His altar, standing around the Prince of Life, [Peace] to whom they have given a bed, is a lovely idea." It may also be observed here, with reference to Dr. Macdonald's and our note on the place : [See page 70] that our present Laureate uses the technical ' *in fee* ' in his immortal 'In Memoriam', in a passage dear to many hearts and in myriad memories :

" More than my brothers are to me ".
Let not this vex thee, noble heart !
I know thee of what force thou art,
To hold the costliest love in fee.'

Equally if not surpassingly original, is lordly Jerusalem lifting up high its signal-lights from tower and palace—in vain: while the lowly manger-cradle is accepted. I can't resist also quoting in this place the beautiful little poem "Vpon the two great Feasts of the Annunciation and Resurrection":

> "Thrice happy day, which sweetly do'st combine
> Two hemispheres in th' Equinoctiall line:
> The one debasing God to earthly paine,
> The other raising man to endlesse raigne.
> Christ's humble steps declining to the wombe,
> Touch heau'nly scales erected on His tombe:
> We first with Gabriel must this Prince conuay
> Into His chamber on the marriage day,
> Then with the other angels cloth'd in white,
> We will adore Him in this conqu'ring night:
> The Sonne of God assuming humane breath,
> Becomes a subiect to His vassall Death,
> That graues and Hell laid open by His strife,
> May giue vs passage to a better life.
> See for this worke how things are newly styl'd,
> Man is declar'd, Almighty, God, a child;
> The Word made flesh, is speechlesse, and the Light
> Begins from clouds, and sets in depth of night;
> Behold the sunne eclips'd for many yeeres,
> And eu'ry day more dusky robes He weares,
> Till after totall darknesse shining faire,
> No moone shall barre His splendour from the aire.

Let faithfull soules this double feast attend
In two processions : let the first descend
The temple's staires, and with a downe-cast eye
Vpon the lowest pauement prostrate lie ;
In creeping violets, white lilies, shine
Their humble thoughts, and eu'ry pure designe ;
The other troope shall climbe, with sacred heate,
The rich degrees of Salomon's bright seate,
In glowing roses feruent zeale they beare,
And in the azure flowre de-lis appeare
Celestiall contemplations, which aspire
Aboue the skie, vp to th' immortall quire."[1]

Milton might have worked the close into 'Comus'
or even 'Paradise Lost'. The reader of GILES
FLETCHER will recognize his influence in the above
poem, in the paradoxes of the Divinely-human
and humanly-Divine life, and elsewhere, as in
"Of Sinne" there are evident recollections of
"Christs's Victorie"—the first edition of which
was published in 1610. Nearly all the 'Sacred
Poems' are similarly markedly genuine, markedly
evangelic, and finished in workmanship. Like the
'wise man' of old, he had sought out 'many in-
ventions' and to 'intermeddle' with 'all knowledge', but the deeper hunger went unsatisfied,

---

1 See our Volume, pp. 67—68.

and he looked UP.   There was no common experience in this cry ' of the miserable state of man ' :

> " But these are ends which draw the meanest hearts :
> Let vs search deepe and trie our better parts :
> O knowledge, if a heau'n on earth could be.
> I would expect to reape that blisse in thee :
> But thou art blind, and they that haue thy light
> More clearely know, they liue in darksome night.
> See, man, thy stripes at schoole, thy paines abroad,
> Thy watching and thy palenesse well bestow'd :
> These feeble helpes can scholers neuer bring
> To perfect knowledge of the plainest thing :
> And some to such a height of learning grow,
> They die perswaded that they nothing know.
> In vaine swift houres spent in deep study slide,
> Vnlesse the purchast doctrine curbe our pride.
> The soule perswaded, that no fading loue
> Can equall her imbraces, seekes aboue :
> And now aspiring to a higher place,
> Is glad that all her comforts here are base.''[1]

At the opposite pole, are his " In spirituall
Comfort ", " Act of Hope" and " True Liberty,"
which tell of the very rapture of Christian fellow-
ship.

Of his pursuit after Knowledge in less prominent and less urgent departments we are informed

---

1 See our Volume, pp. 92—95.

in the Letter to Edmund Bolton already given, and there are acknowledgments of help rendered by him to the good old Historian of Leicestershire, BURTON, who writes thus gratefully concerning him as "a gentleman of great learning, gravity and worthiness : the remembrance of whom I may not here omit, for many worthy respects."[1] Similarly, Anthony a-Wood wakes up from his usual Dr. Dry-as-dust style, to say of him : "The former part of his life he had fully employed in poetry : and the latter he as happily bestowed on more serious and beneficial studies : [Innocent Dr. Dry-as-dust!] and had not death untimely cut him off in his middle age, he might have prov'd a patriot, being accounted at the time of his death a person of great knowledge, gravity and worth."[2] That word 'patriot' from the pen of Anthony a-Wood was a synonym for Royalist or one for the King as against the Kingdom, for Privilege as above Law : and perchance he was right—though personally, as in innumerable cases, the loyalty of our Worthy was pure and unselfish, if blinded.

In 1626 he was made a 'Baronet' : and he evidently stood high in favour at Court. We may

---

1 Quoted by Nichols, as before. Burton was brother of *the* Burton of 'Melancholy'.

2 As before.

agree with his poet-friend DRAYTON that it was
good he was gone before the Tempest crashed
over England :

> " Heau'n was kinde, and would not let thee see
> The plagues that must vpon this Nation be."[1]

His son and heir—Sir John—adhered to the king,
and as already told, was killed at the siege of
Gloucester.   He but followed in what would
have been his father's footsteps.   The family and
the family-property, direct and collateral, suffered
as in all Civil Wars, and especially the losing side.
I am enabled by the spontaneous courtesy of the
present Sir George H. Beaumont, Bart., of Cole-
orton Hall—another branch of the Beaumont-stock,
destined to share for ever the glory of WORDS-
WORTH—to print for the first time a melancholy
memorial of the ravage of the period, in the form
of a " Petition," in his possession.   The Bishop
addressed was Humphrey Henchman, Bishop of
London from 1663 to 1675 : which chronological
fact convicts the Petitioners of—shall I say ?—
fibbing, seeing that Naseby was fought in 1645,
thirty (*not* ' above forty ') years only before the
latest date at which the petition could have been
written :

---

1 See our Volume, pp. 17—18.

"To the Righte Reverend Father in God Humphrey, now Lord Bishop of London.

The humble Petition of the inhabitants of Coleorton, in the Countye of Leicester, Humbly sheweth, that in the reign of that sacred martyr, Charles the I (of ever blessed memorye) above 40 years agoe, the house of the righte Honourable Thomas Beamonte, Viscounte Swords, was made a Garrison, and the Parish Churche was also included within their Bulwarks, where, whilst these rude Oliverians stayed, they made greate spoyle and committed many outrages, keeping sentinell in the Church, which they defaced, with a stately monument of the Beaumonts' noble familye, broke down all the windows, threw down the battlements, caused all the lead from off all the 3 Ifles[1] to be carried away and embessled, and pluck'd down many houses adiacent, whereof a fine parsonage-house, new built, was one; by this rude action, ever since the fatal battle at Nasebye; we have been exposed to all inconveniences of storms and tempests, so that many times, to our unspeakable griefe, we have been driven from our devotions, and now the roofes, havinge so long laine without coveringe, are all rotten. and the walls which should have supported them being in many places fallen downe, we are afraide to enter the Church, when there is any highe windes, least it should fall upon oure heads and entombe us quicke. We being a lamentable poore parishe, most consisting of colliers, and so despairinge ever to repaire it, have formerly made our addresses to

---

1 Query—isles = aisles?   G.

the General Sessions, and did procure their informatione
and request to his sacred Majestye to grant us his letters
pattant, without which it will falle to rubbishe speedily.
We had 4 able workmen, a mason, a plumber, a carpenter,
and a joiner, who upon their oaths certified that 1391
pounds would not complete it as formerly it had been :
therefore we jointly begg your gracious assistance, so
shall we be bound all to pray for your Lordship['s] health
and everlasting happinesse hereafter."

It were very idle to start a controversy out of
this old Petition, as it were easy to bandy words
as between Cavalier and Roundhead.   Either side,
in the alternation of triumph and defeat, could
shew the same ordeal of suffering and wrong.
War is too realistic to leave one side less at fault
than the other.   But all the shame and sorrow of
the internecine Contest, our Poet was spared.   He
died according to Anthony a-Wood " in the Win-
ter-time of 1628 :" and so all the old authorities,
probably following him.   But as the *Athenæ*
mistakes in adding " and was buried in the
Church at Grace-dieu ", we may safely regard
1628 as a mistake for 1627.   This entry from the
Register of Burials from Westminster Abbey,
cannot be disputed :

" 1627.   Sr. John Beaumont bd in ye broad Ile on ye
south s.   April 29. "

Our Worthy departed not without the 'meed of some melodious tear.' I am fortunate enough to have secured from the Bodleian, an 'Elegy' by WILLIAM COLEMAN,—one of those appended to his excessively rare "*La Dance Machabre* or Death's Duell" It is as follows :

"*An Elegie*
VPON THE HONORABLE
SIR IOHN BEAVMONT.
Knight Baronet.

A Beaumont dead ; he forfeiteth his pen
That writeth not an elegie. For when
The Muses' darlings, whose admir'd numbers
Recorded are amongst our ages wonders,
Exchange this dull earth for a crowne of glorie,
All are ingag'd t' immortalize their storie.
But thou hast left vs sacred poesie
Reduc'd vnto her former infancie.
Hauing—as all things else by long gradation—
Lost her first lustre, till thy reformation,
Forcing her backe into the ancient streame
Taught's[t] thy chast muse diuinitie : a theame
So farre neglected, we did hardly know
If there were any—but a name—or no.
Mirror of men, who left'st vs not a line
Wherein thy liuing honor doth not shine
Equall with that of the celestiall globe,
Clad in the splendor of her midnight robe,
Onely that Venus neuer did appeare

Within the circle of thy hemispheare ;
Which so much addes to thy religious verse,
Succeeding ages shall not dare reherse
Without some sacred ceremonie, sent
Beforehand, as a diuine complement."

Again the ' Crowne of Thornes ' seems designa-
ted in these allusions to his ' religious verse.'

Such is what we have to tell of our Worthy.
It is to be regretted that very much fuller though
our Memoir be, than any preceding, after all so little
should have been transmitted concerning him. On
reading the many noble and eminent names
celebrated by him, one wistfully asks, Where is
his Correspondence ?   Where his Manuscripts ?
Turning to Mrs. Thomson's " Life and Times of
George Villiers, Duke of Buckingham " (3 vols.
8vo.) it is vexatious to find a single passing allusion to him and a reference for more to 'the
Appendix', while not a syllable is given there.
However his Poetry remains ' in part, ' if the
record of the Life be dim and inadequate : and so
we may comfort ourselves as did Ia. Cl.—whoever
he was—in these ingenious lines :

" *I knew thee not*, I speake it to my shame :
But by that cleare, and equall voyce of Fame,
Which—with the sunne's bright course—did **ioyntly beare**
Thy glorious name about each hemisphere !

While I who had confin'd my selfe to dwell
Within the straite bounds of an obscure cell,
Tooke in those pleasing beames of wit and worth,
Which, where the sunne could neuer shine, breake forth :
Wherewith I did refresh my weaker sight,
When others bath'd themselues in thy full light.
But when the dismall rumour was once spred,
That struck all knowing soules, of Beaumont dead :
Aboue thy best friends, 'twas my benefit
To know thee onely by thy liuing wit ;
And whereas others might their losse deplore,
Thou liu'st to me iust as thou didst before.
In all that we can value great or good,
Which were not in these cloathes of flesh and blood
Thou now hast laid aside ; BUT IN THAT MIND
THAT ONELY BY ITSELFE COULD BE CONFIN'D,
THOU LIU'ST TO ME."[1]

Even more widely, must we say with LEOPOLD
SCHEFER, of such outwardly-oblivionized Lives :

" Out of all poets since the hoary eld,—
Out of the poems and the legends all,—
Out of all sages that have said their word,
Out of their words themselves and prophecies,—
Out of all painters, who haue wrote their sketch,
Out of all pictures, *even of those passed by,*—
OUT OF ALL GOOD MEN WHO HAUE DONE THEIR WORK,
Out of all champions who haue fought the fight

---

1 See our Volume, pp. 20—21.

4

With bodies, souls, dragons, and despotisms,
Down to this hour, and out of all the treasures
Which all shall still to the last day of earth
Conspire to swell with godlike energies,—
Out of all these comes MAN ! the only one
Among all beings, THAT FOR EVER GROWS.
While rock and cloud, lion and cypress-tree,
Are all alike, the latest and the first,
Just as one egg is like all other eggs."1

Of the Poetry of Sir John Beaumont as now brought together, little more requires to be said. The commendatory Verses prefixed to the ' Metmorphosis of Tabacco ' (1602) and to the volume of 1629, shew that independent of partialities of friendship, he had made his mark on his contemporaries : while later, even the blundering and frigid WINSTANLEY is stirred to write of him thus : " Sir John Beaumont was one who drank as deep draughts of Helicon as any of that age : and though not many of his works are extant, yet those we have be such as are displayed on the flags of highest invention, and may justly style him to be one of those great souls of numbers."2 Later still, WORDSWORTH—' one whose praise is

---

1 " The Layman's Breviary " translated by Brooks : Boston, U.S. 1867, pp. 427—28.

2 Quoted in Nichols, as before, p. 657.

fame '—justly observes Dyce, in quoting the words
—praises him for " spirit, elegance and harmony,"[1]
and CAMPBELL remarks that he " deserves notice
as one of the earliest polishers of what is called
the heroic couplet."[2] Darley—himself a genuine
poet—is amusingly irate with certain critics for
their over-praise of Francis Beaumont's verse-
letter to Ben Jonson on his Fox.[3] I think it
clear that those critics must have mixed up in
their memories, our poet's thoughtful and sonorous
address " To his late Majesty, concerning the true
forme of English Poetry,"[4] with his brother's
verses, and perhaps his son's " Congratulation to
the Muses, for the immortalizing of his deare
father, by the sacred vertue of poetry."[5] The
" Metamorphosis of Tabacco " is more remarkable for its smoothness of versification—so early as
1602—than substantively. The youthful poet to a
considerable extent paraphrases Ovid and Virgil.
He turns aside with every possible opportunity, to
glorify Elizabeth. I give a single specimen of the

---

1 Note on the Song at the Feast of Brougham Castle.
2 Specimens, *s.n.*
3 Introduction to Beaumont and Fletcher, as before.
4 See our Volume, pp 118—121.
5 *Ibid.* pp. 10—12.

'Metamorphosis,' which King James would have read with horror and Joshua Sylvester with loathing. You have in the following passage, a fair example of the serio-comic exaggeration of the poem : but it will be hard to discover anywhere the 'philosophie' for which I. P. eulogises him in his commendatory lines :

"The marrow of the world, starre of the West,
The pearle, whereby this lower orbe is blest,
The ioy of mortals, vmpire of all strife,
Delight of nature, Mithridate of life,
The daintiest dish of a delicious feast,
By taking which man differs from a beast.
Thrice happie Isles, which steale the world's delight,
And doe produce so rich a Margarite!
Had but the old heroicke spirits knowne
The newes, which Fame vnto our eares hath blowne,
Colchis, and the remote Hesperides
Had not been sought for halfe so much as these ;
Nor had the fluent wits of ancient Greece
Prais'd the rich apples or the Golden Fleece ;
Nor had Apolloe's garland been of bayes,
Nor Homer writ of sweete Nepenthe's praise :
Nor had Anacreon with a sugred glose
Extold the vertues of the fragrant rose ;
Nor needed Hermes with his fluent tongue
Haue ioyn'd in one a rude vnciuil throng,
And by perswasions made that companie
An order'd politike societie,

When this dumbe oratour would more perswade
Then all the speeches Mercurie had made ;
Nor honour'd Ceres been create diuine,
And worshipt so at curious Eleusine :
Whom blinder ages did so much adorne
For the inuention of the vse of corne :
Nor Saturne s feast had been the ioyfull day
Wherein the Romanes washt their cares away,
But in the honour of great Trinidade
A new Tobacconalia had been made."[1]

The Battle of "Bosworth Field" deserves the encomium of Campbell, and apart from its workmanship is a very striking poem, although all must shew pale before the mighty pages of Shakespeare's Richard III. One incident, admirably told, viz., the meeting of BYRON and Clinton, in its apologetic introduction :

" If in the midst of such a bloody fight,
The name of friendship be not thought too light "[2]

reminds us of a curious parallel in Byron's ' Childe Harold,' wherein he turns aside from the general carnage of Waterloo to celebrate young Howard. Leaving the prominent dead, the noble Poet exclaims,

---

1 See our Volume, pp, 304—306.
2 See our present Volume p. 56.

" Their praise is hymn'd by loftier harps than mine :
Yet one I would select from that proud throng,
Partly because they blend me with his line,
And partly that I did his sire some wrong,
And partly that bright names will hallow song ;
And his was of the bravest, and when shower'd
The death-bolts deadliest the thinn'd files along,
Even where the thickest of War's tempest lower'd,
They reach'd no nobler breast than thine, young,
    gallant Howard."[1]

Some of the similes and separate lines, are
vivid and memory-haunting, as of the sleeping
sentinel killed by the King :

" I leaue him as I found him, fit to keepe
The silent doores of euerlasting Sleepe."[2]

and this of the infamous Tyrell, under the threat
of Richard :

" The wretch astonisht, hastes·away to slide,
As damned ghosts themselues in darknesse hide."[3]

and this of the troubled night-dreams :

" If some resistlesse strength my cause should crosse,
Feare will increase, and not redeeme the losse :

---

1 Childe Harold, c. iii., st. xxix.
2 See our present Volume p. 28.
3 *Ibid* p. 25.

All dangers, clouded with the mist of feare,
Seem great farre off, but lessen comming neare."1

and this of the fully-armed hero :

. . . ." he takes his helmet bright
Which like a trembling starre, with twinkling light
Sends radiant lustre through the darksome aire."2

and this of the doomed monarch :

" Then putting on his crowne, a fatall signe
—So offer'd beasts neere death in garlands shine."3

and this of Richmond's view of the army:

" He sees their motion like to rolling fires,
Which by the winde along the fields are borne
Amidst the trees, the hedges and the corne : ·
Where they the hopes of husbandmen consume,
And fill the troubled ayre with dusky fume."4

The death of Richard has often been quoted
for its power and keeping :

' The king growes weary, and begins to faint,
It grieues him that his foes perceiue the taint :
Some strike him that till then durst not come neare,
With weight and number they to ground him beare,
Where trampled down, and hew'd with many swords,

---

1 *Ibid* p. 26   2 *Ibid* p. 27.   3 *Ibid* p. 34.
4 *Ibid* p. 53.

He softly vtter'd these his dying words :
' Now strength no longer Fortune can withstand,
I perish in the center of my Land.'
His hand he then with wreathes of grasse infolds,
And bites the earth, which he so strictly holds,
As if he would haue borne it with him hence,
So loth he was to lose his right's pretence."[1]

On this the Biographia Britannica remarks : " A moderate Poet would have been contented with the King's biting the earth ; but it belonged to a sublimer imagination to paint the reluctance with which he quitted his usurped possession, even in death."[2] The same authority praises his Translations. They are pretty close to the original, occasionally somewhat clumsy : occasionally also bits shew that considerable pains must have been spent on them. The version of the City and Country Mouse, after Horace, has arch touches The Satires of Juvenal and Persius lack the pungency, the burning passion of the Latin : and yet now and again there are flashes of the true rage. His Elegies—like some of his Royal and Courtly poems —are unequal and task-work, on the face of them. Nevertheless there are scattered up and down, felicities brilliant as dew-drops gleaming on the

---

1 *Ibid* pp. 62—63.   2 As before, pp. 622.

spider's web in the hedge-row. A few must have
been heart-felt: for they go right to one's heart still.
His religious poetry,—all too disproportionate in
amount, in the (present) loss of the 'Crowne of
Thornes'—is his supreme gift to our Literature.
The more it is read and returned on, the higher
will be the estimate of the Poet and the man. I
have already given examples of his originality and
beauty in this department: but the slightest will
reward study.

I think THOMSON may have read the Poems of
our Worthy. In the 'Ode of the blessed Trinity'
we have this,

> "Then praise with humble silence heavenly things
> And what is more then this, to still deuotion leaue."[1]

The Hymn at the close of The Seasons ends,

> " ....I lose
> Myself in Him, in light ineffable!
> Come, then, expressive silence, muse His praise."

Every one knows the fine rapture in the Castle
of Indolence :

> " I care not Fortune, what you me deny :
> You cannot rob me of free Nature's grace,

---

1 *Ibid* p. 77.

> You cannot shut the windows of the sky,
> Through which Aurora shews her brightening face ;
> You cannot bar my constant feet to trace
> The woods and lawns, by living stream at eve ;
> Let health my nerves and finer fibres brace,
> And I their toys to the great children leave ;
> Of fancy, reason, vertue, nought can me bereave."

Fainter perhaps, but in the same line of thought, is this of our Poet in his 'True Liberty : '

> " In these delights, though freedome show more high,
> Few can to things aboue their thoughts apply.
> *But who is he that cannot cast his looke*
> *On earth, and reade the beauty of that booke ?*
> *A bed of smiling flow'rs, a trickling spring,*
> *A swelling riuer, more contentment bring,*
> *Then can be shadow'd by the best of Art :*
> THUS STILL THE POORE MAN HATH THE BETTER PART."[1]

I believe another anticipation of THOMSON, but later than our Poet herein, has escaped our literary Critics and Commentators : I refer to Randolph's " Ode to Mr. Anthony Stafford, to hasten him into the Country ", which has these noticeable lines :

> " Where every word is thought and every thought is pure :
>   Our's is the skie

---

1 See our Volume pp. 97—98.

Whereat what fowl we please our hauk shall flye :
    Nor will we spare
To hunt the crafty fox or timorous hare ;
    And let our hounds run loose
    In any ground they'l choose ;
      The buck shall fall,
      The stag and all :
Our pleasure must from their own warrants be,
    FOR TO MY MUSE, IF NOT TO MEE,
    I'M SURE ALL GAME IS FREE :
HEAVEN, EARTH, ARE ALL BUT PARTS OF HER GREAT
    ROYALTY."[1]

This reference to RANDOLPH, reminds me of another parallel with our Beaumont, as Beaumont suggests that Milton may have read him. In his Lines "Upon report of the King of Sweden's death" he exclaims grandly :

"If I had seen *a comet in the air*
With glorious eye, and bright dishevell'd hair
All on a suddain with his gilded train
Drop down."[2]

Nearer to Milton is our Poet thus, of base Loue :

"A vapor first extracted from the stewes
—Which with new fewell still the lampe renewes—

---

1 My edition is the 3rd, 1640 ; pp. 62—65.
2 *Ibid* p. 77.

And with a pander's sulph'rous breath inflam'd,
Becomes a meteor for distinction fram'd.
*Like some prodigious comet which foretells
Disasters to the realme on which it dwells.*"[1]

I note one Shakesperian parallel and one golden little bit that has been worked in finely into an imperishable Hymn. The former is " soule of goodness " (p. 186) which occurs also in Henry V. (IV. i.). The latter is Keble's " Sun of my soul," as in our Poet's " Abused Love " :

" *Sunne of the soule*, cleare beauty, liuing fire,
Celestiall Light, which dost pure hearts inspire."[2]

Bibliographically, there is one curious circumstance connected with the volume of 1629. Nichols in his *Leicestershire* states that he had examined no fewer than twenty copies without finding pp. 181—182: and so Anthony a-Wood, and all the leading authorities. From the Grenville copy in the British Museum I give in our volume, what is there inserted for the cancelled leaf viz., Verses on the death of ' Marquesse of Hamilton' and others, on a ' Funeralle '. There is nothing in these to suggest a motive for their suppression :

---

1 See our Volume, p. 103
2 *Ibid* p. 101.

and if a ' forgery ' as written by Grenville, it is
equally difficult to understand their insertion.
Probably these two unimportant pieces are genuine,
and taken from some copy wherein they had
been inserted contemporaneously, either in print
or in manuscript.　But be this as it may, on ex-
amining another copy of the volume in the British
Museum [1077, b. 26] and that in the Bodleian,
I find the leaf has been in each case so hastily
or clumsily cut out, that a fragment is left, sufficient to prove another than the first piece at any
rate in the Grenville copy, had been printed and
cancelled.　In the former these are the first letters
of the successive lines left—the catchword on
p. 180 being ' Of ' :

Broken I, N or M.

R

D

T [apparently ' To ']

B [　　　,,　　　' Bu ']　　　.

Se

W

Fo　　　　　　　　　　　.

A

In [or ' Im ']

T [apparently ' Th ']

T [,,   'Th ']

So

A

W

W

A

In the latter, less fully but in agreement :

T

T

S

A

V [half W]

V [half W]

A, and on reverse, what looks like half an N. This does not agree as the catchword of p. 183, which is 'Ivvenall', but the first word of the Poem is 'In'.   Comparison will reveal that these first letters of the lines, differ altogether from those that would have been there, had the Verses in the Grenville copy on the death of the Marquesse of Hamilton really been on that side of the cancelled leaf.   So that the leaf has been over-successfully suppressed.

And so I close my little Memorial-Introduction to one in very truth a Worthy, albeit he bulks not before the world.   Living and dying unobtrusively, he finely confirms Mrs. Browning in her Aurora Leigh (B. iv.)

............" the best men, doing their best
Know peradventure least of what they do :
Men usefullest in the world, are simply used.
The nail that holds the wood, must pierce it first,
And he alone who wields the hammer sees
The work advanced by the earliest blow.   Take heart."

ALEXANDER B. GROSART.

St. George's, Blackburn.

Poems

of

Sir John Beaumont Bart.

A

Note.

The following is the original title-page of the principal volume of our Poet:

" Bosworth-field:

WITH

A TASTE OF

THE VARIETY OF

OTHER POEMS, LEFT

by Sir *John Beaumont*, Baronet, deceased:

SET FORTH BY HIS

SONNE, SIR IOHN BEAV-

MONT, Baronet;

And dedicated to the Kings most
Excellent Maiestie.

———

LONDON,

Printed by *Felix Kyngston* for *Henry Seile,* and are
to be sold at the Tygers head in Saint *Pauls*
Churchyard, 1629."   (18o)

Collation—Title-page—Dedication and preliminary Verses, 10 leaves—Poems, pp. 208. As explained in our Memorial-Introduction, pp. 181—182 were cancelled by excision after the volume was printed: but we have been fortunate enough to recover the leaf from the Grenville copy. 'Bosworth Field' was re-printed in 1710 and in Nichols' Leicestershire, Chalmers' (so-called) 'British Poets', and in the United States of America, by SANFORD, in his dainty little collection of the Poets (1819). We give the Epistle-Dedicatory and other preliminary matter in the order of the original edition. For slight changes in the arrangement of the Poems, and considerable additions, see our Prefatory Note. G.

Epistle Dedicatory.

TO THE KING'S MOST EXCELLENT MAIESTIE.[1]

Most Gracious Soueraigne,

I HERE present at the feet of your Sacred Maiesty, these orphan Verses, whose Author—had hee suruiued—might haue made this gift somewhat more correspondent to so great a Patron. I haue only endeauoured without art, to set this iewell, and render it apt for your Maiestie's acceptance; to which boldnes I am led by a filiall duty in performing the will of my father, who, whil'st he liued, did ever intend to your Maiesty these Poems: Poems in which no obscene sport can bee found—the contrary being too frequent a crime among Poets—while these—if not too bold I speake—will challenge your Maiestie for their Patron, since it is most

---

conuenient, that the purest of Poems should be directed to you, the vertuousest and most vntoucht of Princes, the delight of Brittaine, and the wonder of Europe; at the altar of whose iudgement, bright erected flames, not troubled fumes, dare approach. To your Maiestie must bee directed the most precious off-springs of each Muse, which though they may well bee esteemed starres, yet how can they subsist without the aspect of you their sun? Receiue then, great King, these my father's Verses, and let them find—what his son hath found—your princely clemency. Effect on them—I beseech your Maiesty—a kingly worke: giue them life, and withal graciously please to accept the sincere wishes for your felicity, and the humble vowes of

Your Maiestie's euer loyall subject,

IOHN BEAUMONT.[1]

---

1 On this Sir John Beaumont, see our Memorial-Introduction: and for Poems by him, our Appendix. G.

Preliminary Verses.

AN ELEGY TO THE LIUING MEMORY
OF HIS DECEASED FRIEND, SIR
JOHN BEAUMONT, KNIGHT, BARONET.

 O tell the World what it hath lost in thee,
 Were but in vaine ; for such as cannot see,
 Would not be grieu'd to heare, the morn-
  ing light
Should neuer more succeed the gloomy night.
Such onely whom thy vertue made, or found
Worthy to know thee, can receiue this wound :
Of these each man will duly pay his teares
To thy great memory, and when he heares
One fam'd for vertue, he will say, so blest,
So good his Beaumont was, and weepe the rest.
If knowledge shall be mention'd, or the Arts,
Soone will he reckon up thy better parts :
At naming of the Muses, he will streight
Tell of thy workes, where sharpe and high conceit,

Cloath'd in sweet verse, giue thee immortall fame,
Whil'st Ignorance doth scorne a poet's name :
And then shall his imagination striue,
To keepe thy gratefull memory aliue,
By poems of his owne ; for that might bee
Had he no Muse, by force of knowing thee.
This maketh me—who in the Muses' quire
Sing but a meane—thus boldly to aspire,
To pay sad duties to thy honor'd herse,
With my unpolish'd lines, and ruder verse.
Yet dreame I not of raysing amongst men
A lasting fame to thee by my fraile pen :
But rather hope, something may liue of me,
—Perhaps this paper—hauing mention'd thee.

THOMAS NEUILL.[1]

AN ELEGY, DEDICATED TO THE MEMORY OF HIS MOST HONOURED FRIEND, SIR IOHN BEAUMONT, KNIGHT AND BARONET:

 WRITE not Elegies, nor tune my verse,
To waite in mourning notes upon thy
herse

For vaine applause, or with desire to rank

---

1 Cf. our Phineas Fletcher, Vol. I. lxxi.   Probably
the Master of Trinity College, Cambridge.   G.

My slender Muse 'mongst those, who on the bank
Of Aganippe's streame can better sing,
And to their words more sence of sorrow bring,
That stirres my genius, which should excite
Those pow'rfull wits to doe a pious right
To noble vertue, and by verse conuay
Truth to posterity, and shew the way
By strong example, how in mortall state
We heau'nly worth may loue, and imitate.
Nay, 'twere a great iniustice not to saue
Him from the ruines of a silent graue,
Who others from their ashes sought to raise,
To weare—giu'n from his hand—eternall bayes.
It is by all confess'd, thy happy straines,
Distill'd from milky streames of natiue veines,
Did like the liuing source of Naso's[1] song,
Flow to the eare, thence gently glide along
Downe to the heart, in notes so heau'nly-sweet,
That there the sister-Graces seem'd to meet,
And make thy brest their seate for soft retire
And place from whence they fetch'd Promethean
    fire,
To kindle other hearts with purest flame
Of modest verse, and unaffected fame :
While pedant poetasters of this age

---

1 Ovid. **G.**

—Who stile their saucy rimes, poëtique rage—
Loose humours vent, and ballad-lines extrude,
Which grieue the wise, captiue the multitude.
And that thy Poems might the better take,
Not with vaine sound, or for the Author's sake,
Which often is by seruile spirits tryde,
Whil'st heau'n-bred soules are left vnsatisfyde ;
Like to the bee, thou didd'st those flow'rs select,
That most the tastefull palate might affect,
With pious relishes of things diuine,
And discomposèd sence with peace combine,
Which—in thy Crowne of Thornes—we may dis-
    cerne,
Fram'd as a modell for the best to learne
That verse may Vertue teach, as well as prose,
And minds with natiue force to good dispose,
Deuotion stirre, and quicken cold desires,
To entertaine the warmth of holy fires.
There may we see thy soule exspaciate,
And with true feruour sweetly meditate,
Vpon our Sauiour's sufferings ; that while
Thou seek'st His painefull torments to beguile,
With well-tun'd accents of thy zealous song,
Breath'd from a soule transfix'd, a passion strong,
We better knowledge of His woes attaine,
Fall into teares with thee, and then againe,
Rise with thy verse to celebrate the flood

Of those eternall torrents of His blood.[1]
Nor lesse delight—things serious set apart—
Thy sportiue poems yeeld, with heedfull art
Composèd so, to minister content,
That though we there thinke onely wit is meant,
We quickly by a happy error, find
In cloudy words, cleare lampes to light the mind.
Then blesse that Muse, which by vntrodden wayes
Pursuing Vertue, meetes deseruèd bayes
To crowne it selfe, and wandring souls reduce
From paths of Ignorance, and wit's abuse ;
And may the best of English laureats striue,
Thus, their owne fun'rall ashes to suruiue.

THOMAS HAWKINS.[2]

1 See Memorial-Introduction on the 'Crowne of Thornes' described *supra*. **G.**

2 Sir Thomas Hawkins, of Nash, Kent, well known as among our earliest translators of Horace : also of Caussin's 'Holy Court.' For our Sir John Beaumont's over-looked Lines to Hawkins, see in its place. **G.**

TO THE WORTHY MUSE OF HIS NOBLE FRIEND, SIR IOHN BEAUMONT, KNIGHT BARONET.

E doe not usher forth thy Verse with these,
That thine may by our prayse the better please :
That were impertinent, and we too weake,
To adde a grace, where eu'ry line doth speake,
And sweetly eccho out in this rich store,
All we can any way pretend, and more.
Yet since we stand engag'd, we this make knowne,
Thy layes are vnaffected ; free ; thine owne ;
Thy periods, cleare ; expressions, genuine ;
Muse most emphaticall ; and wit, diuine.

THOMAS HAWKINS.[1]

A CONGRATULATION TO THE MUSES, FOR THE IMMORTALIZING OF HIS DEARE FATHER, BY THE SACRED VERTUE OF POETRY.

E heau'nly Sisters, by whose sacred skill,
Sweet sounds are rays'd vpon the fork-
èd hill
Of high Parnassus : you, whose tunèd strings

---

1 See preceding ' Elegy ' and relative foot-note.   G.

Can cause the birds to stay their nimble wings,
And silently admire : before whose feet,
The lambs, as fearelesse, with the lions meet.
You whom the harpe of Orpheus so inspir'd,
That from the Stygian Lake he safe retir'd ;
You could Amphion's harp with vertue fill,
That euen the stones were pliant to his will.
To you, you therefore I my verse direct,
From whom such beames celestiall can reflect
On that deare Author of my life, inspir'd
With heauenly heate, and sacred fury fir'd ;
Whose vigour, quencht by death, you now reuiue,
And in this booke conserue him still aliue.
Here liues his better part, here shines that flame,
Which lights the entrance to eternall fame.
These are his triumphs ouer death, this spring
From Aganippe's fountaines he could bring
Cleare from all drosse, through pure intentions
      drain'd,
His draughts no sensual waters euer stain'd.
Behold, he doth on euery paper strow
The loyall thoughts he did his Sou'raigne owe.
Here rest affections to each nearest friend,
And pious sighs, which noble thoughts attend ;
Parnassus him containes, plast in the quire
With Poets : what then can we more desire
To haue of him ?   Perhaps an empty royce,

While him we wrong with our contentlesse choyce:
To you I this attribute, Sisters nine,
For onely you can cause this worke diuiue;
By none but you could these bright fires be found;
Prometheus is not from the rocke vnbound,
No Æsculapius still remaines on earth,
To giue Hippolitus a second birth.
Since then such god-like pow'rs in you remaine,
To worke these wonders, let some soule containe
His spirit of sweet musicke, and infuse
Into some other brest his sparkling Muse.
But you, perhaps, that all your pow'r may speake,
Will chuse to worke on subiects dull and weake:
Chuse me, inspire my frozen brest with heat,
No deed you euer wrought, can seeme more great.

IOHN BEAUMONT.[1]

VPON THE FOLLOWING POEMS OF MY DEARE FATHER, SIR IOHN BEAUMONT, BARONET, DECEASED.

OU who prepare to reade graue Beaumont's
    verse,
    And at your entrance view my lowly
    straines,

---

[1] See our Memorial-Introduction and Appendix, as before. G.

Expect no flatt'ring prayses to reherse
The rare perfections, which this booke containes.

But onely here in these few lines, behold
The debt which I vnto a parent owe ;
Who, though I cannot his true worth vnfold,
May yet at least a due affection show.

For should I striue to decke the vertues high,
Which in these poems—like faire gemmes—appeare ;
I might as well adde brightnesse to the skie,
Or with new splendour make the sunne more cleare.

Since eu'ry line is with such beauties grac'd,
That nothing farther can their prayses sound :
And that deare name which on the front is plac'd
Declares what ornaments within are found :

That name, I say, in whom the Muses meete,
And with such heate his noble spirit raise,
That kings admire his verse, whil'st at his feete,
Orpheus his harpe, and Phœbus casts his bayes.

Whom, though fierce death hath taken from our
    sights,
And caus'd that curious[1] hand to write no more ;

---

1 = skilful.   See Mr. W. A. Wright's Bible Word-
Book *s. v.* for excellent illustrations.   **G.**

Yet maruell not if from the fun'rall rites
Proceed these branches neuer seene before.

For from the corne arise not fruitfull eares,
Except at first the earth receiue the same :
Nor those rich odors which Arabia beares,
Send forth sweet smells, vnlesse consum'd with
    flame.

So from the ashes of this phœnix, flye
These off-springs, which with such fresh glory
    shine ;
That whil'st Time runneth, he shall neuer dye,
But still be honour'd in this famous shrine:
  To which this verse alone I humbly giue ;
  He was before : but now begins to liue
              FRANCIS BEAUMONT.[1]

VPON THESE POEMS OF HIS DEAREST BROTHER, SIR IOHN BEAUMONT, BARONET.

HEN lines are drawn greater then Nature, Art
  Commands the obiect, and the eye to part,
Bids them to keepe at distance, know their place,

---

1 This ' Francis ' Beaumont became a Jesuit.   Dyce's

Where to receiue, and where to giue their grace ;
I am too neere thee, Beaumont, to define
Which of those lineaments is most diuine,
And to stand farther off from thee, I chuse
In silence rather to applaude thy Muse,
And lose my censure ;[1] tis enough for mee
To ioy, my pen was taught to moue by thee.

GEORGE FORTESCUE.[2]

ON THE HONOR'D POEMS OF HIS HONORED FRIEND, SIR IOHN BEAUMONT, BARONET.

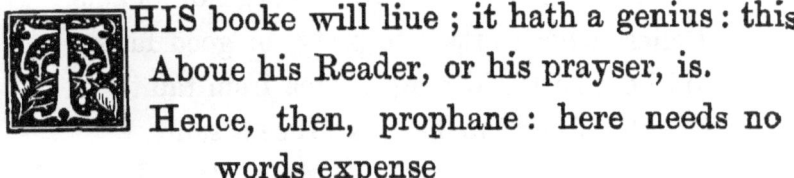 HIS booke will liue ; it hath a genius : this
Aboue his Reader, or his prayser, is.
Hence, then, prophane : here needs no
words expense
In bulwarkes, rau'lins, ramparts, for defense,

Beaumont and Fletcher, I., xxiii. A portrait of him is given in Nichols's Leicestershire : Vol. iii, pt. ii, p.* 662 : but see our Memorial-Introduction. G.

1 Judgment, opinion, *not* as now, condemnation. G.

2 *Brother*-in-law to Sir John Beaumont. Cf. Chalmers's Biogr. Dict. *s. n.* and Nichols's Leicestershire. From the latter it would appear that the Fortescues, and so the mother of our Poet, descended from Edward IV. G.

Such, as the creeping common pioners vse
   When they doe sweat to fortifie a Muse.
Though I confesse a Beaumont's booke to bee
   The bound, and frontire of our Poëtrie;
And doth deserue all muniments of praise,
   That Art, or ingine,[1] on the strength can raise.
Yet who dares offer a redoubt to reare?
   To cut a dike? or sticke a stake vp here,
Before this worke? where Enuy hath not cast
   A trench against it, nor a battry plac't?
Stay, till she make her vaine approches. Then
   If maymèd, she come off, tis not of men
This fort of so impregnable accesse,
   But higher power, as spight could not make
     lesse,
Nor flatt'ry! but secur'd by the Author's name,
   Defies, what's crosse to piety, or good fame.
And like a hallow'd temple, free from taint
   Of ethnicisme,[2] makes his Muse a saint.

                        BEN. IONSON.[3]

---

1 Genius or wit. G.

2 Heathenism. G.

3 To annotate this immortal name were superfluity of pains: but it may be worth-while to call attention to the frequency and fulness of the praise of Jonson for his contemporaries. He is generous in his recognition everywhere. G.

TO THE DEARE REMEMBRANCE OF HIS NOBLE FRIEND, SIR JOHN BEAU-MONT, BARONET.

HIS posthumus, from the braue parent's
    name,
  Likely to be the heire of so much fame,
Can haue at all no portion by my prayse :
Onely this poore branch of my with'ring bayes
I offer to it ; and am very glad,
I yet haue this ; which if I better had,
My loue should build an altar, and thereon
Should offer vp such wreaths as long agone
Those daring Grecians, and proud Romans crownd :
Giuing that honour to their most renown'd.
But that braue world is past, and we are light,
After those glorious dayes, into the night
Of these base times, which not one heroe haue,
Onely an empty title, which the graue
Shall soone deuoure ; whence it no more shall
    sound,
Which neuer got vp higher then the ground.
Thy care for that which was not worth thy breath,
Brought on too soone thy much lamented death.[1]

---

1 On these two lines see our Memorial-Introduction.
They have been dealt with as enigmatical and even mysterious. G.

B

But Heau'n was kinde, and would not let thee see
The plagues that must vpon this Nation be,
By whom the Muses haue neglected bin,
Which shall adde weight and measure to their
     sinne ;
And haue already had this curse from vs,
That in their pride they should grow barbarous.

   There is no splendor which our pens can giue
By our most labor'd lines, can make thee liue
Like to thine owne, which able is to raise
So lasting pillars to prop vp thy prayse,
As Time shall hardly shake, vntil it shall
Ruine those things, that with it selfe must fall.

               MI. DRAYTON[1].

---

   1 Equally unnecessary with Jonson is it to annotate this eminent name. See the dedication-verses prefixed to the Metamorphosis of Tabacco, onward. By a curious inadvertence, in text and index alike, the late Mr. Robert Bell, in his ' Lives of the Poets' in the Cabinet Cyclopædia, quotes these lines as by Dryden, to the perplexity of his un-informed Readers. G.

AD POSTHUMUM OPUS D. IO. BELLO-
MONTIJ EQUITIS AURATI ET BARON-
ETTI, VIRI NOBLISSIMI: HENDECAS-
YLLABON.

ECTUM discubui; biceps gemello
　　Parnassus bijugo imminębat: vnde
　　Fontes desiliunt leues, loquaces;
Pellucent vitreo liquore fontes.
Sudo sub Iouē, sydere et secundo
Discumbo.　Teneras rosas pererro
Narcissum, violas odore gratas,
Vnguento ambrosio has et has refectas.
Quas inter philomela cantitillat
Præpes, blandula, mellilinguis ales.
Quas inter volitant Apollinesque,
Et musæ Veneresque mille, mille.
　　Insomne hoc sibi somnium quid audet?
Altum effare noëma bello-montis:
Effatum euge! Poëma Bello-montî est
Dium, castalium nitens, politum;
Libatum salibus, lepore tinctum.
Decurrens velut amnis alti monte
Feruet delicijs, ruit profundo
Beaumontus latice.　Altius resultat
Fertur, nec tenui nec vsitatâ
Pennâ per liquidam ætheram, biformis.

Hic Phœbi deus est, decus cohortis
Summum Palladiœ iubar sororum,
Ipse et flos Venerum, resurgo ; legi.

PH. KIN.[1]

VPON THE HONORED POEMS OF HIS VNKNOWNE FRIEND, SIR IOHN BEAUMONT BARONET.

 KNEW thee not, I speake it to my shame :
But by that cleare, and equall voyce of
Fame,
Which—with the sunne's bright course—did
ioyntly beare
Thy glorious name, about each hemisphere.

---

1 Philip King, the youngest son of Dr. John King, Bishop of London, 1611—1621 : born in London 1603, Died at Langley, 4th March 166⅔. He has Latin verses in Jacobi Ara, 1617, and Annæ Fvnebria, 1619. Wood (A. O. ii. 435) had evidently not seen above Verses, nor Hannah, as they mis-describe them as 'English'. Cf. Poems and Psalms by Henry King D.D. edited by HANNAH (1843) p xcvii, and my Memoir of Bishop King, prefixed to reprint of his commentary on Jonah. It may be noted that it was quite customary to abbreviate names, as above, at the period e.g. FRANCIS QUARLES in title-page of his 'Mildreiados' is Fr. Qua. (1638). G.

Whiles I who had confin'd my selfe to dwell
Within the straite bounds of an obscure cell,
Tooke in those pleasing beames of wit and worth,
Which, where the sunne could neuer shine, breake
 forth :
Wherewith I did refresh my weaker sight,
When others bath'd themselues in thy full light.
But when the dismall rumour was once spred,
That struck all knowing soules, of Beaumont dead :
Aboue thy best friends, 'twas my benefit,
To know thee onely by thy liuing wit;
And whereas others might their losse deplore,
Thou liu'st to me iust as thou didst before.
In all that we can value great or good,
Which were not in these cloathes of flesh and
 blood
Thou now hast laid aside, but in that mind,
That onely by itselfe could be confind,
Thou liu'st to me, and shalt for euer raine,
In both the issues of thy blood and braine.

       Ia. Cl.

Bosworth Field:

WITH

Certaine other Poems, &c.

THE Winter's storme of Ciuill Warre I
sing,
Whose end is crown'd with our eternall
Spring,
Where Roses ioyn'd, their colours mixe in one,
And armies fight no more for England's Throne.[1]
Thou gracious Lord, direct my feeble pen,
Who—from the actions of ambitious men,—
Hast by Thy goodnesse drawne our ioyfull good,
And made sweet flowres and oliues, grow from
blood,
While we delighted with this faire release,

---

1 'Bosworth Field' was the end of the Wars of the
Roses.   Similarly in Drayton we read of Bosworth:
. . . . "the last of that long war
Entitled by the name of York and Lancaster."   G.

May clime Parnassus, in the dayes of peace.[1]

    The King[2]—whose eyes were neuer fully clos'd,
Whose minde opprest, with feareful dreames sup-
        pos'd
That he in blood had wallow'd all the night—
Leaps from his restlesse bed, before the light :
Accursèd Tirell[3] is the first he spies
Whom threatning with his dagger, thus he cries ;
' How dar'st thou, villaine, so disturbe my sleepe,
Were not the smother'd children buried deepe ?

---

1 Christopher Brooke in his remarkable " Ghost of
Richard III[d]." puts a like compliment to James into the
mouth of the dying king :
    " Now England's chaos was reduc't to order
      By god-like Richmond whose successive stems
    The hand of Time hath brancht, in curious border,
      Unto the mem'rie of thrice-royall James :
    An angel's trumpe be his true fame's recorder,
      And may that Brittaine Phœbus from his beames,
    In glorie's light his in-fluence extend
      His offspring countles ; peace, nor date, nor end."
      (Collier's reprint : [1844] Shakespeare Society) G.
2 Richard III.   G.
3 Christopher Brooke, as before, thus refers to the
infamous Sir James Tyrrell, by whom the princes in the
Tower were murdered :
    —" Of this ranke one Tyrell, I did frame
    To doe this deed, whose horror wants a name."
(p 48) Cf. Sir Thomas More's History of Henry VII. G.

And hath the ground againe beene ript by thee,
That I their rotten carkases might see?
The wretch astonisht, hastes away to slide,
—As damnèd ghosts themselues in darkenesse
    hide—
And calls vp three, whose counsels could asswage
The sudden swellings of the prince's rage:
Ambitious Louell,[1] who to gaine his grace,
Had stain'd the honour of his noble race:
Perfidious Catesby,[2] by whose curious skill,
The Law was taught to speak his Master's will:
And Ratcliffe,[3] deepely learn'd in courtly art,

---

1 Francis, Lord Lovell, created Viscount by Richard III, to whom he was chamberlain. See Notes and Queries 2nd Series, vi, 396; vii, 17; xii, 234; 3d Series ix. 523. G.

2 Sir William Catesby, executed after Bosworth. Brooke, as before, makes Richard thus delineate him:
"My blood-hound Catesby foyl'd him in the chase,
Who, earst by him being rais'd, cherisht and bred
    Knowing himselfe too weake to stand for right
    Proves treacherously wise, and friend to might:
(p 36) G.

3 Sir Richard Ratcliffe, like Catesby, a Privy-councillor. It is to Ratcliffe and Catesby, and Lovell, the popular distich of the time referred:
    "The rat, the cat, and Lovell the dog
    Rule all England under the hog"
The 'hog' is an allusion to Richard's crest of the boar, on which see onward. G.

Who best could search into his Sou'raigne's hart;
Affrighted Richard, labours to relate
His hideous dreames, as signes of haplesse Fate:
' Alas '—said they—' such fictions children feare,
These are not terrors, shewing danger neare,
But motiues sent by some propitious power,
To make you watchfull at this early hower;
These proue that your victorious care preuents,[1]
Your slouthfull foes, that slumber in their tents;
This precious time must not in vaine be spent,
Which God—your helpe—by heau'nly meanes
    hath lent.'
He—by these false coniectures—much appeas'd,
Contemning fancies, which his minde diseas'd,[2]
Replies : ' I should haue been asham'd to tell
Fond[3] dreames to wise men: whether Heau'n or
    Hell,
Or troubled Nature these effects hath wrought,
I know, this day requires another thought;
If some resistlesse strength my cause should crosse,
Feare will increase, and not redeeme the losse:
All dangers, clouded with the mist of feare,

---

1 Anticipates. G.

2 = dis-cased or disturbed. Cf. our Phineas Fletcher,
Vol. iii. page 194.

3 Foolish. G.

Seeme great farrè off, but lessen comming neare.
Away, ye blacke illusions of the night,
If ye combin'd with Fortune, haue the might
To hinder my designes : ye shall not barre
My courage, seeking glorious death in Warre.'
Thus being chear'd, he calles aloud for armes,
And bids that all should rise, whom Morpheus
    charmes.
' Bring me '—saith he—' the harnesse that I wore
At Teuxbury,[1] which from that day no more
Hath felt the battries of a ciuill strife,
Nor stood betweene destruction and my life.'
Vpon his brest-plate he beholds a dint,
Which in that field young Edward's sword did
    print :
This stirres remembrance of his heinous guilt,
When he, that prince's blood so foulely spilt.
Now fully arm'd, he takes his helmet bright,
Which like a twinkling starre, with trembling
    light
Sends radiant lustre through the darksome aire ;
This maske will make his wrinkled visage faire.
But when his head is couer'd with the steele,
He telles his seruants, that his temples feele
Deepe-piercing stings, which breed vnusuall paines,

---

1 Tewkesbury. G.

And of the heauy burden much complaines.
Some marke his words, as tokens fram'd t' expresse
The sharpe conclusion of a sad successe.
Then going forth, and finding in his way
A souldier of the Watch, who sleeping lay ;
Enrag'd to see the wretch neglect his part,
He strikes a sword into his trembling heart ;
The hand of death, and iron dulnesse takes
Those leaden eyes, which nat'rall ease forsakes :
The King this morning sacrifice commends,
And for example, thus the fact[1] defends ;
I leaue him as I found him, fit to keepe
The silent doores of euerlasting Sleepe.[2]

   Still Richmond[3] slept : for wordly care and feare
Haue times of pausing, when the soule is cleare,
While Heaun's Directer, Whose reuengefull[4] brow
Would to the guilty head no rest allow,
Lookes on the other part with milder eyes :
At His command an angell swiftly flies
From sacred Truth's perspicuous[5] gate, to bring

---

1 Deed. Cf. our edn. of Joseph Fletcher, page 15. **G.**

2 **A** reminiscence and reproduction of a well-known classical incident, variously assigned. **G.**

3 Earl of Richmond, after Bosworth, Henry VII. **G.**

4 = Avenging. **G.**

5 = transparent. Cf. Troilus and Cressida i. 3. **G.**

A crystall vision on his golden wing.
This lord thus sleeping, thought he saw and knew
His lamblike vnkle, whom that tiger slew,
Whose powerfull words encourage him to fight:
' Goe on iust scourge of murder, Vertue's light,
The combate which thou shalt this day endure,
Makes England's peace for many ages sure,
Thy strong inuasion cannot be withstood,
The earth assists thee with the cry of blood,
The heau'n shall blesse thy hopes, and crowne
    thy ioyes,
See how the fiends with loud and dismall noyse,
—Presaging vultures, greedy of their prey—
On Richard's tent their scaly wings display.'
The holy King then offer'd to his view
A liuely[1] tree, on which three branches grew:
But when the hope of fruit had made him glad,
All fell to dust: at which the Earle was sad;
Yet comfort comes againe, when from the roote
He sees a bough into the North to shoote,
Which nourisht there, extends it selfe from thence
And girds this Iland with a firme defence:
There he beholds a high and glorious Throne,
Where sits a king by lawrell garlands knowne,

---

1 =living. Consult Mr W. A. Wright's inestimable
Bible Word-Book s. v. G.

Like bright Apollo in the Muses' quires,
His radiant eyes are watchfull heauenly fires,
Beneath his feete pale Enuie bites her chaine,
And snaky Discord whets her sting in vaine.
'Thou   seest'—said Henry—'wise and potent
      Iames,[1]
This, this is he, whose happy Vnion tames
The sauage feudes, and shall those lets[2] deface,
Which keepe the Bord'rers from a deare imbrace ;
Both nations shall in Britaine's royall crowne,
Their diff'ring names, the signes of faction drowne ;
The siluer streames which from this spring increase,
Bedew all Christian hearts with drops of peace ;
Obserue how hopefull Charles[3] is borne t' asswage
The winds that would disturbe this golden age.
When that great king shall full of glory leaue
The earth as base, then may this prince receiue
The diadem, without his father's wrong,
May take it late, and may possesse it long ;
Aboue all Europe's princes shine thou bright,
O God's selected care, and man's delight.'
Here gentle sleepe forsooke his clouded browes,
And full of holy thoughts, and pious vowes,
He kist the ground assoone as he arose,

---

1 James VI of Scotland, Ist of England. G.
2 Hindrances. G.   3 Charles Ist. G.

When watchfull Digby,[1] who among his foes
Had wanderd vnsuspected all the night,
Reports that Richard is prepared to fight.

   Long since the King had thought it time to send
For trusty Norfolke,[2] his vndaunted friend,
Who hasting from the place of his abode,
Found at the doore, a world of papers strow'd ;
Some would affright him from the tyrant's aide,
Affirming that his master was betray'd ;
Some laid before him all those bloody deeds,
From which a line of sharp reuenge proceeds
With much compassion that so braue a knight
Should serue a lord, against whom angels fight,
And others put suspicions in his minde,
That Richard most obseru'd,[3] was most vnkind.
The duke awhile these cautious words reuolues
With serious thoughts, and thus at last resolues ;
' If all the campe proue traytors to my lord,
Shall spotlesse Norfolke falsifie his word ;
Mine oath is past : I swore t'vphold his crowne,

---

1 Sir Simon Digby, Knt of Coleshill, c : Warwick, who
with his six valiant brothers contributed mainly to the
Earl of Richmond's success at Bosworth. See Burke's
Peerage *s. n.* G

   2 John, Lord Howard, created duke of Norfolk by
Richard III in 1483. G.

   3 = obeyed, served : frequent in Shakespeare. G.

And that shall swim, or I with it will drowne.
It is to late now to dispute the right ;
Dare any tongue, since Yorke[1] spread forth his
    light,
Northumberland,[2] or Buckingham[3] defame,
Two valiant Cliffords,[4] Roos,[5] or Beaumonts'
    name,[6]
Because they in the weaker quarrell die ?
They had the king with them, and so haue I.
But eu'ry eye the face of Richard shunnes,
For that vile murder of his brother's sonnes :
Yet lawes of knighthood gaue me not a sword
To strike at him, whom all with ioynt accord
Haue made my prince, to whom I tribute bring :
I hate his vices, but adore the king.
Victorious Edward, if thy soule can heare

---

1 Edward, duke of York, afterwards Edward IV. G.

2 Henry Percy, earl of Northumberland, slain at
Towton, 29th March, 1461. G.

3 Humphrey Stafford, duke of Buckingham, slain at
Northampton, 10th July, 1460. G.

4 Lord Clifford, slain at the battle of St. Alban's 23d
May 1455, and his son, who fell at Towton. G.

5 Thomas Manners, Lord Roos, slain at Towton. G.

6 John Beaumont of Overton and his cousin John,
Viscount Beaumont, both slain at Northampton, and Lord
Beaumont slain at Towton. G.

Thy seruant Howard, I devoutly sweare,
That to haue sav'd thy children from that day,
My hopes on earth should willingly decay ;
Would Glouster then, my perfect faith haue tryed,
And made two graues, when noble Hastings[1] died.'
This said, his troopes he into order drawes,
Then double haste redeemes his former pause :
So stops the sayler for a voyage bound,
When on the sea he heares the tempests sound,
Till pressing hunger to remembrance sends,
That on his course his houshold's life depends :
With this he cleares the doubts that vext his
          minde,
And puts his ship to mercy of the winde.
    The duke's stout presence and couragious lookes,
Were to the king as falls of sliding[2] brookes,
Which bring a gentle and delightfull rest
To weary eyes, with grieuous care opprest :
He bids that Norfolke and his hopefull sonne,[3]

---

1 Edward, Lord Hastings, put to death by Richard
III. Brooke, as before, thus speaks of Hastings through
Richard :
    " Now good Lord Hastings, great in all mens' grace
    —Of th' adverse faction, fautor and chiefe head
    I heav'd at, and remov'd. (p 36). G.
    2 Cf. our Phineas Fletcher iii. 199, 240. G.
    3 Thomas Howard, earl of Surrey. On the accession
of Henry VII, he was committed to the tower, where he

        C

—Whose rising fame in armes this day begun—
Should leade the vantguard : for so great command,
He dare not trust in any other hand ;
The rest he to his owne aduice referres,
And as the spirit, in that body stirres ;
Then putting on his crowne, a fatall signe,
—So offer'd beasts neere death in garlands shine—
He rides about the rankes, and striues t' inspire
Each brest with part of his vnwearied fire ;
To those who had his brother's seruants been,
And had the wonders of his valour seene,
He saith : ' My fellow-souldiers, though your
          swords
Are sharpe, and need not whetting by my words ;
Yet call to minde those many glorious dayes,
In which we treasur'd up immortall prayse ;
If when I seru'd, I euer fled from foe,
Fly ye from mine, let me be punisht so :
But if my father, when at first he try'd,
How all his sonnes, could shining blades abide,
Found me an eagle, whose vndazled eyes

---

remained for about three years and a half : but in 1489 he
was restored to his earldom, of which he had been de-
prived by attainder.   On the 9th of September, 1513, he
defeated the gallant James IV of Scotland, at Flodden ;
for which he was restored to the dukedom of Norfolk.
He died 21st May, 1524.   G.

Affront the beames, which from the steele arise,
And if I now in action, teach the same,
Know then, ye haue but chang'd your gen'rall's
 name;
Be still your selues, ye fight against the drosse
Of those, that oft haue runne from you with losse :
How many Somersets,[1]—Dissention's brands !—
Haue felt the force of our reuengefull hands !
From whome this youth, as from a princely floud,
Deriues his best, yet not vntainted bloud ;
Haue our assaults made Lancaster to droupe ?
And shall this Welshman with his ragged troupe,
Subdue the Norman, and the Saxon line,
That onely Merlin may be thought diuine ?
See what a guide, these fugitiues haue chose !
Who bred among the French, our ancient foes,
Forgets the English language, and the ground,
And knowes not what our drums and trumpets
 sound.'
To others' minds, their willing othes he drawes,
He tells his iust decrees, and healthfull lawes,
And makes large proffers of his future grace.
Thus hauing ended, with as chearefull face,
As Nature, which his stepdame still was thought,

---

1 Edmund Beaufort, duke of Somerset, beheaded after
the battle of Tewkesbury, May 1471. G.

Could lend to one, without proportion wrought,—
Some with loud shouting, make the valleyes ring,
But most with murmur sigh : 'God saue the King.'
    Now carefull Henry sends his seruant Bray[1]
To Stanl[e]y[2] who accounts it safe to stay,
And dares not promise, lest his haste should bring
His sonne to death, now pris'ner with the Kiug.
About the same time, Brakenbury[3] came,
And thus, to Stanley saith, in Richard's namc :
' My Lord, the King salutes you, and commands
That to his ayde, you bring your reddy bands,
Or else he sweares by Him that sits on high,
Before the armies ioyne, your sonne shall die'.
At this the lord stood, like a man that heares
The Iudge's voyce, which condemnation beares :
Till gath'ring vp his spirits he replies :
My fellow Hastings' death hath made me wise,
More then my dreame could him, for I no more
Will trust the tushes[4] of the angry bore ;[5]

---

1 Sir Reginald Bray, steward to the countess of Richmond.   See Nichols' Leicestershire and Gentleman's
Magazine 1789 Vol lxix.   G.

2 Thomas, Lord Stanley, afterwards earl of Derby :
died 1504.   G.

3 Sir Robert Brackenbury, Governor of the Tower.   G.

4 Tusks.   Curiously enough ' tushes ' is now the mother's name given to young children's first teeth.   G.

5 As before, the allusion is to the crest of Richard.   G.

If with my George's[1] bloud, he staine his throne,
I thanke my God, I haue more sonnes then one :
Yet to secure his life, I quiet stand,
Against the King not lifting vp my hand.'
The messenger departs, of hope deny'd.
Then noble Stanley, taking Bray aside,
Saith : ' Let my sonne proceede, without dispaire
Assisted by his mother's almes, and prayre ;
God will direct both him, and me to take,
Best courses, for that blessed woman's sake.'
The Earl by this delay, was not inclin'd,
To feare nor anger, knowing Stanleye's mind,
But calling all his chiefe commanders neare,
He boldly speakes, while they attentiue heare :
' It is in vaine, braue friends, to show the right
Which we are forc'd to seeke by ciuill fight.
Your swords are brandish't in a noble cause,
To free your country from a tyrant's iawes.
What angry planet ? what disastrous signe
Directs Plantagenet's afflicted line ?
Ah, was it not enough, that mutuall rage
In deadly battels should this race ingage,

---

1 George Stanley, Lord Strange, died before his father
in 1497 (?) The countess of Richmond, mother of Henry
VII. being married to Lord Stanley, her son George was
Henry's half-brother. G.

Till by their blowes themselves they fewer make,
And pillers fall, which France could neuer shake?
But must this crooked monster now be found,
To lay rough hands on that vnclosèd wound?
His secret plots haue much increast the flood;
He with his brothers' and his nephewes' blood,
Hath stain'd the brightnesse of his father's flowres,
And made his owne white Rose as red as ours.
This is the day whose splendour puts to flight
Obscuring clouds, and brings an age of light;
We see no hindrance of those wishèd times,
But this vsurper, whose depressing crimes
Will driue him from the mountaine where he stands,
So that he needs must fall without our hands.
In this we happy are, that by our armes,
Both Yorke and Lancaster reuenge their harmes.
Here Henrie's seruants ioyne with Edward's friends,
And leaue their priuat griefes for publike ends.'
Thus ceasing, he implores th' Almightie's grace,
And bids, that euery captaine take his place.
His speach was answer'd with a gen'rall noyse
Of acclamations, doubtlesse signes of ioyes:
Which souldiers vtterd, as they forward went,
The sure forerunners of a faire euent;
So when the Winter to the Spring bequeathes
The rule of time, and milde Fauonius breathes,
A quire of swans, to that sweet musicke sings,

The ayre resounds the motion of their wings,
When ouer plaines, they flie in orderd rankes,
To sport themselues, upon Caïster's[1] bankes,
    Bold Oxford[2] leades the vantguard vp amaine,
Whose valiant offers, heretofore were vaine,
When he his loue to Lancaster exprest,
But now, with more indulgent fortune blest,
His men he toward Norfolke's quarter drew,
And straight the one, the other's ensignes knew ;
For they in seu'rall armies, were display'd,
This oft in Edward's, that in Henrie's ayde :
The sad remembrance of those bloudy fights,
Incenst new anger, in these noble knights ;
A marish[3] lay betweene, which Oxford leaues
Vpon his right hand, and the sunne receiues
Behind him, with aduantage of the place :
For Norfolke must endure it on his face,
And yet his men, aduance their speares, and swords,
Against this succour, which the heau'n affords ;
His horse and foote possest the field in length,

---

1 Cayster. Cf. Homer's Iliad, ii., 461 ; and Virgil,
vii. 699, and Georg. i., 383. G.

2 This is the "warlike Vere" of this Poem, viz. John de
Vere, earl of Oxford, who commanded the van at Bosworth. G.

3 Marsh. Cf. Mr. W. A. Wright's ' Word-Book ' as
before, s. v. G.

While bowmen went before them, for their strength :
Thus marching forth, they set on Oxford's band ;
He feares their number ; and with strict command,
His souldiers closely to the standard drawes :
Then Howard's troupes amaz'd, begin to pause,
They doubt the slights[1] of battell, and prepare
To guard their valour with a trench of care.
This sudden stop made warlike Vere more bold
To see their fury in a moment cold ;
His rankes he in a larger forme displayes,
Which all were archers, counted in those dayes
The best of English souldiers ; for their skill
Could guide their shafts according to their will ;
The featherd wood they from their bowes let flie,
No arrow fell but caus'd some man to die ;
So painefull[2] bees, with forward gladnesse striue
To ioyne themselues in throngs before the hiue,
And with obedience, till that houre, attend,
When their commander shall his watchword send :
Then to the winds their tender sailes they yield,
Depress the flowres, depopulate the field :
Wise Norfolke, to auoyde these shafts the more,
Contriues his battaile thin and sharpe before ;

---

1 Sleights. Cf. our Phineas Fletcher, ii., 90, 93. 104,
142, 167, 187, 199 ; iv., 187, 199, 287, 308, 420. G.
 2 Painstaking. G.

He thus attempts to pierce into the hart,
And breake the orders of the adverse part,
As when the cranes direct their flight on high,
To cut their way, they in a trigon flie ;
Which pointed figure may with ease diuide
Opposing blasts, through which they swiftly glide.
  But now the wings make haste to Oxford's ayde ;
The left by valiant Sauage[1] was display'd:
His lusty souldiers were attir'd in white ;
They move like drifts of snow, 'whose sudden
    fright[2]
Constraines the weary passenger to stay ;
And beating on his face, confounds the way.
Braue Talbot[3] led the right, whose grandsire's
    name
Was his continuall spurre, to purchase fame :
Both these rusht in, while Norfolke, like a wall,
Which oft with engines crackt, disdaines to fall,
Maintains his station by defensiue fight,
Till Surrey, pressing forth, with youthfull might,
Sends many shadowes to the gates of death,
When dying mouths had gaspt forth purple breath :
His father followes : age and former paines

---

1 Sir John Savage, commanded the left wing. G.
2 Query = freight ? or is it ' flight ' or descent ? G.
3 Sir Gilbert Talbot commanded the right wing. G.

Had made him slower, yet he still retaines
His ancient vigour ; and, with much delight
To see his sonne do maruailes in his sight,
He seconds him, and from the branches cleaues
Those clusters, which the former vintage leaues.
Now Oxford flyes—as lightning—through his
    troupes,
And with his presence cheares that part that
  · droupes :
His braue endeuours Surreye's force restraine
Like bankes,[1] at which the ocean stormes in vaine.
The swords and armours shine as sparkling coales,
Their clashing drownes the grones of parting
    soules.
The peacefull neighbours, who had long desir'd
To find the causes of their feare expir'd,
Are newly grieu'd, to see this scarlet flood,
And English ground bedew'd with English blood.
Stout Rice and Herbert leade the power of Wales[2]
Their zeale to Henry, moues the hills and dales
To sound their country-man's belouèd name,
Who shall restore the British offspring's fame ;

---

1 Embankments. G.
2 Rice ap Thomas and Sir Walter Herbert. See
Shakespeare's Richard IIId., Act iv : scene 5. G.

These make such slaughter with their glaues[1] and
    hooks,[2]
That carefull bardes may fill their precious bookes
With prayses, which from warlike actions spring,
And take new themes, when to their harpes
    they sing.
Besides these souldiers borne within this Ile,
We must not of their part, the French beguile,
Whom Charles for Henrie's succour did prouide,[3]
A Lord of Scotland, Bernard,[4] was their guide,
A blossome of the Stuart's happy line,
Which is on Brittaine's throne ordain'd to shine :
The sun, whose rayes, the heau'n with beauty
    crowne,
From his ascending, to his going downe,
Saw not a brauer leader, in that age ;
And Bosworth field must be the glorious stage,
In which this Northerne eagle learnes to flie,
And tries those wings, which after raise him high,

---

1 Broad-swords. G

2 Curved instrument—long used in reaping grain. G.

3 Charles VIII., King of France, 1483—98, who had
assisted Henry in fitting out his expedition. G.

4 Bernard the renowned Lord D'Aubigny. He visited
the court of James more than once. He died at Edinburgh
in 1508 : and according to tradition was buried in Corstor-
phine Church, not far from Edinburgh. G

When he beyond the snowy Alpes renown'd,
Shall plant French lilies in Italian ground,
And cause the craggy Appenine to know,
What fruits on Caledonian mountaines grow.
Now in this ciuill warre, the troupes of France,
Their banners dare on English soil aduance,
And on their launces points, destruction bring,
To fainting seruants of the guilty King;
When heretofore they had no powre to stand
Against our armies in their natiue land,
But melting fled, as waxe before the flame,
Dismayd with thunder of Saint George's name.

Now Henry, with his vncle Pembroke[1] moues,
The rereward on; and Stanley then approues
His loue to Richmond's person and his cause;
He from his army of three thousand, drawes
A few choyse men, and bids the rest obay
His valiant brother, who shall proue this day
As famous as great Warwick, in whose hand,

---

1 Jasper Tudor, earl of Pembroke, afterwards Duke of
Bedford. He was a son of Catherine, widow of Henry
V., by her marriage with Owen Tudor, and uncle to
Henry VII. Drayton thus notices Pembroke:
"With him the noble earl of Pembroke, who commands
Their countrymen the Welsh,—of whom it mainly stands
For their great numbers found to be a greatest force." G.

The fate of England's crowne, was thought to
    stand :[1]
With these he closely steales to helpe his friend,
While his maine forces stirre not, but attend
The younger Stanley, and to Richard's eye
Appeare nót parties, but as standers by.
Yet Stanleye's wordes so much the King incense,
That he exclames, ' This is a false pretense :
His doubtfull answere shall not saue his sonne,
Yong Strange shall die : see, Catesby, this be
    done.'
Now like a lambe, which, taken from the folds,
The slaughter-man with rude embraces holds,
And for his throte prepares a whetted knife,
So goes this harmlesse lord, to end his life;
The axe is sharpen'd, and the blocke prepar'd,
But worthy Ferrers,[2] equall portion shar'd,
Of griefe and terrour which the pris'ner felt,
His tender eyes in teares of pitty melt,
And hasting to the King, he boldly said :
' My Lord, too many bloody staines are laid
By enuious tongues vpon your peacefull raigne,

---

1 Richard Nevile, the ' great ' earl of Warwick 1453-
70 : or Edward Plantagenet, son of George, duke of
Clarence. **G.**

2 Sir Walter Devereux, Lord Ferrers. G.

O may their malice euer speake in vaine :
Afford not this aduantage to their spite,
None should be kill'd to-day, but in the fight;
Your crowne is strongly fixt ; your cause is good ;
Cast not vpon it drops of harmelesse blood ;
His life is nothing, yet will dearely cost,
If while you seeke it, we perhaps haue lost
Occasions of your conquest ; thither flie,
Where rebels arm'd with cursèd blades shall die,
And yeeld in death to your victorious awe :
Let naked bands be censur'd[1] by the Law.'
Such pow'r his speech and seemely action hath
It mollifies the tyrant's bloody wrath,
And he commands, that Strange's death be stay'd.
The noble youth—who was before dismay'd
At Death's approaching sight—now sweetly cleares
His cloudy sorrowes, and forgets his feares.
As when a steare[2] to burning altars led,
Expecting fatall blowes to cleaue his head,
Is by the priest, for some religious cause
Sent backe to liue, and now in quiet drawes
The open ayre, and takes his wonted food,
And neuer thinkes how neere to death he stood :
  The King, though ready, yet his march delayd,
To haue Northumberland's expected ayde.

---

1 Adjudged. G.   2 Steer. G.

To him industrious Ratcliffe swiftly hies;
But Percy greetes him thus : ' My troubled eyes
This night beheld my father's angry ghost,
Advising not to ioyne with Richard's host :
Wilt thou '—said he—' so much obscure my shield,
To beare mine azure lion to the field
With such a gen'rall ? Aske him, on which side
His sword was drawne, when I at Towton¹ died.'
When Richard knew that both his hopes were
    vaine,
He forward set with cursing and disdaine,
And cries, ' Who would not all these lords detest
When Percy changeth, like the moone his crest ? '
This speech the heart of noble Ferrers rent :
He answers, ' Sir, though many dare repent,
That which they cannot now without your wrong,
And onely grieue they haue been true too long,
My brest shall neuer beare so foule a staine ;
If any ancient blood in me remaine,
Which from the Norman Conqu'rours tooke des-
    cent,
It shall be wholly in your seruice spent ;
I will obtaine to day aliue or dead,
The crownes that grace a faithfull souldier's head.'

---

1 This battle in which Edward IVth was victorious, was
fought on March 29th, 1461. G.

‘ Blest be thy tongue ’—replies the King—‘ in thee
The strength of all thine ancestors I see,
Extending warlike armes for England's good,
By thee their heire, in valour as in blood.’

But here we leaue the King, and must reuiew
Those sonnes of Mars, who cruell blades imbrue
In riuers sprung from hearts that bloodlesse lie,
And staine their shining armes in sanguine die.
Here valiant Oxford and fierce Norfolke meete,
And with their speares each other rudely greete ;
About the ayre the shiuerd pieces play,
Then on their swords their noble hands they lay,
And Norfolke first a blow directly guides
To Oxford's head, which from his helmet slides
Vpon his arme, and biting through the steele,
Inflicts a wound, which Vere disdaines to feele ;
He lifts his fauchion with a threatning grace,
And hewes the beuer off from Howard's face.
This being done, he with compassion charm’d,
Retires, asham’d to strike a man disarm’d :
But straight a deadly shaft sent from a bow,
—Whose master, though farre off, the Duke could
      know—
Vntimely brought this combat to an end,
And pierc’d the braine of Richard's constant friend.
When Oxford saw him sinke, his noble soule
Was full of griefe, which made him thus condole :

' Farewell, true knight, to whom no costly graue
Can giue due honour : would my teares might saue
Those streames of blood, deseruing to be spilt
In better seruice : had not Richard's guilt
Such heauy weight vpon his fortune laid,
Thy glorious vertues had his sinnes outwaigh'd.'
Couragious Talbot had with Surrey met,
And after many blowes begins to fret,
That one so young in armes should thus vnmou'd,
Resist his strength, so oft in warre approu'd.
And now the Earle beholds his father fall ;
Whose death, like horri'd darkenesse, frighted all :
Some giue themselues as captiues, others flie,
But this young lion casts his gen'rous eye
On Mowbraye's lion,[1] painted in his shield,
And with that king of beasts, repines to yeeld :
' The field '—saith he—' in which the lion stands,
Is blood, and blood I offer to the hands
Of daring foes ; but neuer shall my flight
Die blacke my lion, which as yet is white.'
His enemies—like cunning huntsmen—striue
In binding snares, to take their prey aliue,
While he desires t'expose his naked brest,

---

1 An allusion to the arms of the Dukes of Norfolk,
descended from the Mowbrays. G.

D

And thinkes the sword that deepest strikes, is
    best.
Young Howard single with an army fights;
When, mou'd with pitie, two renownèd knights,
Strong Clarindon,[1] and valiant Coniers[2] trie
To rescue him, in which attempt they dié;
For Sauage, red with blood of slaughter'd foes,
Doth them in midst of all his troopes inclose,
Where, though the captain for their safetie striues,
Yet baser hands depriue them of their liues;
Now Surrey fainting, scarce a sword can hold,
Which makes a common souldier grow so bold,
To lay rude hands vpon that noble flower;
Which, he disdaigning,—anger giues him power—
Erects his weapon with a nimble round,
And sends the peasant's arme to kisse the ground.
This done, to Talbot he presents the blade,
And saith, ' It is not hope of life hath made
This my submission, but my strength is spent;
And some, perhaps, of villaine blood, will vent
My weary soule: this fauour I demand,
That I may die by your victorious hand.'

---

1 Sir Richard Clarendon. **G.**

2 Sir William Coniers, or Conyers. These were two
of tho king's most courageous knights: they vowed to
rescue him or perish in the attempt. **G.**

' Nay, God forbid that any of my name '
—Quoth Talbot—' should put out so bright a
    flame
As burnes in thee—braue youth—where thou hast
    err'd,
It was thy father's fault, since he preferr'd
A tyrant's crowne before the iuster side.'
The Earle, still mindfull of his birth, replied,
' I wonder—Talbot—that thy noble hart
Insults on ruines of the vanquisht part :
We had the right, if now to you it flow,
The fortune of your swords hath made it so :
I neuer will my lucklesse choyce repent,
Nor can it staine mine honour or descent.
Set England's royall wreath vpon a stake,
There will I fight, and not the place forsake ;
And if the will of God hath so dispos'd,
That Richmond's brow be with the crowne in-
    clos'd,
I shall to him, or his, give doubtlesse signes
That duty in my thoughts, not faction, shines.'
The earnest souldiers still the chase pursue,
But their commanders grieue they should imbrue
Their swords in blood which springs from English
    veines ;
The peacefull sound of trumpets them restraines
From further slaughter, with a milde retreat,

To rest contented in this first defeate.

  The king intended, at his setting out,
To helpe his vantguard ; but a nimble scout
Runnes crying, ' Sir, I saw not farre from hence,
Where Richmond houers with a small defence,
And like one guilty of some heynous ill,
Is couer'd with the shade of yonder hill.'
The rauen, almost famisht, ioyes not more,
When restlesse billowes tumble to the shore
A heape of bodies shipwrackt in the seas,
Then Richard with these newes himselfe doth
    pleuse :
He now diuerts his course another way,
And with his army led in faire array,
Ascends the rising ground, and taking view
Of Henric's army, sees they are but few :
Imperiall courage fires his noble brest,
He sets a threatning speare within his rest,
Thus saying, 'All true knights on me attend,
I soone will bring this quarrell to an end;
If none will follow, if all faith be gone,
Behold, I goe to try my cause alone.'
He strikes his spurres into his horse's side,
With him stout Louell and bold Ferrers ride;
To them braue Ratcliffe, gen'rous Clifton haste,
Old Brakenbury scornes to be the last :
As borne with wings, all worthy spirits flye,

Resolu'd for safety of their prince to dye ;
And Catesby to this number addes his name,
Though pale with fear, yet ouercomne with shame.
Their boldnesse Richmond dreads not, but admires ;
He sees their motion like to rolling fires,
Which, by the winde, along the fields are borne
Amidst the trees, the hedges and the corne :
Where they the hopes of husbandmen consume,
And fill the troubled ayre with dusky fume.
Now as a carefull lord of neighb'ring grounds,
He keepes the flame from entering in his bounds ;
Each man is warn'd to hold his station sure,
Prepar'd with courage strong assaults t' endure ;
But all in vaine : no force, no warlike art,
From sudden breaking can preserue that part,
Where Richard, like a dart from thunder falles :
His foes giue way, and stand as brazen walles
On either side of his inforcèd path ;
While he neglects them, and reserues his wrath
For him whose death these threatning cloudes
        would cleare,
Who now with gladnes he beholdeth neere,
And all those faculties together brings,
Which moue the soule to high and noble things.
Eu'n so a tyger hauing follow'd long
The hunter's steps that robb'd her of her young :
When first she sees him is by rage inclin'd

Her steps to double, and her teeth to grind.
　　Now horse to horse, and man is ioyn'd to man
So strictly, that the souldiers hardly can
Their aduersaries from their fellowes know :
Here each braue champion singles out his foe.
In this confusion Brakenbury meetes
With Hungerford,[1] and him thus foulely greetes :
' Ah traytor, false in breach of faith and loue,
What discontent could thee and Bourchier[2] moue,
Who had so long my fellowes beene in armes,
To flie to rebels ? What seducing charmes
Could on your clouded minds such darknesse bring,
To serue an outlaw, and neglect the king ?'
With these sharpe speeches Hungerford enrag'd,
T' vphold his honour, thus the battaile wag'd :
'Thy doting age '—saith he—' delights in words,
But this aspersion must be try'd by swords.'
Then leauing talke, he by his weapon speakes,
And driues a blow, which Brakenbury breakes,
By lifting vp his left hand, else the steele
Had pierc'd his burgonet, and made him feele

---

1 "Stout Hungerford." Drayton. **G.**

2 "Braue Bourchier." Drayton. Sometimes the name
is written Boucher. Hungerford and Bourchier deserted
Brakenbury their leader, a little beyond Stony Stratford.
Brakenbury was killed by Hungerford at Bosworth. **G.**

The pangs of death: but now the fury fell
Vpon the hand that did the stroke repell,
And cuts so large a portion of the shield,
That it no more can safe protection yeeld.
Bold Hungerford disdaines his vse to make
Of this aduantage, but doth straight forsake
His massy target, render'd to his squire,
And saith : ' Let cowards such defence desire.'
This done, these valiant knights dispose their
    blades,
And still the one the other's face inuades,
Till Brakenburie's helmet giving way
To those fierce strokes that Hungerford doth lay,
Is brus'd and gapes ; which Bourchier, fighting
    neare,
Perceiues, and cries, ' Brave Hungerford, forbeare.
Bring not those siluer haires to timelesse end ;
He was, and may be once againe our friend.'
But oh too late ! The fatall blow was sent
From Hungerford, which he may now repent
But not recall, and digges a mortall wound
Into Brackenburie's head, which should be crown'd
With precious metals, and with bayes adorn'd
For constant truth appearing, when he scorn'd
To staine his hand in those young princes' blood,
And like a rocke amidst the ocean stood
Against the tyrant's charmes, and threats vnmoud

Though death declares how much he Richard
   lou'd.
Stout Ferrers aimes to fix his mighty launce
In Pembroke's heart, which on the steele doth
   glaunce,
And runnes in vaine the empty ayre to presse ;
But Pembroke's speare, obtaining wisht successe,
Through Ferrer's brest-plate and his body sinkes,
And vitall blood from inward vessels drinkes.
Here Stanley, and braue Louel trie their strength,
Whose equall courage drawes the strife to length,
They thinke not how they may themselues defend,
To strike is all their care, to kill their end.
So meete two bulls vpon adioyning hills
Of rocky Charnwood, while their murmur fills
The hollow crags, when striuing for their bounds,
They wash their piercing hornes in mutuall
   wounds.
   If in the midst of such a bloody fight,
The name of friendship be not thought too light,
Recount my Muse how Byron's faithfull loue[1]
To dying Clifton[2] did it selfe approue :

---

1 Sir John Byron, of Clayton, in Lancaster, knighted
by Henry VIII., died third May, 1488. See our Memorial-Introduction for a curious parallel in Byron's 'Childe
Harold,' c III. st, 29-30. G.
   2 "An interesting incident is montioned of Sir John

For Clifton fighting brauely in the troope,
Receiues a wound, and now begins to droope :
Which Byron seeing, though in armes his foe,
In heart his friend, and hoping that the blow
Had not been mortall, guards him with his shield
From second hurts, and cries, ' Deare Clifton, yeeld ;
Thou hither cam'st, led by sinister fate,
Against my first aduice, yet now though late,
Take this my counsell.'   Clifton thus replied :
' It is too late, for I must now prouide
To seeke another life : liue thou, sweet friend,
And when thy side obtains a happy end,
Vpon the fortunes of my children looke ;

Byron and Sir Gervaso Clifton, friends and neighbours in
Nottinghamshire.   Byron joined Henry ; Clifton fought
with Richard : they agreed that whichever party triumphed,
the supporter of that should intercede with the victor for
his friend's estate, for the benefit of his family.   In the
midst of the battle, Byron saw Clifton fall, in the opposite
ranks.   He ran to him, sustained him on his shield, and
entreated him to surrender.   Clifton faintly exclaimed,
' All is over : remember your promise : use all your
interest that my lands be not taken from my children ;'
and expired.   Byron performed this promise, and the
estate was preserved to the Clifton family.   Hutton's
Bos. Field, 117, 9.   There are grants to Clifton, in the
Harl. MSS. 433, as pp 81, 96."   Sharon Turner's History
of England (1839) Vol. vi. p 526 (note).   G.

Remember what a solemne oath we tooke,
That he whose part should proue the best in fight,
Would with the conqu'rour trie his vtmost might,
To saue the other's lands from rau'nous pawes,
Which seaze on fragments of a lucklesse cause.
My father's fall our house had almost drown'd,
But I by chance a boord in shipwracke found :
May neuer more such danger threaten mine,
Deale thou for them, as I would doe for thine.'
This said, his senses faile, and powr's decay,
While Byron calles ; ' Stay, worthy Clifton, stay,
And heare my faithfull promise once againe,
Which if I breake, may all my deeds be vaine.'
But now he knowes, that vitall breath is fled,
And needlesse words are vtter'd to the dead :
Into the midst of Richard's strength he flies,
Presenting glorious acts to Henrie's eyes,
And for his scruice he expects no more,
Then Clifton's sonne from forfeits to restore.

   While Richard bearing downe with eager mind,
The steps by which his passage was confin'd,
Laies hands on Henrie's standard as his prey;
Strong Brandon[1] bore it, whom this fatall day

---

1 Sir William Brandon, Henry's Standard-bearer,
father to Charles Brandon, created duke of Suffolk, by
Henry VIII. G.

Markes with a blacke note, as the onely knight,
That on the conqu'ring part forsakes the light.
But Time, whose wheels with various motion
    runne,
Repayes this seruice fully to his sonne,
Who marries Richmond's daughter, borne betweene
Two royall parents, and endowed a Queene,[1]
When now the King perceiues that Brandon striues
To saue his charge, he sends a blow that riues
His skull in twaine, and by a gaping hole,
Giues ample scope to his departing soule.
And thus insults; 'Accursed wretch, farewell,
Thine ensignes now may be display'd in hell :
There thou shalt know, it is an odious thing,
To let thy banner flie against thy King.'
With scorne he throwes the standard to the
    ground,
When Cheney[2] for his height and strength renown'd
Steps forth to couer Richmond, now expos'd
To Richard's sword : the King with Cheney clos'd,
And to the earth this mighty giant fell'd.
Then like a stag whom fences long with-held
From meddowes, where the Spring in glory raignes :

---

1 By marriage. G.

2 " Sir Ihon Cheinye, a man of great force and strength
by hym [Richard] manfully overthrowen. [Hall]. G.

—Now hauing leuell'd those vnpleasing chaines,
And treading proudly on the vanquisht flowres,
He in his hopes a thousand ioyes deuoures :—
For now no pow'r to crosse his end remaines,
But onely Henry, whom he neuer daines
To name his foe, and thinkes he shall not braue,
A valiant champion, but a yeelding slaue.
Alas! how much deceiu'd, when he shall find
An able body and couragious minde :
For Richmond boldly doth himselfe oppose
Against the King, and giues him blowes for
       blowes,
Who now confesseth with an angry frowne,
His riuall, not vnworthy of the crowne.

  The younger Stanley then no longer staid,
The Earle in danger needs his present aide,
Which he performes as sudden as the light :
His comming turnes the ballance of the fight.
So threatning clouds, whose fall the ploughmen
       feare,
Which long upon the mountaine's top appeare,
Dissolue at last, and vapours then distill
To watry showres that all the valley fill.
The first that saw this dreadfull storme arise,
Was Catesby, who to Richard loudly cries,
' No way but swift retreate your life to saue,

It is no shame with wings t' auoide the graue.'
This said, he trembling turnes himselfe to flie,
And dares not stay, to heare the King's replie,
Who scorning his aduice, so foule and base,
Returnes this answer with a wrathfull face ;
' Let cowards trust their horse's nimble feete,
And in their course with new destruction meete ;
Gain thou some houres to draw thy fearefull breath,
To me ignoble flight is worse then death.'
But at th' approach of Stanleye's fresh supply,
The King's side droopes : so gen'rous horses lie
Vnapt to stirre, or make their courage knowne,
Which vnder cruell masters sinke and grone.
There at his Prince's foote stout Ratcliffe dies,
Not fearing, but despairing, Louell flies,
For he shall after end his weary life
In not so faire, but yet as bold a strife.
The King maintaines the fight, though left alone :
For Henrie's life he faine would change his owne,
And as a lionesse, which compast round
With troopes of men, receiues a smarting wound
By some bold hand, though hinder'd and opprest
With other speares, yet slighting all the rest,
Will follow him alone that wrong'd her first :
So Richard pressing with reuengefull thirst,
Admits no shape, but Richmond's to his eye,

And would in triumph on his carcase die :[1]
But that great God, to whom all creatures yeeld
Protects His seruant with a heau'nly shield ;
His pow'r, in which the Earle securely trusts,
Rebates[2] the blowes, and falsifies the thrusts.
The King growes weary, and begins to faint,
It grieues him that his foes perceiue the taint :
Some strike him that till then durst not come neare,
With weight and number they to ground him beare,
Where trampled down, and hew'd with many
          swords
He softly vtter'd these his dying words ;
' Now strength no longer Fortune can withstand,
I perish in the center of my Land.'
His hand he then with wreathes of grasse infolds ;
And bites the earth : which he so strictly holds,

---

1 So Charles Alleyn in his " Redmoore or Bosworth "
(1638) :

> " He like a Bore—his bearing was a Bore
> A cognizance which with his mind agrees,—
> Broke up the rankes to Richmond's selfe, and tore
> Men up like trees."

                    (Nichols's Leicestershire, as before p 564). G.
2 = Beats back. Cf. remarks on ' rebate ' in Memorial-
Introduction to our Joseph Fletcher, pages 9—10. G.

As if he would haue borne it with him hence,
So loth he was to lose his right's pretence.[1]

---

1 Compare the end of Richard, as described by our
Poet, with Alleyn's, as before:

"And now to see him sinke: his eyes did make
A shot like falling starres: flash out and done:
Groaning he did a stately farewell take,
And in his night of death set like the sunne:
    For Richard in his West seem'd greater, than
    When Richard shin'd in the Meridian,
Three yeares he acted ill, these two houres well,
And with unmatchèd resolution strove:
He fought as bravely, as he justly fell.
As did the Capitoll to Manlius prove
    So Bosworth did to him, the monument
    Both to his glory and his punishment."   G.

Sacred Poems.

Sacred Poems.

VPON THE TWO GREAT FEASTS OF THE ANNUNCIATION AND RESURRECTION FALLING ON THE SAME DAY, MARCH 25TH, 1627.

HRICE happy day, which sweetly do'st combine
    Two hemispheres in th' Equinoctiall line :
The one debasing God to earthly paine,
The other raising man to endlesse raigne.
Christ's humble steps declining to the wombe,
Touch heau'nly scales erected on His tombe :
We first with Gabriel must this Prince conuay
Into His chamber on the marriage day,
Then with the other angels cloth'd in white,
We will adore Him in this conqu'ring night :
The Sonne of God assuming humane breath,
Becomes a subiect to His vassall Death.
That graues and Hell laid open by His strife.

May giue vs passage to a better life.
Sec for this worke how things are newly styl'd,
Man is declar'd, Almighty, God, a child ;
The Word made flesh, is speechlesse, and the Light
Begins from clouds, and sets in depth of night;
Behold the sunne eclips'd for many yeeres,
And eu'ry day more dusky robes He weares,
Till after totall darknesse shining faire,
No moone shall barre His splendor from the aire.
Let faithfull soules this double feast attend
In two processions : let the first descend
The temple's staires, and with a downe-cast eye
Vpon the lowest pauement prostrate lie ;
In creeping violets, white lilies, shine
Their humble thoughts, and eu'ry pure designe ;
The other troope shall climbe, with sacred heate,
The rich degrees[1] of Salomon's bright seate,
In glowing roses feruent zeale they beare,
And in the azure flowre de-lis appeare
Celestiall contemplations, which aspire
Aboue the skie, vp to th' immortall quire.

---

1 Steps = ascents.   See Mr. W. A. Wright's Biblo
Word-book, as before.   G.

OF THE EPIPHANY.

FAIRE Easterne starre, that art ordain'd
    to runne
    Before the sages, to the rising Sunne,
Here cease thy course, and wonder that the cloud
Of this poore stable can thy Maker shroud :
Ye heauenly bodies, glory to be bright,
And are esteem'd, as ye are rich in light :
But here on earth is taught a diff'rent way,
Since vnder this low roofe the Highest lay ;
Ierusalem erects her stately towres,
Displayes her windowes, and adornes her bowres ;
Yet there thou must not cast a trembling sparke :
Let Herod's palace still continue darke ;
Each schoole and synagogue thy force repels,
There Pride enthron'd in misty errours, dwels.
The temple, where the priests maintaine their
    quire,
Shall taste no beame of thy celestiall fire ;
While this weake cottage all thy splendor takes,
A joyfull gate of eu'ry chinke it makes.
Here shines no golden roofe, no iu'ry staire,
No king exalted in a stately chaire,
Girt with attendants, or by heralds styl'd,
But straw and hay inwrap a speechlesse child :
Yet Sabae's lords before this Babe vnfold

Their treasures, off'ring incense, myrrh and gold.
The cribbe becomes an altar ; therefore dies
No oxe nor sheepe ; for in their fodder lies
The Prince of Peace, who thankfull for His bed,
Destroyes those rites, in which their blood was
    shed :
The quintessence of earth, He takes and fees,[1]
And precious gummes distill'd from weeping trees :
Rich metals and sweet odours now declare
The glorious blessings, which His lawes prepare
To cleare vs from the base and lothsome flood
Of sense, and make vs fit for angels' food,
Who lift to God for vs the holy smoke
Of feruent pray'rs, with which we Him inuoke,
And trie our actions in that searching fire,
By which the seraphims our lips inspire :
No muddy drosse pure min'ralls shall infect,

---

1 Dr. George Macdonald, in ' Antiphon ' as before, asks
" Should this be " *in* fees ;" that is, in acknowledgemement
of His feudal sovreignty ?" (p 143) But the technical
term proper would be ' in *fee* '. The rhyme might necessi-
tate ' in fees.' Perhaps ' *and* fees ' is really the Poet's
idea. He describes a two-fold act, taking *and* taking as
' in fee.' The allusion may be as Dr. Macdonald suggests, albeit a corruption must be very evident to warrant
change of au author's text. **G.**

We shall exhale our vapours vp direct :
No stormes shall crosse, nor glitt'ring lights deface
Perpetuall sighes, which seeke a happy place.

OF THE TRANSFIGURATION OF OUR LORD.

EE that in lowly valleyes weeping sate,
 And taught your humble soules to mourne
  of late
For sinnes, and suff'rings breeding griefes and
 feares,
And made the riuers bigger with your teares ;
Now cease your sad complaints, till fitter time,
And with those three belou'd Apostles clime
To lofty Thabor, where your happy eyes
Shall see the Sunne of glory brightly rise :
Draw neere, and euer blesse that sacred hill,
That there no heate may parch, no frost may kill
The tender plants, nor any thunder blast
That top, by which all mountaines are surpast.
By steepe and briery paths ye must ascend :
But if ye know to what high scope ye tend,
No let[1] nor danger can your steps restraine,

---

1 Hindrance or obstacle. G.

The crags will easie seeme, the thickets plaine.
Our Lord there stands, not with His painefull crosse
Laid on His shoulders, mouing you to losse
Of precious things or calling you to beare
That burden, which so much base worldlings feare.
Here are no promist hopes obscur'd with clouds,
No sorrow with dim vailes true pleasure shrowds,
But perfect ioy, which here discouer'd shines,
To taste of heauenly light your thoughts inclines,
And able is to weane deluded mindes
From fond[1] delight, which wretched mortals
    blinds :
Yet let not sense so much your reason sway,
As to desire for euer here to stay,
Refusing that sweet change which God prouides,
To those whom with His rod and staffe He guides :
Your happinesse consists not now alone
In those high comforts which are often throwne
In plenteous manner from our Sauiour's hand,
To raise the fall'n, and cause the weake to stand :
But ye are blest, when being trodden downe,
Ye taste His cup, and weare His thorny Crowne.

---

1 Foolish. G.

ON ASCENSION DAY.

E that to heau'n direct your curious eyes,
    And send your minds to walk the spac-
      ious skies,
See how the Maker to your selues you brings,
Who sets His noble markes on meanest things :
And hauing man aboue the angels plac'd,
The lowly earth more then the heau'n hath grac'd.
Poore clay, each creature Thy degrees admires ;
First, God in thee a liuing soule inspires,
Whose glorious beames hath made thee farre more
    bright,
Then is the sunne, the spring of corp'rall light :
He rests not here, but to Himselfe thee takes,
And thee diuine by wondrous vnion makes.
What region can afford a worthy place
For His exalted flesh ? Heau'n is too base,
He scarce would touch it in His swift ascent,
The orbes fled backe—like Iordan—as He went :
And yet He daign'd to dwell a while on earth,
As paying thankefull tribute for His birth :
But now this body all God's workes excels,
And hath no place, but God, in Whom it dwels.

AN ODE OF THE BLESSED TRINITIE.

VSE, that art dull and weake,
  Opprest with worldly paine,
  If strength in thee remaine.
Of things diuine to speake :
Thy thoughts awhile from vrgent eares restraine,
And with a cheareful voice-thy wonted silence
  breake.

  No cold shall thee benumme,
  Nor darknesse taint thy sight ;
  To thee new heate, new light,
  Shall from this obiect come,
 Whose praises if thou now wilt sound aright,
My pen shall giue thee leaue hereafter to be dumbe.

  Whence shall we then begin
  To sing, or write of this,
  Where no beginning is ?
  Or if we enter in,
 Where shall we end ? The end is endlesse blisse ;
Thrice happy we, if well so rich a thread we spinne.

  For Thee our strings we touch,
  Thou that are Three, and One,
  Whose essence though vnknowne

Beleeu'd is to be such ;   .
To Whom what ere we giue, we giue Thine owne,
And yet no mortall tongue can giue to Thee so
    much.

See how in vayne we trie
To find some tipe, t'agree
With this great One in Three,
Yet can none such descrie ;
If any like, or second were to Thee,
Thy hidden nature then were not so deepe and high.

Here faile inferiour things ;
The sunne whose heate and light
Make creatures warme and bright,
A feeble shadow brings :
The sunne shewes to the world his Father's might.
With glorious raies, from both our fire—the spirit—
    springs.

Now to this toplesse hill,
Let vs ascend more neare,
Yet still within the spheare
Of our connat'rall skill,
We may behold how in our soules we beare
An vnderstanding pow'r, ioyn'd with effectuall will.

We can no higher goe
To search this point diuine ;

Here it doth chiefly shine,
This image must it show :
These steppes as helpes our humble minds incline,
T" embrace those certaine grounds, which from true
    faith must flow.

To Him these notes direct,
Who not with outward hands,
Nor by His strong commands,
Whence creatures take effect :
While perfectly Himselfe He vnderstands,
Begets another selfe, with equall glory deckt.

From these, the spring of loue,
The Holy Ghost proceeds,
Who our affection feeds,
With those cleare flames which moue
From that eternall essence which them breeds,
And strikes into our soules, as lightning from aboue.

Stay, stay, Parnassian girle,
Heere thy descriptions faint,
Thou humane shapes canst paint,
And canst compare to pearle
White teeth, and speak of lips which rubies taint,
Resembling beauteous eies to orbs that swiftly whirle.

But now thou mayst perceiue
The weakenesse of thy wings ;

And that thy noblest strings
To muddy obiects cleaue :
Then praise with humble silence heau'nly things,
And what is more then this, to still deuotion leaue.

A DIALOGUE BETWEENE THE WORLD,
A PILGRIM, AND VERTUE.

PILGRIM.

HAT darknes clouds my senses? Hath the
    day
    Forgot his season, and the sunne his way?
Doth God withdraw His all-sustaining might,
And works no more with His faire creature Light,
While heau'n and earth for such a losse com-
    plaine,
And turne to rude vnformèd heapes againe?
My paces with intangling briers are bound,
And all this forrest in deepe silence drownd ;
Here must my labour and my iourney cease,
By which in vaine I sought for rest and peace :
But now perceiue that man's vnquiet mind,
In all his waies can only darkenesse find.
Here must I starue and die, vnlesse some light
Point out the passage from this dismall night.

WORLD.

Distressèd pilgrim, let not causelesse feare
Depresse thy hopes, for thou hast comfort neare,
Which thy dull heart with splendor shall inspire,
And guide thee to thy period of desire.
Cleare vp thy browes, and raise thy fainting eyes,
See how my glitt'ring palace open lies
For weary passengers, whose desp'rate case
I pitie, and prouide a resting place.

PILGRIM.

O thou whose speeches sound, whose beauties
        shine!
Not like a creature but some pow'r diuine,
Teach me thy stile, thy worth and state declare,
Whose glories in this desart hidden are.

WORLD.

I am thine end, Felicity my name;
The best of wishes, Pleasures, Riches, Fame,
Are humble vassals, which my throne attend,
And make you mortals happy when I send:
In my left hand delicious fruits I hold,
To feede them who with mirth and ease grow old;
Afraid to lose the fleeting dayes and nights,
They seaze on times, and spend it in delights.
My right hand with triumphant crownes is stor'd,
Which all the kings of former times ador'd:

These gifts are thine : then enter where no strife,
No griefe, no paine shall interrupt thy life.

VERTUE.

Stay, hasty wretch, here deadly serpents dwell,
And thy next step is on the brinke of Hell :
Wouldst thou, poore weary man, thy limbs repose ?
Behold my house, where true contentment growes :
Not like the baites, which this seducer giues,
Whose blisse a day, whose torment euer liues.

WORLD.

Regard not these vaine speeches, let them goe,
This is a poore worme, my contemnèd foe,
Bold thredbare Vertue ; who dare promise more
From empty bags, then I from all my store ;
Whose counsels make men draw vnquiet breath,
Expecting to be happy after death.

VERTUE.

Canst thou now make, or hast thou euer made
Thy seruants happy in those things that fade ?
Heare this my challenge, one example bring
Of such perfection ; let him be the king
Of all the world, fearing no outward check,
And guiding others by his voice or beck :
Yet shall this man at eu'ry moment find
More gall then hony in his restlesse mind.

Now monster, since my words haue struck thee
  dumb,
Behold this garland, whence such vertues come,
Such glories shine, such piercing beames are
  throwne,
As make thee blind, and turne thee to a stone.
And thou, whose wand'ring feet were running
  downe
Th'infernall steepenesse, looke vpon this crowne :
Within these folds lie hidden no deceits,
No golden lures, on which perdition waites :
But when thine eyes the prickly thornes haue past,
See in the circle boundlesse ioyes at last.

PILGRIM.

  These things are now most cleare, thee I imbrace :
Immortall wreath, let worldlings count thee base,
Choyce is thy matter, glorious is thy shape,
Fit crowne for them who tempting dangers scape.

AN ACT OF CONTRITION.

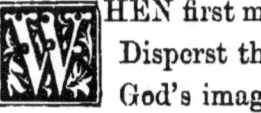HEN first my reason, dawning like the day,
        Disperst the clouds of childish sense away :
        God's image fram'd in that superior tow'r,
Diuinely drew mine vnderstanding pow'r
To thinke vpon His greatnesse, and to feare

His darts of thunder, which the mountaines teare.
And when with feeble light my soule began
T'acknowledge Him a higher thing then man,
My next discourse erected by His grace,
Conceiues Him free from bounds of time or place,
And sees the furthest that of Him is knowne,
All spring from Him, and He depends of none.
The steps which in His various workes are seal'd,
The doctrines in His sacred Church reueal'd,
Were all receiu'd as truths into my mind,
Yet durst I breake His lawes, O strangely blind :
My festring wounds are past the launcing cure
Which terrour giues to thoughts at first impure :
No helpe remaines these vlcers to remoue,
Vnlesse I scorch them with the flames of loue.
Lord, from Thy wrath my soule appeales, and flyes
To gracious beames of those indulgent eyes,
Which brought me first from nothing, and sustaine
My life, lest it to nothing turne againe,
Which in Thy Sonne's blood washt my parents'
    sinne,
And taught me waies eternall blisse to winne.
The starres which guide my bark with heau'nly
    calls,
My boords in shipwrack after many falls : [1]

---

1 Cf. Acts xxvii. 44.   G.

F

In these I trust, and wing'd with pleasing hope,
Attempt new flight to come to Thee, my scope,
Whom I esteeme a thousand times more deare,
Then wordly things which faire and sweet appeare.
Rebellious flesh, which Thee so oft offends,
Presents her teares : alas, a poore amends,
But Thou accept'st them.   Hence they precious
     grow,
As liuing waters which from Eden flow.
With these I wish my vitall blood may runne,
Ere new eclipses dimme this glorious sunne :
And yeeld my selfe afflicting paines to take
For thee my Spouse, and onely for Thy sake.
Hell could not fright me with immortall fire,
Were it not arm'd with Thy forsaking ire :
Nor should I looke for comfort and delight
In heau'n, if heau'n were shadow'd from Thy sight.

IN DESOLATION.

THOU, Who sweetly bend'st my stub-
          borne will,
Who send'st Thy stripes to teach, and not
     to kill !
Thy chearefull face from me no longer hide ;
Withdraw these clouds, the scourges of my pride ;

I sinke to hell, if I be lower throwne :
I see what man is, being left alone.
My substance, which from nothing did begin,
Is worse then nothing by the waight of sin :
I see my selfe in such a wretched state,
As neither thoughts conceiue, [n]or words relate.
How great a distance parts vs ! for in Thee
Is endlesse good, and boundlesse ill in mee.
All creatures proue me abiect, but how low
Thou onely know'st, and teachest me to know :
To paint this basenesse, Nature is too base ;
This darknesse yeelds not but to beames of grace.
Where shall I then this piercing splendor find ?
Or found, how shall it guide me, being blind ?
Grace is a taste of blisse, a glorious gift,
Which can the soule to heau'nly comforts lift :
It will not shine to me, whose mind is drown'd
In sorrowes, and with worldly troubles bound :
It will not daigne within that house to dwell,
Where drinesse raignes, and proud distractions
    swell.
Perhaps it sought me in those lightsome dayes
Of my first feruour, when few winds did raise
The waues, and ere they could full strength obtaine,
Some whisp'ring gale straight charm'd them downe
    again :
When all seem'd calme, and yet the virgin's Child

On my deuotions in His manger smild ;
  While then I simply walkt, nor heed could take
Of Complacence, that slye deceitfull snake ;
  When yet I had not dang'rously refus'd
So many calls to vertue, nor abus'd
  The spring of life, which I so oft enioy'd,
Nor made so many good intentions voyd ;
  Deseruing thus that grace should quite depart,
And dreadfull hardnesse should possesse my heart
  Yet in that state this onely good I found,
That fewer spots did then my conscience wound,
  Though who can censure,[1] whether in those times,
The want of feeling seem'd the want of crimes ?
  If solid vertues dwell not but in paine,
I will not wish that golden age againe
  Because it flow'd with sensible delights
Of heauenly things : God hath created nights
  As well as dayes, to decke the varied globe ;
Grace comes as oft clad in the dusky robe
  Of desolation, as in white attire,
Which better fits the bright celestiall quire.
  Some in foule seasons perish through despaire,
But more through boldnesse when the daies are
      faire.
  This then must be the med'cine for my woes,

---

1 Judge, decide. G.

To yeeld to what my Sauiour shall dispose :
To glory in my basenesse, to reioyce
In mine afflictions, to obey His voyce,
As well when threatnings my defects reproue
As when I cherisht am with words of loue,
To say to Him in eu'ry time and place,
' Withdraw Thy comforts, so thou leaue Thy grace.'

IN SPIRITUALL COMFORT.

NOUGH delight, O mine eternall good !
I feare to perish in this fiery flood :[1]
And doubt, lest beames of such a glorious
light
Should rather blind me, then extend my sight :
For how dare mortals here their thoughts erect
To take those ioyes, which they in heau'n expect ?
But God inuites them in His boundlesse love,
And lifts their heauy minds to things aboue.
Who would not follow such a pow'rfull guide

---

1 Is this a reminiscence of the passionate-hearted
Father ? " Restrain O Lord ! the floods of Thy grace !
My Saviour depart a little way from me : for it is not
possible for me to bear the torrents. of Thy consola-
tion "? G.

Immidst of flames, or through the raging tide?
What carelesse soule will not admire the grace
Of such a Lord, who knowes the dang'rous place
In which His seruants liue; their natiue woes,
Their weake defence, and fury of their foes :
And casting downe to earth these golden chaines,
From Hel's steepe brinke their sliding steps
    restraines?
His deare affection flies with wings of haste ;
He will not stay till this short life be past :
But in this vale where teares of griefe abound,
He oft with teares of ioy His friends hath drown'd.
Man, what desir'st thou? wouldst thou purchase
    health,
Great honour, perfect pleasure, peace and wealth?
All these are here, and in their glory raigne :
In other things these names are false and vaine.
True wisdome bids vs to this banquet haste,
That precious nectar may renew the taste
Of Eden's dainties, by our parents lost
For one poore apple, which so deare would cost,
That eu'ry man a double death should pay ;
But Mercy comes the latter stroke to stay,
And—leauing mortall bodies to the knife
Of Iustice—striues to saue the better life.[1]

---

1 Cf. our Phineas Fletcher, Vol. I. pp ccclii-ccclxi. G.

No sou'raigne med'cine can be halfe so good
Against destruction, as this angels' food,
This inward illustration, when it finds
A seate in humble, and indiff'rent[1] minds.
If wretched men contemne a sunne so bright,
Dispos'd to stray, and stumble in the night,
And seeke contentment where they oft haue
    knowne
By deare experience that there can be none :
They would much more neglect their God, their
    end,
If ought were found whereon they might depend,
Within the compasse of the gen'rall frame :[2]
Or if some sparkes of this celestiall flame
Had not ingrau'd this sentence in their brest :
In Him that made them is their onely rest.[3]

---

1 = unprejudiced, unbiassed. G.

2 As below, our Poet is here versifying one of the *memorabilia* of St. Augustine, on the fascinations of our world even as cursed and thorny. G.

3 " O Lord ! Thou hast made us for Thyself ; and our souls are restless until they rest in Thee." : St. Augustine. G.

AN ACT OF HOPE.

WEET Hope is soueraigne comfort of our
    life :
    Our ioy in sorrow, and our peace in
    strife :
The dame of beggers and the queene of kings :
Can these delight in height of prosp'rous things,
Without expecting still to keepe them sure ?
Can those the weight of heauy wants endure,
Vnlesse perswasion instant paine allay,
Reseruing spirit for a better day ?
Our God, who planted in His creature's brest,
This stop on which the wheeles of passion rest,
Hath rays'd by beames of His abundant grace,
This strong affection to a higher place.
It is the second vertue which attends
That soule, whose motion to His sight ascends.
Rest here, my mind, thou shalt no longer stay
To gaze vpon these houses made of clay :
Thou shalt not stoope to honours, or to lands,
Nor golden balles, where sliding fortune stands :
If no false colours draw thy steps amisse,
Thou hast a palace of eternall blisse,
A paradise from care, and feare exempt,
An obiect worthy of the best attempt.
Who would not for so rich a country fight ?

Who would not runne that sees a goale so bright ?
O Thou Who art our author and our end,
On Whose large mercy, chaines of hope depend ;
Lift me to Thee by Thy propitious hand,
For lower I can find no place to stand.

OF TEARES.

EHOLD what riuers feeble nature spends,
And melts vs into seas at losse of friends:
Their mortall state this fountaine neuer
dries,
But fills the world with worlds of weeping eies.
Man is a creature borne, and nurst in teares,
He through his life the markes of sorrow beares ;
And dying, thinkes he can no off'ring haue
More fit then teares distilling on his graue.
We must these floods to larger bounds extend ;
Such streames require a high and noble end.
As waters in a chrystall orbe contain'd
Aboue the starry firmament, are chain'd
To coole the fury of those raging flames,
Which eu'ry lower spheare by motion frames :
So this continuall spring within thy head,
Must quench the fires in other members bred.
If to our Lord our parents had been true,

Our teares had beene like drops of pleasing dew :
But sinne hath made them full of bitter paines,
Vntimely children of afflicted braines :
Yet they are chang'd, when we our sinnes lament,
To richer pearles, then from the East are sent.

OF SINNE.

HAT pencil shall I take, or where begin
To paint the vgly face of odious Sinne?
Man sinning oft, though pardon'd oft
    exceeds
The falling angels in malicious deeds :
When we in words would tell the sinner's shame,
To call him diuell is too faire a name :
Should we for euer in the chaos dwell,
Or in the lothsome depth of gaping hell :
We there no foule and darksome formes shall find
Sufficient to describe a guilty mind.
Search through the world, we shall not know a
    thing,
Which may to Reason's eye more horrour bring,
Then disobedience to the highest cause,
And obstinate auersion from His Lawes :
The sinner will destroy God, if He can.
O what hath God deseru'd of thee, poore man,

That thou should'st boldly striue to pull Him
    downe
From His high throne, and take away His crowne ?[1]
What blindnesse moues thee to vnequall fight ?
See how thy fellow creatures scorne thy might,
Yet thou prouok'st thy Lord, as much too great,
As thou too weake for His imperiall seate.
Behold a silly wretch distracted quite,
Extending towards God his feeble spite,
And by his poys'nous breath his hopes are faire
To blast the skies, as it corrupts the aire.
Vpon the other side thou mayst perceiue
A mild commander, to whose army cleaue
The sparkling starres, and each of them desires
To fall and drowne this rebell in their fires.
The cloudes are ready this proud foe to tame,
Full fraught with thunderbolts, and lightnings'
    flame.
The earth, his mother, greedy of his doome,
Expects to open her vnhappy wombe,
That this degen'rate sonne may liue no more,
So chang'd from that pure man, whom first she
    bore.

---

1 Jonathan Edwards of America, works out this idea
very grandly in several of his burning Sermons. Very
solemn and 'weighty' are his appeals to those who would
if they could 'pull God from His throne.' G.

The sauage beasts, whose names his father gaue,
To quell this pride, their Maker's licence craue.
The fiends his masters in this warlike way,
Make sute to seaze him as their lawfull prey.
No friends are left: then whither shall he flie ?
To that offended King, Who sits on high,
Who hath deferr'd the battell, and restrain'd
His souldiers like the winds in fetters chain'd :
For let the sinner leaue his hideous maske,
God will as soone forgiue, as he shall aske.

OF THE MISERABLE STATE
OF MAN.

S Man, the best of creatures, growne the
        worst ?
    He once most blessèd was, now most
        accurst :
His whole felicity is endlesse strife,
No peace, no satisfaction crownes his life ;
No such delight as other creatures take,
Which their desires can free, and happy make :
Our appetites, which seeke for pleasing good,
Haue oft their wane and full ; their ebbe and floud ;
Their calme and stormes : the neuer-constant moone,
The seas, and nimble winds not halfe so soone

Incline to change, while all our pleasure rests
In things which vary, like our wau'ring brests.
He who desires that wealth his life may blesse,
Like to a iayler, counts it good successe,
To haue more pris'ners, which increase his care ;
The more his goods, the more his dangers are :
This sayler sees his ship about to drowne,
And he takes in more wares to presse it downe.
Vaine honour is a play of diuers parts,
Where fainèd words and gestures please our hearts ;
The flatt'red audience are the actor's friends,
But lose that title when the fable ends.
The faire desire that others should behold,
Their clay well featur'd, their well temperd mould ;
Ambitious mortals make their chiefe pretence,
To be the objects of delighted sense :
Yet oft the shape and hue of basest things,
More admiration moues, more pleasure brings.
Why should we glory to be counted strong ?
This is the praise of beasts, the pow'r of wrong :
And if the strength of many were inclos'd
Within one breast, yet when it is oppos'd
Against that force, which Art or Nature frame,
It melts like waxe, before the scorching flame.
We cannot in these outward things be blest ;
For we are sure to lose them ; and the best
Of these contentments no such comfort beares,

As may waigh equall with the doubts and feares,
Which fixe our minds on that vncertaine day,
When these shall faile, most certaine to decay.
From length of life no happinesse can come,
But what the guilty feele, who after doome
Are to the lothsome prison sent againe,
And there must stay to die with longer paine.
No earthly gift lasts after death, but Fame ;
This gouernes men, more carefull of their name
Then of their soules, which their vngodly taste
Dissolues to nothing, and shall proue at last
Farre worse then nothing : prayses come too late,
When man is not, or is in wretched state.
But these are ends which draw the meanest hearts :
Let vs search deepe and trie our better parts :
O knowledge, if a heau'n on earth could be,
I would expect to reape that blisse in thee :
But thou art blind, and they that haue thy light,
More clearely know, they liue in darksome night.
See, man, thy stripes at schoole, thy paines abroad,
Thy watching, and thy palenesse well bestow'd :
These feeble helpes can scholers neuer bring
To perfect knowledge of the plainest thing :
And some to such a height of learning grow,
They die perswaded, that they nothing know.[1]

---

1 Socrates, Plato, Aristotle, and later than our Poet,
Newton in his fine modesty. G.

In vaine swift houres spent in deep study slide,
Vnlesse the purchast doctrine curbe our pride.
The soule perswaded, that no fading loue
Can equall her imbraces, seekes aboue :
And now aspiring to a higher place,
Is glad that all her comforts here are base.

OF SICKNESSE.

HE end of sicknesse, health or death declare
The cause as happy, as the sequels are.
Vaine mortals, while they striue their
sense to please,
Endure a life worse then the worst disease :
When sports and ryots of the restlesse night,
Breede dayes as thicke, possest with fenny light[1] :
How oft haue these — compell'd by wholsome
paine—
Return'd to sucke sweet Nature's brest againe,
And then could in a narrow compasse find
Strength for the body, clearenesse in the mind ?
And if Death come, it is not he, whose dart,
Whose scalpe and bones afflict the trembling heart :
—As if the painters with new art would striue

---

1 Qu : ignis fatuus ?　G.

For feare of bugs[1] to keepe poore men aliue—
But one, who from thy mother's wombe hath been
Thy friend and strict companion, though vnseene,
To lead thee in the right appointed way,
And crowne thy labours at the conqu'ring day.
Vngratefull men, why doe you sicknesse loath,
Which blessings giue in Heau'n, or Earth, or both ?

OF TRUE LIBERTY.

E that from dust of worldly tumults flies,
May boldly open his vndazled eyes,
To reade wise Nature's booke ; and with
delight
Surueyes the plants by day, and starres by night.
We need not trauaile, seeking wayes to blisse,
He that desires contentment, cannot misse :
No garden walles this precious flowre imbrace,
It common growes in eu'ry desart place.
Large scope of pleasure drownes vs like a flood,
To rest in little, is our greatest good.
Learne ye that clime the top of Fortune's wheele,
That dan'grous state which ye disdaine to feele :
Your highnesse puts your happinesse to flight,

---

1 Bug-bears : in the Puritans, fray-bugs.   G.

Your inward comforts fade with outward light ;
Vnlèsse it be a blessing not to know
This certaine truth, lest ye should pine for woe,
To see inferiours so diuinely blest
With freedome, and yourselues with fetters prest ;
Ye sit like pris'ners barr'd with doores and chaines
And yet no care perpetuall care restraines.
Ye striue to mixe your sad conceits with ioyes,
By curious[1] pictures, and by glitt'ring toyes,
While others are not hind'red from their ends,
Delighting to conuerse with bookes or friends,
And liuing thus retir'd, obtaine the pow'r
To reigne as kings, of euery sliding houre :
They walke by Cynthiae's light, and lift their eyes
To view the ord'red armies in the skies.
The heau'ns they measure with imagin'd lines,
And when the Northerne hemisphere declines,
New constellations in the South they find,
Whose rising may refresh the studious mind.
In these delights, though freedome show more high
Few can to things aboue their thoughts apply.
But who is he that cannot cast his looke
On earth, and reade the beauty of that booke ?
A bed of smiling flow'rs, a trickling spring,

---

1 See Mr. Wright's Bible Word-Book, as before.   G.

G

A swelling riuer, more contentment bring,
Then can be shadow'd by the best of Art:
Thus still the poore man hath the better part.[1]

AGAINST INORDINATE LOUE OF CREATURES.

H ! who would loue a creature ? who would
    place
His heart, his treasure in a thing so base ?
Which Time consuming, like a moth destroyes,
And stealing Death will rob him of his ioyes.
Why lift we not our minds aboue this dust ?
Haue we not yet perceiu'd that God is iust,
And hath ordain'd the obiects of our loue
To be our scourges, when we wanton proue ?
Go, carelesse man, in vaine delights proceed,
Thy fansies, and thine outward senses feede,
And bind thy selfe, thy fellow-seruants thrall :
Loue one too much, thou art a slaue to all.
Consider when thou follow'st seeming good,
And drown'st thy selfe too deepe in flesh and
    blood,

---

1 See our Memorial-Introduction for remarks on these
fine closing lines—together with parallels. G.

Thou making sute to dwell with woes and feares,
Art sworne their souldier in the vale of teares :
The bread of sorrow shall be thy repast ;
Expect not Eden in a thorny waste,
Where grow no faire trees, no smooth riuers swell ;
Here onely losses and afflictions dwell.
These thou bewayl'st with a repining voyce,
Yet knew'st before that mortall was thy choyse.
Admirers of false pleasures must sustaine
The waight and sharpenesse of insuing paine.

AGAINST ABUSED LOUE.

HALL I stand still, and see the world on
fire,
    While wanton writers ioyne in one
desire,
To blow the coales of loue, and make them burne,
Till they consume, or to the chaos turne
This beautious frame by them so foully rent ?
That wise men feare, lest they those flames pre-
    uent,[1]
Which for the latest day th'Almightie keepes
In orbes of fire, or in the hellish deepes.

---

1 Anticipate = hasten. G.

Best wits, while they possesst with fury, thinke
They taste the Muses' sober well, and drinke
Of Phœbus' goblet—now a starry signe—
Mistake the cup, and write in heat of wine.
Then let my cold hand here some water cast,
And drown their warmth, with drops of sweeter
　　taste;
Mine angry lines shall whip the purblind page,
And some will reade them in a chaster age;
But since these most diuine, I know,
How can I fight with loue, and call it so?
Is it not loue? It was not now:—O strange!—
Time and ill custome, workers of all change,
Haue made it loue: Men oft impose not names
By Adam's rule, but what their passion frames.
And since our childhood taught vs to approue
Our father's words, we yeeld and call it loue.
Examples of past times our deeds should sway,
But we must speake the language of to day:
Vse hath no bounds, it may prophane once more
The name of God, which first an idoll bore.
How many titles fit for meaner groomes,
Are knighted now, and marshal'd in high roomes!
And many which once good and great were thought,
Posterity, to vice and basenesse brought,
As it hath this of loue; and we must bow,
As States, vsurping tyrants' raignes allow,

And after-ages reckon by their yeeres :
Such force possession, though iniurious, beares ;
Or as a wrongfull title, or foule crime
Made lawfull by the statute for the time,
With reu'rend estimation blindes our eies,
And is call'd iust, in spite of all·the wise :
Then heau'nly Loue, this loathèd name forsake,
And some of thy more glorious titles take :
Sunne of the soule, cleare beauty, liuing fire,
Celestiall light, which dost pure hearts inspire,
While lust, thy bastard brother, shal be knowne
By Loue's wrong'd name, that louers may him
    owne.
So oft with hereticks such tearmes we vse,
As they can brooke, not such as we would chuse :
And since he takes the throne of Loue exil'd,
In all our letters he shall Loue be stil'd :
But if true Loue vouchsafe againe his sight,
No word of mine shall preiudice his right :
So kings by caution with their rebels treate,
As with free States, when they are growne too
    great.
If common drunkards onely, can expresse
To life the sad effects of their excesse :
How can I write of Loue, who neuer felt
His dreadfull arrow, nor did euer melt
My heart away before a female flame,

Like waxen statues, which the witches frame?
I must confesse if I knew one that had
Bene poyson'd with this deadly draught, and mad,
And afterward in Bedlem well reclaym'd
To perfect sence, and in his wits not maym'd:
I would the feruour of my Muse restraine,
And let this subiect for his taske remaine:
But aged wand'rers sooner will declare
Their Eleusinian rites, then louers dare
Renounce the deuil's pompe, and Christians die:
So much preuailes a painted idol's eye.
Then since of them, like Iewes, we can conuert
Scarce one in many yeeres, their iust desert,
By selfe confession, neuer can appeare;
But on presumptions wee proceed, and there
The Iudge's innocence most credit winnes:
True men trie theeues, and saints describe foule
      sinnes.
This monster, Loue by day, and Lust by night,
Is full of burning fire, but voyde of light;
Left here on earth to keepe poore mortals out
Of errour, who of Hell-fire else would doubt.
Such is that wandring nightly flame, which leades
Th'vnwary passenger, vntill he treades
His last step on the steepe and craggy walles
Of some high mountaine, whence he headlong
      falles.

A vapor, first extracted from the stewes,
—Which with new fewell still the lampe renewes—
And with a pandar's sulph'rous breath inflam'd,
Became a meteor, for destruction fram'd :
Like some prodigious comet which foretells
Disasters to the realme on which it dwells.
And now hath this false light preuail'd so farre ·
That most obserue[1] it as a fixèd starre,
Yea, as their load-starre ; by whose beames impure,
They guide their ships, in courses not secure ;
Bewitcht and daz'led with the glaring sight
Of this proud fiend, attir'd in angel's light ;
Who still delights his darksome smoke to turne
To rayes, which seeme t'enlighten, not to burne :
He leades them to the tree, and they beleeue
The fruite is sweete ; so he deluded Eue.
But when they once haue tasted of the feasts,
They quench that sparke, which seuers men from
    beasts,
And feele effects of our first parents' fall
Depriu'd of reason, and to sence made thrall.
Thus is the miserable louer bound

---

1 Misprinted 'obserue, it is a fixed starre.' The 'yea,
as their loadstarre' seems to shew a needed correction, as
in our text. G.

With fancies, and in fond[1] affection drown'd .
In him no faculty of man is seene,
But when he sighes a sonnet to his queene :
This makes him more then man, a poet fit
For such false poets, as make passion wit :
Who lookes within an emptie caske,[2] may see,
Where once a soule was, and againe may be ;
Which by this diffrence from a corse is knowne,
One is in pow'r to haue life, both haue none :
For louers slipp'ry soules—as they confesse,
Without extending racke, or straining presse—
By transmigration to their mistresse flow :
Pithagoras instructs his schollers so,
Who did for penance lustfull minds confine
To leade a second life in goates, and swine :
Then Loue is death, and driues the soule to dwell
In this betraying harbour, which like Hell
Giues neuer backe her bootie, and containes
A thousand firebrands, whips, and restlesse paines:
And which is worse, so bitter are those wheeles,
That many hells at once, the louer feeles,
And hath his heart dissected into parts,
That it may meete with other double harts.
This loue stands neuer sure, it wants a ground,
It makes no ordred course, it findes no bound,

---

1 Foolish. G.   2 Casket ? G.

It aymes at nothing, it no comfort tastes,
But while the pleasure, and the passion lasts.
Yet there are flames, which two hearts one can
        make,
Not for th' affections, but the obiect's sake ;
That burning glasse, where beames disperst, incline
Vnto a point, and shoot forth in a line.
This noble Loue hath axletree, and poles
Wherein it moues, and gets eternall goales :
These resolutions, like the heau'nly spheres,
Make all the periods equall as the yeeres :
And when this time of motion finisht is,
It ends with that great yeere of endlesse blisse.

A DESCRIPTION OF LOUE.

OUE is a region full of fires,
    And burning with extreme desires ;
    An obiect seekes, of which possest,
The wheeles are fixt, the motions rest,
The flames in ashes lie opprest :
This meteor striuing high to rise,
—The fewell spent—falles downe and dies.

Much sweeter, and more pure delights
Are drawne from faire alluring sights,

When rauisht minds attempt to praise
Commanding eyes, like heau'nly rayes ;
Whose force the gentle heart obayes :
Then where the end of this pretence
Descends to base inferiour sense.

Why then should louers—most will say—
Expect so much th'enioying day ?
Loue is like youth, he thirsts for age,
He scornes to be his mother's page :
But when proceeding times asswage
The former heate, he will complaine,
And wish those pleasant houres againe.

We know that Hope and Loue are twinnes ;
Hope gone, fruition now beginnes :
But what is this ? vnconstant, fraile,
In nothing sure, but sure to faile :
Which, if we lose it, we bewaile ;
And when we haue it, still we beare
The worst of passions, daily Feare.

When Loue thus in his center ends,
Desire and Hope, his inward friends
Are shaken off : while Doubt and Griefe,
The weakest giuers of reliefe,
Stand in his councell as the chiefe :

And now he to his period brought,
From Loue becomes some other thought.

These lines I write not, to remoue
Vnited soules from serious loue :
The best attempts by mortal made,
Reflect on things which quicky fade ;
Yet neuer will I men perswade
To leaue affections, where may shine
Impressions of the Loue diuine.

AN EXPRESSION OF SIBYLL'S ACROSTICHS.[1]

I n signe that iudgement comes, the Earth shall
· sweat :
E xpected times, behold the Prince, whose might
S hall censure[2] all within His kingdome great :
V ntrue and faithfull shall approach His sight,
S hall feare this God, by His high glory knowne,

---

1 Cf. Ovid: Met. 14, 104 *seqq* : 154: 15, 712: Virgil:
Aeneid vi., 10. G.
2 Judge, as before. G.

Combin'd with flesh, and compast with His saints ;
His words diuiding soules before His throne,
Redeeme the world from thornes and barren taints.
In vaine then mortals leaue their wealth, and sinne :
Strong force the stubborne gates of Hell shall tame :
The saints, though dead, shall light and freedome
    winne :

So thriue not wicked men, with wrathfull flame
Opprest : Whose beames can scarch their words
    and deeds ;
No darkesome brest can couer base desires ;
New sorrow, gnashing teeth, and wailing, breeds ;
Exempt from sunny rayes, or starry quires,

O heau'n thou art roll'd vp, the moone shall die ;
From vales He takes their depth, from hilles their
    height.

Great men no more arc insolent and high ;
On seas no nimble ships shall carry weight ;
Dire thunder arm'd with heat, the Earth confounds ;

Sweet springs and bubbling streames their course
    restraine ;
A heau'nly trumpet sending dolefull sounds,
Vpbraydes the World's misdeeds, and threatens
    paine :

𝕴 n gaping earth infernall depths are seenc ;
𝕺 ur proudest kings are summon'd by His call
𝖁 nto his seate ; from heau'n, with anger keene,
𝖄 euengefull floods of fire and brimstone fall.

VIRGIL. ECLOG. IV.[1]

ICILIAN Muses, sing we greater things,
     All are not pleas'd with shrubs and lowly
       springs;
More fitly to the consull,[2] woods belong :
Now is fulfild Cumæan sibyl's song :
Long chaines of better times begin againe ;[3]
The Maide[4] returnes, and brings backe Saturne's
     raigne,
New progenies from lofty Heau'n descend ;[5]
Thou chaste Lucina, be this Infant's friend,
Whose birth the dayes of ir'n shall quite deface,
And through the world the golden age shall place :[6]
Thy brother Phœbus weares his potent crowne,
And thou—O Pollio[7]—know thy high renowne ;

---

1 Cf. Pope's ' Messiah '. G.   2 Pollio, as onward. G.
3 Cf. Isaiah lxi. G.   4 Cf. Isaiah vii., 14. G.
5 Cf. Hesiod : Op. 256 et 109. G.
6 Cf. Isaiah ix., 6, 7. G.
7 Cf. Aeneid 6, 86 ; and 9. 47. G.

Thy consulship this glorious change shall breed,
Great moneths shall then endevour to proceed :
Thy rule the steps of threatning sinne shall cleare,
And free the Earth from that perpetuall feare :[1]
He with the gods shall liue,[2] and shall behold,
With heauenly spirits noble soules enroll'd,
And scene by them shall guide this worldly frame,
Which to His hand His father's strength doth
    tame.
To Thee—sweet child—the Earth brings natiue
    dowres,[3]
The wandring iuy,[4] with faire bacchar's[5] flowres,
And colocasia,[6] sprung from Egypt's ground,
With smiling leaues of greene acanthus crown'd ;
The gotes their swelling vdders home shall beare,
The droues no more shall mighty lions feare :[7]
For Thee, Thy cradle, pleasing flowres shall bring ;
Imperious Death shall blunt the serpent's sting ;

---

1 Cf. Isaiah lx., 18. **G.**   2 Cf. Hesiod, Op. 118. **G.**
3 Cf. Isaiah xxxv., 1 ; and lx., 13. **G.**
4 = ivy. **G.**
5 Baccar = βάκχαρις, a plant having a fragrant root, which produced a kind of oil. Is our abbreviation (vulgarly) 'bacca = tobacco, from this ? **G.**
6 = Casia, *i.e.* Laurus Cassia. **G.**
7 Cf. Isaiah xi., 6. **G.**

No herbes shall with deceitfull poyson flow,
And sweet amomum eu'ry where shall grow :
But when Thou able art to reade the facts[1]
Of worthies,[2] and thy father's famous acts,
To know what glories Vertue's name adorne,
The fields to ripenesse bring the tender corne ;[3]
Ripe grapes depend on carelesse brambles' tops,
Hard oakes sweat hony, form'd in dewy drops ;
Yet some few steps of former fraudes remaine,
Which men to trie, the sea with ships constraine,
With strengthening walles their cities to defend,
And on the ground long furrowes to extend ;
A second Tiphys, and new Argo then,
Shall leade to braue exploits the best of men ;
The warre of Troy that town againe shall burne,
And great Achilles thither shall returne :
But when firme age a perfect man Thee makes,
The willing sayler straight the seas forsakes,
The pine no more the vse of Trade retaines ;
Each countrie breeds all fruits, the Earth dis-
    daines
The harrowes weight, and vines the sickle's
    strokes;
Strong ploughmen let their bulls go free from
    yokes,

---

1 Deeds, as before. G   2 Cf. Isaiah vii. 16. G.
3 Cf. Isaiah lv., 13 ; et xxxv. 7. G.

Woolll feares not to dissemble colours strange,
But rammes their fleeces then in pastures change
To pleasing purple, or to saffron die,
And lambes turne ruddy, as they feeding lie.
The Fates—whose wills in stedfast end agree,
Command their wheeles to run such daies to see—
Attempt great honours, now the time attends ;
Deare Childe of gods, whose line from Ioue descends.
See how the world with weight declining lies ;
The Earth, the spacious seas, and archèd skies :
Behold againe, how these their griefe asswage
With expectation of the future age :
O that my life and breath so long would last
To tell Thy deeds ! I should not be surpast
By Thracian Orpheus, nor if Linus sing,
Though they from Phœbus and the muses spring :
Should Pan—Arcadia iudging—striue with me,
Pan by Arcadia's doome would conquer'd be.
Begin Thou, little Childe ; by laughter owne
Thy mother, who ten mon'ths hath fully knowne
Of tedious houres : begin, Thou little Childe,
On Whom as yet thy parents neuer smil'd ;
The God with meate hath not Thy hunger fed,
Nor goddesse laid thee in a little bed.[1]

---

1 Cf. Horace. Od. 4. 8. 30.   G.

Royal and Courtly Poems.

Royal and Courtly Poems.

ON THE ANNIUERSARY DAY OF HIS MAIESTIE'S REIGNE OUER ENGLAND MARCH THE 24. WRITTEN AT THE BEGINNING OF HIS TWENTIETH YEERE.[1]

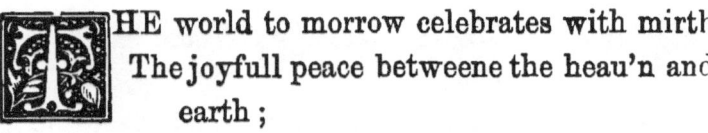

HE world to morrow celebrates with mirth
   The joyfull peace betweene the heau'n and
      earth ;
To day let Britaine praise that rising light, ─
Whose titles, her diuided parts vnite.
The time since Safety triumph'd ouer Feare,
Is now extended to the twenti'th yeere.
Thou happy yeere with perfect number blest,
O slide as smooth and gentle as the rest:
That when the sunne dispersing from his head,
The clouds of Winter on his beauty spred,

---

   1 James came to the Crown on the death of Elizabeth in 1603. G.

Shall see his equinoctiall point againe,
And melt his dusky maske to fruitfull raine,
He may be loth our climate to forsake,
And thence a patterne of such glory take,
That he would leaue the Zodiake, and desire
To dwell for euer with our northerne fire.

A THANKSGIUING FOR THE DELIUER-ANCE OF OUR SOUERAIGNE, KING IAMES, FROM A DANGEROUS ACCI-DENT, JANUARY 8.

GRACIOUS Maker, on Whose smiles or
frownes
Depends the fate of scepters and of crownes!
Whose hand not onely holds the hearts of kings,
But all their steps are shadow'd with Thy wings!
To Thee immortall thanks three sisters giue,
For sauing him, by whose deare life they liue.
First, England crown'd with roses of the Spring,
An off'ring like to Abel's gift will bring:
And vowes that she for Thee alone will keepe
Her fattest lambes and fleeces of her sheepe.
Next, Scotland triumphs, that she bore and bred
This Ile's delight; and wearing on her head

A wreath of lilies gather'd in the field,
Presents the min'rals which her mountaines yeeld.
Last, Ireland like Terpischore attir'd
With neuer-fading lawrell, and inspir'd
By true Apollo's heat, a pæan sings,
And kindles zealous flames with siluer strings.
This day a sacrifice of praise requires,
Our brests are altars, and our ioyes are fires.
That sacred head, so oft, so strangely blest
From bloody plots, was now—O feare!—deprest
Beneath the water, and those sunlike beames
Were threat'ned to be quencht in narrow streames.
Ah! who dare thinke, or can indure to heare
Of those sad dangers, which then seem'd so neare?
What Pan would haue preseru'd our flocks' increase
From wolues? What Hermes could with words of
    peace,
Cause whetted swords to fall from angry hands,
And shine the starre of calmes in christian Lands?
But Thou, Whose eye to hidden depths extends,
To shew that he was made for glorious ends,
Hast rays'd him by thine All-commanding arme,
Not onely safe from death, but free from harme.

TO HIS LATE MAIESTY, CONCERNING THE TRUE FORME OF ENGLISH POETRY.[1]

GREAT king, the sou'raigne ruler of this
  Land,
By whose graue care, our hopes securely
  stand :
Since you descending from that spacious reach,
Vouchsafe to be our Master, and to teach
Your English poets to direct their lines,
To mixe their colours, and expresse their signes :
Forgiue my boldnesse, that I here present
The life of Muses yeelding true content
In ponder'd numbers, which with ease I try'd,
When your iudicious rules haue been my guide.

 He makes sweet musick, who in serious lines,
Light dancing tunes, and heauy prose declines :
When verses like a milky torrent flow,
They equall temper in the poet show.
He paints true formes, who with a modest heart,
Giues lustre to his worke, yet couers art.[2]

---

1 James Ist., who it must be remembered had so early as
1584, published his "Essayes of a prentise, in the divine
art of poesie." References are made to this quaint and
still quick treatise by Beaumont, *supra*. **G.**

 2 "Ars est celare artem." **G.**

Vneuen swelling is no way to fame,
But solid ioining of the perfect frame :
So that no curious[1] finger there can find
The former chinkes, or nailes that fastly bind.
Yet most would haue the knots of stitches seene,
And holes where men may thrust their hands
  between.
On halting feet the ragged poem goes
With accents, neither fitting verse nor prose :
The stile mine eare with more contentment fills
In lawyers' pleadings, or phisicians' bills.
For though in termes of art their skill they close,
And ioy in darksome words as well as those :
They yet haue perfect sense more pure and cleare
Then enuious Muses, which sad garlands weare
Of dusky clouds, their strange conceits to hide
From humane eyes : and—lest they should be spi'd
By some sharpe Oedipus—the English tongue
For this their poore ambition suffers wrong.
In eu'ry language now in Europe spoke
By Nations which the Roman Empire broke,
The relish of the Muse consists in rime,
One verse must meete another like a chime.
Our Saxon shortnesse hath peculiar grace
In choice of words, fit for the ending place :

---

1 Skilful, as before. G.

Which leaue impression in the mind as well
As closing sounds, of some delightfull bell:
These must not be with disproportion lame,
Nor should an eccho still repeate the same.
In many changes these may be exprest:
But those that ioyne most simply, run the best:
Their forme surpassing farre the fettr'd staues,
Vaine care, and needlesse repetition saues.
These outward ashes keepe those inward fires,[1]
Whose heate the Greeke and Roman works inspires :
Pure phrase, fit epithets, a sober care
Of metaphors, descriptions cleare, yet rare,
Similitudes contracted smooth and round,
Not vext by learning, but with nature crown'd :
Strong figures drawne from deepe inuention's
        springs,
Consisting lesse in words, and more in things :
A language not affecting ancient times,
Nor Latine shreds, by which the pedant climes :
A noble subiect which the mind may lift
To easie vse of that peculiar gift,
Which poets in their raptures hold most deare,
When actions by the liuely sound appeare.
Giue me such helpes, I neuer will despaire,

---

1 " E'en in our ashes live their wonted fires." GRAY. G.

But that our heads which sucke the freezing aire,
As well as hotter braines, may verse adorne,
And be their wonder, as we were their scorne.

TO THE GLORIOUS MEMORY OF OUR LATE SOUERAIGNE LORD, KING IAMES.[1]

EEPE, O ye nymphes: that from your
      caues may flow
Those trickling drops, whence mighty
      riuers gow.[2]
Disclose your hidden store: let eu'ry spring
To this our sea of griefe some tribute bring:
And when ye once haue wept your fountaines dry,
The heau'n with showres will send a new supply.
But if these cloudy treasures prooue too scant,
Our teares shall helpe, when other moystures
      want.
This Ile, nay Europe, nay the World bewailes
Our losse, with such a streame as neuer failes.
Abundant floods from euery letter rise,

---

1 Died 27th March, 1625. G.

2 Misprinted 'flow' as in previous line: but corrected
contemporaneously in my copy, as above. G.

When we pronounce, great Iames, our soueraigne
    dies.
And while I write these words, I trembling stand,
A sudden darkenesse hath possest the Land.
I cannot now expresse my selfe by signes :
All eyes are blinded, none can reade my lines ;
Till Charles ascending, driues away the night,
And in his splendour giues my verses light.
Thus by the beames of his succeeding flame,
I shall describe his father's boundlesse fame.
    The Grecian emp'rours gloried to be borne,
And nurst in purple, by their parents worne.
See here a king, whose birth together twines
The Britan, English, Norman, Scottish lines :
How like a princely throne his cradle stands ;
While[1] diadems become his swathing bands.
His glory now makes all the Earth his tombe,
But enuious fiends would in his mother's wombe
Interre his rising greatnesse, and contend
Against the babe : whom heau'nly troopes defend,
And giue such vigour in his childhood's-state,
That he can strangle snakes, which swell with hate.
This conquest his vndaunted brest declares
In seas of danger, in a world of cares :
Yet neither cares oppresse his constant mind,

---

1 Misprinted white ? G.

Nor dangers drowne his life, for age design'd.
The Muses leaue their sweet Castalian springs
In forme of bees, extending silken wings
With gentle sounds, to keepe this infant still,
While they his mouth with pleasing hony fill.
Hence those large streames of eloquence proceed,
Which in the hearers strange amazement breed :
When laying by his scepters and his swords,
He melts their hearts with his mellifluous words.
So Hercules in ancient pictures fain'd,
Could draw whole Nations to his tongue enchain'd.
He firsts considers in his tender age,
How God hath rays'd him on this earthly stage,
To act a part, expos'd to eu'ry eye :
With Salomon he therefore striues to flie
To Him that gaue this greatnesse, and demands
The precious gift of wisdome from His hands :
While God delighted with this iust request,
Not onely him, with wondrous prudence blest,
But promis'd higher glories, new encrease
Of kingdomes circled with a ring of peace.
He thus instructed by diuine commands,
Extends this peacefull line to other Lands.
When warres are threaten'd by shril trumpets
     sounds,
His oliue stancheth bloud, and binds vp wounds.
The Christian world this good from him deriues,

That thousands had vntimely spent their liues,
If not preseru'd by lustre of his crowne :
Which calm'd the stormes, and layd the billowes
    down :
And dimm'd the glory of that Roman wreath
By souldiers gaiu'd for sauing men from death.
This Denmarke felt, and Swethland, when their
    strife
Ascended to such height, that losse of life
Was counted nothing : for the dayly sight
Of dying men made Death no more then night.
Behold, two potent princes deepe engag'd
In seu'rall int'rests, mutually enrag'd
By former conflicts : yet they downe will lay
Their swords, when his aduice directs the way.
The Northerne climates from dissention barr'd,
Receiue new ioyes by his discreete award.
When Momus could among the godlike-kings,
Infect with poyson those immortall springs
Which flow with nectar; and such gall would
    cast,
As spoyles the sweetnesse of ambrosiac's taste ;
This mighty lord, as ruler of the quire,
With peacefull counsels quencht the rising fire.
The Austrian arch-duke, and Batauian State,
By his endeuours, change their long-bred hate
For twelue yeers truce : this rest to him they owe,

As Belgian shepherds, and poore ploughmen know.
The Muscouites opprest with neighbours, flie
To safe protection of his watchfull eye.
And Germany his ready succour tries,
When sad contentions in the Empire rise.
His mild instinct all Christians thus discerne,
But Christ's malignant foes shall find him sterne.
What care, what charge he suffers to preuent,
Lest infidels their number should augment;
His ships restraine the pirates bloody workes;
And Poland gaines his ayde against the Turkes,
His pow'rfull edicts stretcht beyond the line,
Among the Indians seu'rall bounds designe;
By which his subiects may exalt his throne,
And strangers keepe themselues within their owne.
This Ile was made the sunne's ecliptick way,
For here our Phœbus still vouchsaf'd to stay:
And from this blessed place of his retreat,
In diff'rent zones distinguisht cold and heate,
Sent light or darknesse, and by his commands
Appointed limits to the seas and lands;
Who would imagine, that a prince employ'd
In such affaires, could euer haue enioy'd
Those houres, which drawne from pleasure, and
      from rest,
To purchase precious knowledge, were addrest?
And yet in learning he was knowne t'exceed

Most, whom our houses of the Muses breed.
Ye English sisters, nurses of the Arts,
Vnpartiall iudges of his better parts ;
Raise vp your wings, and to the world declare
His solid iudgement, his inuention rare,
His ready elocution, which ye found
In deepest matters, that your schooles propound.
It is sufficient for my creeping verse,
His care of English language to rehearse.
He leades the lawlesse poets of our times,
To smoother cadence, to exacter rimes :
He knew it was the proper work of kings,
To keepe proportion, eu'n in smallest things.
He with no higher titles can be styl'd,
When seruants name him lib'rall, subiects mild.
Of Antonine's faire time the Romans tell,
No bubbles of ambition then could swell
To forraine warres ; nor ease bred ciuill strife,
Nor any of the senate lost his life.
Our king preserues for two and twenty yeeres,
This realme from inward and from outward feares.
All English peeres escape the deadly stroke,
Though some with crimes his anger durst prouoke.
He was seuere in wrongs, which others felt,
But in his owne, his heart would quickly melt.
For then—like God, from Whom his glories flow—
He makes his mercy swift, his iustice slow.

He neuer would our gen'rall ioy forget,
When on his sacred brow the crowne was set;
And therefore striues to make his kingdome great,
By fixing here his heires' perpetuall seate:
Which eu'ry firme and loyall heart desires,
May last as long as heau'n hath starry fires.
Continued blisse from him this Land receiues,
When leauing vs, to vs his sonne he leaues;
Our hope, our ioy, our treasure: Charles our king,
Whose entrance in my next attempt I sing.

A PANEGYRICK AT THE CORONATION OF OUR SOUERAIGNE LORD, KING CHARLES.[1]

AURORA come: why should thine enuious
    stay
Deferre the ioyes of this expected day?
Will not thy master let his horses runne,
Because he feares to meete another sunne?
Or hath our Northerne starre so dimm'd thine eyes,
Thou knowest not where—at East or West—to
    rise?
Make haste, for if thou shalt denie thy light,

---

1 Succeeded his father, James, in 1625. G.

His glitt'ring crowne will driue away the night.
Debarre not curious Phœbus, who desires
To guild all glorious obiects with his fires.
And could his beames lay open people's harts,
As well as he can view their outward parts;
He heere should find a triumph, such as he
Hath neuer seene, perhaps shall neuer see.

   Shine forth, great Charles, accept our loyall
     words,
Throw from your pleasing eies those conqu'ring
     swords,
That when vpon your name our voyces call,
The birds may feele our thund'ring noise, and fall:
Soft ayre rebounded in a circled ring,
Shall to the gates of heau'n our wishes bring:
For vowes, which with so strong affection flie
Fròm many lips, will doubtlesse pierce the skie:
And God—Who knowes the secrets of our minds,
When in our brests He these two vertues finds,
Sincerity and concord, ioin'd in pray'r
For him,— whom nature made vndoubted heyre
Of three faire kingdomes—will His angels send
With blessings from His throne, this pompe t'
     attend.
Faire citty, England's gemme, the queene of trade,
By sad infection lately desart made:
Cast off thy mourning robes, forget thy teares,

Thy cleare and healthfull Iupiter appeares :
Pale Death, who had thy silent streets possest,
And some foule dampe, or angry planet prest
To work his rage, now from th' Almightie's will
Receiues command to hold his iauelin still.
But since my Muse pretends to tune a song
Fit for this day, and fit t' inspire this throng;
Whence shall I kindle such immortall fires ?
From ioyes or hopes, from prayses or desires ?
To prayse him, would require an endlesse wheele ;
Yet nothing told but what we see and feele.
A thousand tongues for him all gifts intreate
In which Felicity may claime her seate:
Large honour, happy conquest, boundlesse wealth,
Long life, sweete children, vnafflicted health :
But chiefely, we esteeme that precious thing
—Of which already we behold the spring—
Directing Wisdome ; and we now presage
How high that vertue will ascend in age.,
In him, our certaine confidence vnites
All former worthy princes' spreading lights ;
And addes his glorious father to the summe :
From ancient times no greater name can come.
Our hopefull king thus to his subiects shines,
And reades in faithfull hearts these zealous lines ;
This is our Countrie's father, this is hee
In whom we liue, and could not liue so free,

I

Were we not vnder him : his watchfull care
Preuents our dangers : how shall we declare
Our thankfull minds, but by the humble gift
Of firme obedience, which to him we lift ?
As he is God's true image choicely wrought,
And for our ioy to these dominions brought :
So must we imitate celestiall bands,
Which grudge not to performe diuine commands.
His brest, transparent like a liquid flood,
Discouers his aduice for publike good :
But if we iudge it by deceiuing fame,
Like Semele, we thinke Ioue's piercing flame
No more, then common fire in ashes nurst,
Till formelesse fancies in their errors burst.
Shall we discusse his counsels ? We are blest
Who know our blisse, and in his iudgement rest.

OF THE PRINCE'S IOURNEY.[1]

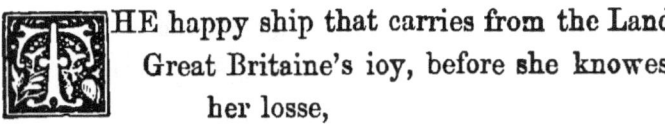HE happy ship that carries from the Land
Great Britaine's ioy, before she knowes
her losse,

---

1 The story of the (intended) Spanish 'Marriage' has
only just been adequately told, in the matter-ful volumes
of Mr. S. R. Gardiner thereon, with abundance of side-
light on the whole events of the period.   G.

Is rul'd by Him, Who can the waues command.

No enuious stormes a quiet passage crosse :

See how the water smiles, the winde breathes
    faire,

The cloudes restraine their frownes, their sighes,
    their teares,

As if the musicke of the whisp'ring ayre

Should tell the sea what precious weight it beares.

A thousand vowes and wishes driue the sayles

With gales of safety to the Neustrian shore.

The ocean, trusted with this pledge, bewailes

That it such wealth must to the Earth restore :

Then France, receiving with a deare imbrace

This Northerne starre, though clouded and dis-
    guis'd,

Beholds some hidden vertue in his face,

And knowes he is a iewell highly priz'd.

Yet there no pleasing sights can make him stay ;

For, like a riuer sliding to the maine,

He hastes to find the period of his way,

And drawne by loue, drawes all our hearts to
    Spaine.

OF THE PRINCE'S DEPARTURE AND RETURNE.

WHEN Charles from vs withdrawes his
glorious light,
The sunne desires his absence to supply:
And that we may nothing in darknesse lie,
He striues to free the North from dreadfull night.
Yet we to Phœbus scarce erect our sight,
But all our lookes, our thoughtes to Charles
apply;
And in the best delights of life we die,
Till he returne and make this climate bright.
Now he ascends and giues Apollo leaue
To driue his horses to the lower part;
We by his presence like content receiue,
As when fresh spirits aide the fainting heart.
Rest here—great Charles—and shine to vs alone,
For other starres are common; Charles our owne.

OF THE PRINCE'S MOST HAPPY RETURNE.

VR Charles, whose horses neuer quencht
their heate,
In cooling waues of Neptune's watry
scate:

Whose starry chariot in the spangled night,
Was still the pleasing obiect of our sight :
This glory of the North hath lately runne
A course as round and certaine as the sunne :
He to the South inclining halfe the yeere,
Now at the Tropike will againe appeare.
He made his setting in the Western streames,
Where weary Phœbus dips his fading beames :
But in this morning our erected eyes
Become so happy as to see him rise.
We shall not euer in the shadow stay,
His absence was to bring a longer day ;
That hauing felt how darknesse can affright,
We may with more content embrace the light,
And call to mind, how eu'ry soule with paine
Sent forth her throwes[1] to fetch him home againe :
For want of him we wither'd in the Spring,
But his returne shall life in Winter bring :
The plants, which, when he went, were growing
    greene,
Retaine their former liu'ries to be seene,
When he reuiewes them : his expected eye
Preseru'd their beauty, ready oft to die.[2]

---

1 Throes = prayers. G.

2 The conceits of our Poet above, are found in a quaintly-exaggerate form in an otherwise sorry volume, viz, N.

What tongue? what hand can to the life display
The glorious ioy of this triumphant day?

Hookes's "Amanda: a Sacrifice to an unknown Goddesse,
or a Free-Will Offering of a loving heart to a Sweet-
heart" (1653).   I give a place to the Lines here:

"TO AMANDA WALKING IN THE GARDEN.

And now what monarch would not gard'ner be,
My faire Amanda's stately gate to see:
How her feet tempt! how soft and light she treads,
Fearing to wake the flowers from their beds!
Yet from their sweet green pillowes ev'ry where,
They start and gaze about to see my faire;
Look at yon flower yonder, how it growes
Sensibly! how it opes its leaves and blowes,
Puts its Easter clothes on, neat and gay!
Amanda's presence makes it holy-day:
Look how on tip-toe that faire lilie stands
To look on thee, and court thy whiter hands
To gather it! I saw in yonder croud
That tulip-bed, of which dame-Flora's proud,
A short dwarfe flower did enlarge its stalk,
And shoot an inch to see Amanda walk;
Nay, look, my fairest, look how fast they grow!
Into a scaffold method spring! as though
Riding to parl'ament were to be seen
In pomp and state some royal am'rous queene:
The gravel'd walks, though ev'n as a die,
Lest some loose pebbles should offensive lie,

When England crown'd with many thousand fires,
Receiues the scope of all her best desires.
She at his sight, as with an earthquake swells,
And strikes the heau'n with sound of trembling
    bells.

Quilt themselves o're with downie mosse for thee,
The walls are hang'd with blossom'd tapestrie ;
To hide her nakednesse when look't upon,
The maiden fig-tree puts Eve's apron on ;
The broad-leav'd sycomore, and ev'ry tree
Shakes like the trembling aspe, and bends to thee,
And each leaf proudly strives with fresher aire,
To fan the curled tresses of thy hair ;
Nay, and the bee too, with his wealthie thigh,
Mistakes his hive, and to thy lips doth flie ;
Willing to treasure up his honey there,
Where honey-combs so sweet and plenty are :
Look how that pretty modest columbine
Hangs down its head to view those feet of thine !
See the fond motion of the strawberrie,
Creeping on th' earth to go along with thee !
The lovely violet makes after too,
Unwilling yet, my dear, to part with you ;
The knot-grasse and the daizes catch thy toes
To kisse my faire one's feet before she goes ;
All court and wish me lay Amanda down,
And give my dear a new green-flower'd gown.
    Come let me kisse thee falling, kisse at rise,
    Thou in the Garden, I in Paradise." (pp 42-44.) G.

The vocall goddesse leauing desart woods,
Slides downe the vales ; and dancing on the floods,
Obserues our words, and with repeating noise
Contends to double our abundant ioyes.
The World's cleare eye is iealous of his name,
He sees this Ile like one continuall flame,
And feares lest earth a brighter starre should breed,
Which might vpon his meate, the vapours, feed.
We maruell not that in his father's land
So many signes of loue and seruice stand :
Behold how Spaine retaines in eu'ry place
Some bright reflection of his chearefull face ;
Madrid, where first his splendor he displayes,
And driues away the clouds that dimm'd his rayes,
Her ioyes into a world of formes doth bring,
Yet none contents her ; while that potent king
Who rules so farre, till now could neuer find
His realmes and wealth too little for his mind.
No words of welcome can such planets greete,
Where in one house they by coniunction meete.
Their sacred concord runnes through many signes,
And to the Zodiake's better portion shines :
But in the Virgin they are scene most farre,
And in the Lyon's heart, the kingly starre.
When towards vs our prince his iourney moues,
And feeles attraction of his seruants loues ;
When—hauing open brests of strangers knowne—

He hastes to gather tribute of his owne ;
The ioyfull neighbours all his passage fill
With noble trophees of his might and skill
In conqu'ring mens affections with his darts ;
Which deepely fixt in many rauisht hearts,
Are like the starry chaines, whose blazes play
In knots of light along the Milkey Way.
He heares the newes of his approaching Fleet,
And will his Nauy see, his seruants greet ;
Thence to the Land returning in his barge,
The waues leape high, as proud of such a charge ;
The Night makes speed to see him, and preuents
The slouthfull twilight, casting duskie tents[1]
On roring streames, which might all men dismay
But him, to whose cleare soule the night is day.
The pressing windes with their officious strife,
Had caus'd a tumult dang'rous to his life :
But their Commander checks them, and restraines
Their hasty feruour, in accustom'd chaines :
This perill—which with feare our words decline—
Was then permitted by the hand diuine,
That good euent might prooue his person deare
To heau'n, and needfull to the people here.
When he resolues to crosse the watry maine,
See what a change his absence makes in Spaine !

---

1 Qu : clouds in shape of tents ?   G.

The earth turnes gray for griefe that she conceiues,
Birds lose their tongues, and trees forsake their
    leaues.
Now floods of teares expresse a sad far[e]well,
Ambitious sayles as with his greatnesse swell;
To him old Nereus on his dolphin rides:
Presenting bridles to direct the tides,
He calles his daughters from their secret caues,
—Their snowy necks are seen aboue the waues—
And saith to them: Behold the onely sonne
Of that great lord, about whose kingdomes run
Our liquid currents, which are made his owne,
And with moyst bulwarks guard his sacred throne:
See how his lookes delight, his gestures moue
Admire and praise, yet flye from snares of loue:
Not Thetes[1] with her beauty and her dowre,
Can draw this Peleus to her watry bowre;
He loues a nymph of high and heau'nly race,
The cu'ning sunne doth homage to her face.
Hesperian orchards yeeld her golden fruit,
He tooke this iourney in that sweet pursuit.
When thus their father ends, the Nereids throw
Their garlands on this glorious prince, and strow
His way with songs, in which the hopes appeare
Of ioyes too great for humane cares to heare.

---

1 Thetis.   G.

UPON THE ANNIUERSARY DAY OF THE PRINCE'S RETURNE, OCTOBER THE FIFTH.

E now admire their doctrine, who main-
taine
The World's creation vnder Autumne's
reigne ;
When trees abound in fruit, grapes swell with iuice,
These meates are ready for the creatures vse :
Old Time resolues to make a new suruay
Of yeeres and ages from this happy day ;
Refusing those accounts which others bring,
He crownes October, as of moneths the king.
No more shall hoary Winter claime the place,
And draw cold proofes from Ianus' double face ;
Nor shall the Ram, when Spring the earth adornes,
Vnlocke the gate of heau'n with golden hornes :
Dry Summer shall not of the dog-starre boast
—Of angry constellations honour'd most—
From whose strong heate Egyptians still begun,
To marke the turning circle of the sunne.
Vertumnus, who hath lordly power to change
The seasons, and can them in order range,
Will from this period fresh beginning take ;
Yet not so much for his Pomonae's sake,
Who then is richly drest to please her spouse,

And with her orchards' treasure deckes her browes.
It is our CHARLES, whose euer louèd name,
Hath made this point of heau'n increase in fame :
Whose long-thought absence was so much deplor'd,
In whom our hopes and all our fruits are stor'd.
He now attaines the shore—O blessed day—
And true Achates waites along his way,
Our wise Anchises for his sonne prouides
This chosen seruant, as the best of guides.
A prince's glory cannot more depend
Vpon his crowne, then on a faithfull friend.

TO THE MOST ILLUSTRIOUS PRINCE CHARLES, OF THE EXCELLENT VSE OF POEMS.

IUINE example of obedient heires,
    High in my hopes, and second in my
      prayers :
True image of your father to the life,
Whom Time desir'd, and Fates in iealous strife,
With chearefull voices taught their wheeles to
    runne,
That such a father might haue such a sonne ;
Since God exalts you on this earthly stage,
And giues you wisedome farre aboue your age,

To iudge of men, and of their actiue pow'rs :
Let me lay downe the fruits of priuate houres
Before your feet : you neuer will refuse
This gift, which beares the title of a Muse.

Among your serious thoughts, with noble care
You cherish poets, knowing that they are
The starres, which light to famous actions giue,
By whom the mem'ries of good princes liue :
You are their prince in a peculiar kind,
Because your father hath their Art refin'd.
And though these priests of greatnesse, quiet sit
Amid'st the silent children of their wit,
Without accesse of sutours, or dispatch
Of high affaires, at which th' ambitious catch ;
They are not idle, when their sight they rayse
Beyond the present time to future daies ;
And braue examples, sage instructions bring
In pleasing verses, which our sonnes may sing.
They oft erect their flight aboue the Land,
When graue Urania ioyning hand in hand
With soft Thalia, mix their diff'rent strings,
And by their musick make celestiall things
More fit for humane eares ; whose winding rounds
Are easly fill'd with well digested sounds.
Pale Enuy and dull Ignorance reproue
This exercise, as onely apt for loue ;
Deuis'd t'allure the sense with curious art,

But not t'enrich the vnderstanding part.
So might they say, the sunne was onely fram'd
To please the eye, and onely therefore nam'd
The eye of heau'n, conceiuing not his wheele
Of liuely heate, which lower bodies feele.
Our Muses striue, that Common-wealths may be
As well from barb'rous deedes, as language free :
The seu'rall sounds in harmony combin'd,
 Knit chaines of vertue in the hearers mind :
And that he still may haue his teacher by,
With measur'd lines, we please his curious eye.
We hold those works of Art, or Nature best,
Where Order's steps most fully are exprest
And therefore all those ciuill men that liue.
By law and rule, will to our numbers giue
The name of good, in which perfection rests ;
And feele their strokes with sympathyzing brests.
Not oratours so much with flowing words,
Can sway the hearts of men, and whet their swords :
Or blunt them at their pleasure, as our straines,
—Whose larger spheare the orbe of prose containes
—Can mens affections lessen or increase,
And guide their passions whisp'ring warre or peace.
Tyrtæus by the vigour of his verse,
Made Sparta conquer, while his lines reherse
Her former glory ; almost then subdude
By stronger foes ; and when the people rude

Contend among themselues with mutuall wrongs,
He tempers discord with his milder songs :
This poore lame poet hath an equall praise
With captaines, and with states-men of his dayes :
The Muses claime possession in those men,
Who first aduentur'd with a nimble pen
To paint their thoughts, in new inuented signes,
And spoke of Nature's workes in numbred lines :
This happy Art, compar'd with plainer wayes,
Was sooner borne, and not so soone decayes :
She safer stands from Time's deuouring wrong,
As better season'd to continue long;
But as the streames of Time, still forward flow,
So wits, more idle and distrustfull grow :
They yeeld this fort, and cowardly pretend
Prose is a castle easier to defend ;
Nor was this change effected in a day,
But with degrees, and by a stealing way ;
They pull the Muse's feathers one by one,
And are not seene till both the wings be gone.
If man injoying such a precious mine,
Esteem'd his nature almost made diuine :
When he beheld th' expression of his thought,
To such a height, and godlike glory brought :
This change may well his fading ioy confound,
To see it naked, creeping on the ground ;
Yet in the Lands that honour'd Learning's name,

Were alwayes some that kept the vestall flame
Of pow'rfull verse, on whose increase or end,
The periods of the soule's chiefe raine depend.
Now in this realme I see the golden age
Returne to vs, whose comming shall asswage
Distracting strife, and many hearts inspire,
To gather fewell for this sacred fire :
On which, if you, great prince, your eyes will cast,
And like Fauonius, giue a gentle blast :
The liuely flame shall neuer yeeld till death,
But gaine immortall spirit by your breath.

TO THE PRINCE.

F eu'ry man a little world we name,
    You are a world most like the greatest
        frame :
Your loue of learning spreads your glory farre,
Lifts you to heau'n, and makes you there a starre.
In actiue sports, and formes of martiall deeds,
Like fire and ayre, your nimble courage breeds
A rare amazement, and a sweet delight
To Brittaines, who behold so deare a sight :
Though higher orbes such glorious signes containe,
Do not—braue prince—this lower globe disdaine.
In pure and fruitfull waters we may see

Your minde from darknesse cleare, in bounty free :
And in the steddy resting of the ground,
Your noble firmenesse to your friend is found :
For you are still the same, and where you loue,
No absence can your constant mind remoue.
So goodnesse spreads itselfe with endlesse lines,
And so the light in distant places shines :
He that aduentures of your worth to sing,
Attempts in vaine, to paint a boundlesse thing.

AN EPITHALAMIUM VPON THE HAPPY MARRIAGE OF OUR SOUERAIGNE LORD, KING CHARLES, AND OUR GRACIOUS LADY, QUEENE MARY.[1]

THE Ocean long contended—but in vaine—
　　To part our shore from France.
　　Let Neptune shake his mace, and swelling
　　　　waues aduance :
The former vnion now returnes againe,
　　This Isle shall once more kisse the maine
oyn'd with a flowry bridge of loue, on which the
　　　　Graces dance.

---

1 The 'queen' was Maria Henrietta of France. Our
Poet was no Seer. G.

X

Leander here no dang 'rous iourney takes,
    To reach his Hero's hand :
Our Hellespont with ships becomes as firme as
    Land,
    When this sweete nymph her place of birth
      forsakes ;
    And England, signes of welcome makes
As many, as our gladsome coasts haue little graines
    of sand.
    That voyce, in which the Continent was blest,
    Now to this Iland calls
The liuing woods and rocks, to frame new rising
    walls :
    The moouing hills salute this happy guest,
    The riuers to her seruice prest,
Seine into Thames, Garonne to Trent, and Loire to
    Seuerne falls.
    The royall payre, the bridegroome and the bride,
    With equall glory shine :
Both full of sparkling light, both sprung from
    race diuine.
    Their princely fathers, Europ's highest pride,
    The westerne world did sweetly guide :
To them as fathers of their realmes, we golden
    crownes assigne.
    Great Henry, neuer vanquisht in the field,
    Rebellious foes could tame.

The wisdome of our James bred terror in his name :
   So that his proudest aduersaries yeeld,
     Glad to be guarded with his shield,
Where Peace with drops of heau'nly dew supprest
     Dissention's flame.
   Our Charles and Mary now their course prepare,
     Like those two greater lights,
Which God in midst of Heau'n exalted to our
     sights,
   To guide our footsteps with perpetuall care ;
     Time's happy changes to declare :
The one affoords vs healthfull daies, the other quiet
     nights.
   See how the planets, and each lesser fire
     Along the Zodiake glide,
And in his stately traine their offices diuide !
   No starre remaines exempted from this quire,
     But all are ioyn'd in one desire,
To mooue, as these their wheeles shall turne, and rest
     where they abide.
   What can these shouts and glitt'ring showes
     portend,
     But neuer-fading ioyes ?
The lords in rich attire, the people with their
     noyse,
   Expresse to what a height their hopes ascend,
     Which like a circle haue no end :

Their strength no furious tempests shake, nor creep-
 ing age destroyes.
On this foundation we expect to build
 The towres of earthly blisse.
Mirth shall attend on Health, and Peace shall
 Plenty kisse :
The trees with fruite, with flowres our gardens
 fill'd,
 Sweete honey from the leaues distill'd ;
For now Astræa's raigne appeares to be a tipe of this.
O may our children with our rauish't eyes
 A race of sonnes behold,
Whose birth shall change our ir'n to siluer, brass
 to gold.
Proceede white houres, that from this stocke
 may rise
 Victorious kings, whom Fame shall prize
More dearely, then all other names within her booke
 enroll'd.

AT THE END OF HIS MAIESTIE'S FIRST YEERE. SONNET FIRST.

OUR royall father Iames, the good and
 great,
 Proclaim'd in March, when first we felt
 the Spring,

A world of blisse did to our Iland bring :
And at his death he made his yeeres compleate,
Although three dayes he longer held his seate,
Then from that houre when he reioyc'd to sing,
Great Brittaine torne before, enioyes a king :
Who can the periods of the starres repeate ?
The sunne, who in his annuall circle takes
A daye's full quadrant from th' ensuing yeere,
Repayes it in foure yeeres, and equall makes
The number of the dayes within his spheare :

Iames was our earthly sunne, who call'd to
heau'n,
Leaues you his heire, to make all fractions eu'n.

SONNET SECOND.

BOUT the time when dayes are longer
made,
When nights are warmer, and the aire
more cleare,
When verdant leaues and fragrant flowres appeare ;
Whose beauty, Winter had constrained to fade.
About the time, when Gabriel's words perswade
The blessed virgin to incline her eare,
And to conceyue that Sonne, whom she shall beare ;
Whose death and rising driue away the shade.

About this time, so oft, so highly blest
By precious gifts of Nature and of Grace,
First glorious Iames, the English crowne possest :
Then gracious Charles succeeded in his place.
    For him his subiects wish with hearty words,
    Both what this world, and what the next affords.

AN EPITHALAMIUM TO MY LORD MAR-QUESSE OF BUCKINGHAM, AND TO HIS FAIRE AND VERTUOUS LADY.[1]

EUERE and serious Muse
    Whose quill, the name of loue
    declines,
Be not too nice, nor this deare worke refuse :
Here Venus stirs no flame, nor Cupid guides thy
    lines,

---

1 George Villiers, ultimately Duke of Buckingham, fills too large a space in English history to need annotation here. Born on August 20th, 1592, he died by the hand of Felton, August 23rd, 1628. The tributes paid to him here and elsewhere, by our poet, seem to vouch for more brain-power and heart than are usually allowed 'The Favourite' of James and Charles. His 'faire and virtuous lady', Lady Catherine Manners, was daughter of Francis, Earl of Rutland, and one of the richest-dowered heiresses in the

But modest Hymen shakes his torch, and chast
    Lucina shines.
    The bridegroome's starres arise !
    Maydes, turne your sight, your faces hide :
  Lest ye be shipwrack't in those sparkling eyes,
Fit to be seene by none, but by his louely bride :
If him Narcissus should behold, he would forget his
    pride.

    And thou faire nymph appeare
    With blushes, like the purple Morne ;
  If now thine eares will be content to heare
The title of a wife, we shortly will adorne
Thee with a ioyfull mother's name, when some sweet
    childe is borne.

    We wish a sonne, whose smile,
    Whose beauty may proclaime him thine ;
  Who may be worthy of his father's stile,
May answere to our hopes, and strictly may com-
    bine

---

kingdom. She is, according to Nichols's Leicestershire,
"The Shepherdesse" of Sir John Beaumont's Poem of
that name : and accordingly I have placed it immediately
after the present. (Vol. iv., pt. 2nd., p 621.) A pedigree
in Nichols's Leicestershire probably explains our Poet's
friendship with the Buckinghams. It appears Anthony
Beaumont, of Glenfield, had a daughter (his 4th) Mary,
who married Sir George Villiers of Brookesby, father of
George Villiers, duke of Buckingham. G.

The happy height of Villier's race, with noble
    Rutland's line.
    Let both their heads be crown'd
  With choycest flowers, which shall presage
  That loue shall flourish, and delights abound ;
Time, adde thou many dayes, nay ages to their
    age ;
Yet neuer must thy freezing arme, their holy fires
    asswage.
    Now when they ioyne their hands,
    Behold, how faire that knot appeares.
  O may the firmenesse of these nuptiall bands
  Resemble that bright line the measure of the
    yeeres,
Which makes a league betweene the poles, and
    ioynes the hemispheres.

THE SHEPERDESSE.

A SHEPERDESSE, who long had kept her
    flocks
  On stony Charnwood's dry and barren rocks,
In heate of Summer to the vales declin'd,
To seeke fresh pasture for her lambes halfe pin'd.
She—while her charge was feeding—spent the
    houres

To gaze on sliding brookes, and smiling flowres.
Thus hauing largely stray'd, she lifts her sight,
And viewes a palace full of glorious light.
She finds the entrance open, and as bold
As countrey maids, that would the Court behold,
She makes an offer, yet again she stayes,
And dares not dally with those sunny rayes.
Here lay a nymph, of beauty most diuine,
Whose happy presence caus'd the house to shine ;
Who much conuerst with mortals, and could know
No honour truly high, that scornes the low :
For she had oft been present, though vnseene,
Among the shepherds' daughters on the greene ;
Where eu'ry homebred swaine desires to proue
His oaten pipe and feet, before his loue,
And crownes the eu'ning, when the daies are
        long,
With some plaine dance, or with a rurall song.
Nor were the women nice to hold this sport,
And please their louers in a modest sort.
There that sweet nymph had seene this countrey
        dame
For singing crown'd, whence grew a world of
        fame
Among the sheepcotes ; which in her reioyce,
And know no better pleasure then her voyce.
The glitt'ring ladies gather'd in a ring,

Intreate the silly[1] shepherdesse to sing :
She blusht and sung, while they with words of
    praise,
Contend her songs aboue their worth to raise.
Thus being chear'd with many courteous signes,
She takes her leaue, for now the sun declines ;
And hauing driuen home her flocks againe,
She meets her loue, a simple shepherd swaine ;
Yet in the plaines he had a poet's name :
For he could roundelayes and carols frame,
Which, when his mistresse sung along the downes,
Was thought celestiall musick by the clownes.
Of him she begs, that he would raise his mind
To paint this lady, whom she found so kind :
You oft—saith she—haue in our homely bow'rs
Discours'd of demi-gods and greater pow'rs :
For you, with Hesiode sleeping, learnt to know
The race diuine from heau'n to earth below.
My deare—said he—the nymph whom thou hast
    seene,
Most happy is of all that liue betweene
This globe and Cynthia, and in high estate,
Of wealth and beauty hath an equall mate ;
Whose loue hath drawne incessant teares in floods,
From nymphs, that haunt the waters and the
    woods.

---

1 Innocent, simple.   G.

And[1] Iris to the ground hath bent her bow
To steale a kisse, and then away to goe :
Yet all in vaine, he no affection knowes
But to this goddesse, whom at first he chose :
Him she enioyes in mutuall bonds of loue :
Two hearts are taught in one small point to moue.
Her father high in honour and descent,
Commands the syluans on the northside Trent.
He at this time for pleasure and retreat,
Comes down from Beluoir, his ascending seate,
To which great Pan had lately honour done :
For there he lay, so did his hopefull sonne.[2]
But when this lord by his accesse desires
To grace our dales, he to a house retires,
Whose walles are water'd with our siluer brookes,
And makes the shepherds proud to view his lookes,
There in that blessed house you also saw
His lady, whose admirèd vertues draw
All hearts to loue her, and all tongues inuite
To praise that ayre where she vouchsafes her light,
And for thy further ioy thine eyes were blest,
To see another lady, in whose brest
True Wisedome hath with Bounty equall place,

---

1 Misprinted 'of.' G.

2 The reference is to the visit of King James and Prince Charles, to Belvoir Castle. G.

As Modesty with Beauty in her face.
She found me singing Florae's natiue dowres,
And made me sing before the heau'nly pow'rs:
For which great fauour, till my voice be done,
I sing of her, and her thrice-noble sonne.

OF HIS MAIESTIE'S VOW FOR THE FELICITY OF MY LORD MARQUESSE OF BUCKINGHAM.

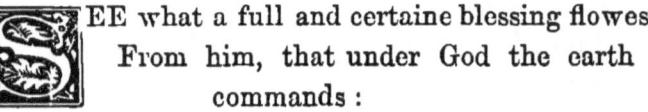EE what a full and certaine blessing flowes
From him, that under God the earth
commands:
For kings are types of God, and by their hands
A world of gifts and honours He bestowes:
The hopeful tree thus blest securely growes,
Amidst the waters in a firtile ground;
And shall with leaues, and flowres, and fruites be
crown'd:
Abundant dew on it the planter throwes.
You are this plant, my lord, and must dispose
Your noble soule, those blossomes to recciue;
Which euer to the roote of Vertue cleaue,
As our Apollo by his skill foreshowes:
    Our Salomon, in wisedome, and in peace,
    Is now the prophet of your faire increase.

MY LORD OF BUCKINGHAM'S WELCOME TO THE KING AT BURLEY.

IR, you haue euer shin'd vpon me bright,
But now, you strike and dazle me with
light :
You England's radiant sunne, vouchsafe to grace
My house, a spheare too little and too base ;
My Burley as a cabinet containes
The gemme of Europe, which from golden veines
Of glorious princes, to this height is growne,
And ioynes their precious vertues all in one :
When I your praise would to the world professe,
My thoughts with zeale, and earnest feruour presse
Which should be first, and their officious strife
Restraines my hand from painting you to life.
I write, and hauing written, I destroy,
Because my lines haue bounds, but not my ioy.

A CONGRATULATION TO MY LORD MARQUESSE OF BUCKINGHAM, AT THE BIRTH OF HIS DAUGHTER.[1]

Y lines describ'd your marriage as the
Spring ;
Now like the reapers, of your fruite I sing,

---

1 The Lady Mary Villiers. G.

And shew the haruest of your constant loue,
In this sweete armefull which your joy shall proue :
Her sexe is signe of plenty, and fore-runnes
The pleasing hope of many noble sonnes :
Who farre abroad their branches shall extend,
And spread their race, till Time receiue an end.
Be euer blest,—faire childe—that hast begunne
So white a threed, by hands of angels spunne :
Thou art the first, and wilt the rest beguile :
For thou shalt rauish with a chearefull smile
Thy parents hearts, not wonted to such blisse :
And steale the first fruites of a tender kisse.

ON TRUE GREATNESSE: TO MY LORD MARQUESSE OF BUCKINGHAM.

IR, you are truely great, and eu'ry eye
    Not dimme with enuy, ioyes to see you
    high :
But chiefely mine, which buried in the night,
Are by your beames rais'd and restor'd to light.
You, onely you haue pow'r to make me dwell
In sight of men, drawne from my silent cell :
Where oft in vaine my pen would haue exprest
Those precious gifts, in which your minde is blest.
But you, as much too modest are to read

Your prayse, as I too weake your fame to spreade.
All curious formes, all pictures will disgrace
Your worth ; which must be studied in your face,
The liuely table, where your vertue shines
More clearely, than in strong and waighty lines.
In vaine I striue to write some noble thing,
To make you nobler; for that prudent king,
Whose words so oft, you happy are to heare;
Hath made instruction needlesse to your eare :
Yet giue me leaue in this my silent song,
To shew true Greatnesse, while you passe along;
And if you were not humble, in each line
Might owne your selfe, and say, This grace is mine.
    They that are great, and worthy to be so,
Hide not their rayes from meanest plants that grow.
Why is the sunne set in a throne so hie,
But to giue light to each inferiour eye ?
His radiant beames distribute liuely grace
To all, according to their worth and place ;
And from the humble ground those vapours draine,
Which are sent[1] downe in fruitfull drops of raine.
As God His greatnesse and His wisdome showes
In kings, whose lawes the acts of men dispose ;
So kings among their seruants those select,
Whose noble vertues may the rest direct :

---

1 Misprinted ' set '.   G.

Who must remember that their honour tends
Not to vaine pleasure, but to publike ends :
And must not glory in their stile or birth ;
The starres were made for man, the heau'n for
    earth.
He whose iust deedes his fellow-seruants please,
May serue his souraigne with more ioy and ease,
Obeying with sincere' and faithfull loue,
That pow'rfull hand, which giues his wheele to
    moue :
His spheare is large ; who can his duty know
To princes ? and respect to vs below ?
His soule is great, when it in bounds confines
This scale, which rays'd so high, so deepe declines:
These are the steps, by which he must aspire
Beyond all things which earthly hearts desire :
And must so farre dilate his noble minde,
Till it in heau'n eternall honour finde.
The order of the blessed spirits there
Must be his rule, while he inhabits here :
He must conceiue that wordly glories are
Vaine shadowes, seas of sorrow, springs of care :
All things which vnder Cynthia leade their life,
Are chain'd in darknesse, borne and nurst in strife :
None scapes the force of this destroying flood,
But he that cleaues to God, his constant good :
He is accurst that will delight to dwell

In this prison, this blacke seditious hell :
When with lesse paine he may imbrace the light,
And on his high Creatour fixe his sight ;
Whose gracious presence giues him perfect rest,
And builds a Paradise within his brest :
Where trees of vertues to their height increase,
And beare the flowres of Ioy, the fruites of Peace.
No enuie, no reuenge, no rage, no pride,
No lust, nor rapine should his courses guide ;
Though all the world conspire to doe him grace :
Yet he is little, and extremely base,
If in his heart, these vices take their seate ;
—No pow'r can make the slaue of passions great.—

VPON MY LORD OF BUCKINGHAM'S ARMES.

EHOLD, the ensignes of a christian knight
Whose field is like his minde, of siluer
bright :
His bloudy crosse supports fiue golden shels,
A precious pearle, in euery scallop dwels :
Fiue vertues grace the middle and the bounds,
Which take their light from Christ's victorious
wounds :
Vpon the top, commanding Prudence shines,

L

Repressing Temp'rance to the foote declines ;
Braue Fortitude and Iustice, are the hands,
And Charity as in the center stands :
Which binding all the ends with strong effect
To euery Vertue, holds the same respect :
May he that beares this shield, at last obtaine
The azure circle of celestiall raigne ;
And hauing past the course of sliding houres,
Enioy a crowne of neuer-fading flow'rs ?

VPON MY LORD BUCKINGHAM'S SHIELD
AT A TILTING, HIS IMPRESSE BEING
A BIRD OF PARADISE.

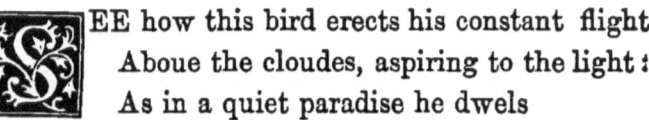EE how this bird erects his constant flight
　　Aboue the cloudes, aspiring to the light :
　　As in a quiet paradise he dwels
In that pure region, where no winde rebels :
And fearing not the thunder, hath attain'd
The palace, where the demigods remaind :
This bird belongs to you, thrice glorious king ;
From you the beauties of his feathers spring :
No vaine ambition lifts him vp so high,
But rais'd by force of your attractiue eye ;
He feedes vpon your beames, and takes delight,
Not in his owne ascent, but in your sight.

Let them, whose motion to the earth declines,
Describe your circle by the baser lines,
And enuy at the brightnesse of your seate :
He cannot liue diuided from your heate.

TO THE DUKE OF BUCKINGHAM AT HIS RETURNE FROM SPAINE.

Y Lord, that you so welcome are to all ;
 You haue deseru'd it, neuer could there
  fall
A fitter way to prooue you highly lou'd,
Then when your selfe you from our sights remou'd :
The clouded lookes of Brittaine sad appeare,
With doubtfull care—ah who can bridle feare ?—
For their inestimable gemme perplext.
The good and gracefull Buckingham is next
In their desires : they to remembrance bring
How oft, by mediation[1] with the king
You mitigate the rigour of the lawes,
And pleade the orphans and the widowes cause.
My Muse, which tooke from you her life and light
Sate like a weary wretch, whome suddaine night
Had ouerspred : your absence casting downe

---

1 Misprinted 'meditation'. G.

The flowr's, and Sirens' feathers from her crowne ;
Your fauour first th' anointed head inclines
To heare my rurall songs and reade my lines :
Your voyce, my reede with lofty musick reares
To offer trembling songs to princely eares.
But since my sou'raigne leaues in great affaires
His trusty seruant, to his subiects pray'rs :
I willing spare for such a noble end
My patron and—too bold I speake—my friend.

TO THE DUKE OF BUCKINGHAM.

HE words of princes iustly we conceiue,
 As oracles inspir'd by pow'r diuine ;
 Which make the vertues of their servants
  shine,
And monuments to future ages leaue.
The sweet consent of many tongues can weaue
 Such knots of honours in a flowry line,
 That no iniurious hands can them vntwine,
Nor enuious blasts of beauty can bereaue.
 These are your helpes, my lord, by these two wings
You lifted are aboue the force of spite :
 For, while the publike quire your glory sings,
The arme that rules them, keepes the musicke right :
 Your happy name with noble prayse to greet
 God's double voyce, the king and kingdome meet.

TO MY GRACIOUS LORD, THE DUKE OF BUCKINGHAM, VPON THE BIRTH OF HIS FIRST SONNE.

GIVE leaue—my lord—to his abounding
    heart,
   Whose faithfull zeale presumes to beare
    · a part
In eu'ry blessing which vpon you shines,
And to your glory consecrates his lines ;
Which rising from a plaine and countrey Muse,
Must all my boldnesse with her name excuse.
Shall Burley onely triumph in this child,
Which by his birth is truly happy stil'd ?
Nay : we will striue, that eccho with her notes,
May draw some ioy into our homely cotes :
While I to solitary hils retire,
Where quiet thoughts my songs with truth inspire,
And teach me to foretell the hopes that flow
From this young lord, as he in yeeres shall grow.
First, we behold—and neede not to presage—
What pleasing comfort in this tender age
He giues his parents, sweetning eu'ry day
With deare contentments of his harmlesse play.
They in this glasse their seu'rall beauties place,
And owne themselues in his delightfull face.
But when this flowry bud shall first beginne

To spread his leaues which were conceal'd within ;
And casting off the dew of childish teares,
More glorious then the rose at noone appeares,
His minde extends it selfe to larger bounds ;
Instinct of gen'rous nature oft propounds :
—Great duke—your actiue graces to his sight,
As obiects full of wonder and delight :
These in his thoughts entire possession keep,
They stop his play, and interrupt his sleepe.
So doth a carefull painter fixe his eyes
Vpon the patterne, which before him lies,
And neuer from the boord his hand withdrawes,
Vntil the type be like th' exemplar cause.
To courtly dancing now he shall incline,
To manage horses, and in armes to shine.
Such ornaments of youth are but the seeds
Of noble vertues, and heroick deeds.
He will not rest in any outward part,
But striues t'expresse the riches of your heart
Within a litle modell, and to frame
True title to succession of your fame :
In riper yeeres he shall your wisedome learne,
And your vndaunted courage shall discerne ;
And from your actions, from your words and
  lookes
Shall gather rules which others read in bookes :

So in Achillis[1] more those lessons wrought,
Which Pelcus show'd then those which Chiron
  taught.

VPON THE EARLE OF COUENTRYE'S DEPARTURE FROM VS TO THE ANGELS.[2]

WEET babe, whose birth inspir'd me with
    a song,
    And call'd my Muse to trace thy dayes
      along ;
Attending riper yeeres, with hope to finde
Such braue endeuours of thy noble minde,
As might deserue triumphant lines, and make
My fore-head bold a lawrell crowne to take :
How hast thou left vs, and this earthly stage,
—Not acting many months—in tender age ?
Thou cam'st into this world a little spie,
Where all things that could please the eare and
  eye,

---

1 Achilles. G.
2 The 'first sonne' of the immediately preceding lines.
He died March 17th, 1626 —27. G.

Were set before thee; but thou found'st them
    toyes,[1]
And flew'st with scornefull smiles t' eternall
    ioyes:
No visage of grim Death is sent t' affright
Thy spotlesse soule, nor darknesse blinds thy sight:
But lightsome angels with their golden wings
Ore-spread thy cradle; and each spirit brings
Some precious balme, for heau'nly phisicke meet,
To make the separation soft and sweet.
The sparke infus'd by God departs away,
And bids the earthly, weake, companion stay
With patience in that nurs'ry of the ground,
Where first the seeds of Adam's limbs were found:
For Time shall come when these diuided friends
Shall ioyne againe, and know no seu'rall ends,[2]
But change this short and momentary kisse,
To strict embraces of celestiall blisse.

---

1 Trifles. **G.**

2 Later, gentle Michael Bruce puts another aspect of
the same sentiment tenderly:

> " A few short years of evil past
>   We reach the happy shore,
> Where death-divided friends at last
>   Shall meet to part no more."

See our edition of the works of Bruce (1865) p. 137, and
Memoir pp. 101—104. **G.**

TO MY LORD VICOUNT PURBECK:[1] A CONGRATULATION FOR HIS HEALTH.

F we inlarge our hearts, extend our voyce,
To shew with what affection we reioyce,
When friends or kinsmen, wealth and
    honour gaine,
Or are return'd to freedome from the chaine:
How shall your seruants and your friends—my
    lord—
Declare their ioy? who find no sound, no word
Sufficient for their thoughts, since you haue got
That iewell health, which kingdomes equall not:
From sicknesse freed, a tyrant farre more fell
Then Turkish pirates, who in gallies dwell.
The Muses to the friend of musicke bring
The signes of gladnesse: Orpheus strikes a string
Which can inspire the dull, can cheare the sad,
And to the dead can liuely motion adde:
Some play, some sing: while I, whose onely skill,
Is to direct the organ of my quill,

---

1 Sir John Villiers, eldest son of Sir George Villiers and his second wife, Mary Beaumont: created 19th June, 1619, Baron Villiers, and Viscount Purbeck, of Purbeck, Dorsetshire. He was eldest brother of *the* Duke of Buckingham. See Banks' Extinct Baronage (1810), Vol. iii., 613. G.

That from my hand it may not runne in vaine,
But keepe true time with my commanding braine :
I will bring forth my Musicke, and will trie
To rayse these dumbe—yet speaking—letters high,
Till they contend with sounds : till arm'd with
　　　wings
My featherd pen surmount Apollo's strings.
We much reiocye that lightsome calmes asswage
The fighting humours, blind with mutuall rage :
So sing the mariners exempt from feare,
When stormes are past, and hopefull signes appeare.
So chaunts the mounting larke her gladsome lay,
When night giues place to the delightfull day.
In this our mirth, the greatest ioy I finde,
Is to consider how your noble minde
Will take true vse of those afflictions past,
And on this ground will fix your vertue fast ;
And hence haue learn't th'vncertaine state of man,
And that no height of glitt'ring honour can
Secure his quiet : for Almighty God,
Who rules the high, can with His powr'full rod
Represse the greatest, and in mercy daignes
With dang'rous ioyes to mingle wholsome paines :
Though men in sicknesse draw vnquiet breath,
And count it worst of euils, next to death :
Yet such His goodnesse is, Who gouernes all,
That from this bitter spring sweete riuers fall :

Here we are truly taught ourselues to know,
To pitty others who indure like woe :
To feele the waight of sinne, the onely cause
Whence eu'ry body this corruption drawes :
To make our peace with that correcting hand,
Which at each moment can our liues command.
These are the blest effects, which sicknesse leaues ;
When these your serious brest aright conceaues,
You will no more repent your former paine
Then we our ioy, to see you well againe.

Elegiac Memorials of Worthies.

Elegiac Memorials of Worthies.

————·

TO THE MEMORY OF THE FAIRE AND THRICE VERTUOUS GENTLEWOMAN, MISTRISS ELIZABETH NEUELL.

 NYMPH is dead, milde, vertuous, young
  and faire ;
Death neuer counts by dayes, or mon'ths,
  or yeeres :
Oft in his sight the infant old appeares,
And to his earthly mansion must repaire.
Why should our sighes disturbe the quiet aire ?
 For when the flood of Time to ruine beares,
 No beauty can preuaile, nor parents teares.
When life is gone, we of the flesh despaire
 Yet still the happy soule immortall liues
 In heauen, as we with pious hope conceiue ;
 And to the Maker endlesse prayses giues,
 That she so soone this lothsome world might leaue.
We iudge that glorious spirit doubly blest,
Which from short life ascends t' eternall rest.

OF THE TRULY NOBLE AND EXCELLENT LADY, THE MARQUESSE OF WINCHESTER.[1]

AN my poore lines no better office haue,
But lie like scritch-owles still about the
    graue ?
When shall I take some pleasure for my paine,
Commending them that can commend againe ?
When shall my Muse in loue-sicke lines recite
Some ladie's worth, which she of whom I write,
With thankfull smiles may reade in her owne
    dayes ?
Or when shall I a breathing woman prayse ?
O neuer ! Mine are too ambitious strings,
They will not sound but of eternall things ;
Such are freed-soules, but had I thought it fit,
T'exalt a spirit to a body knit :
I would confesse I spent my time amisse,
When I was slow to giue due praise to this.
Now when all weepe, it is my time to sing ;
Thus from her ashes must my poem spring :
Though in the race I see some swiftly runne,
I will not crowne them till the goale be won ;

---

1 Lucy, daughter to Thomas, Earl of Exeter, grand-daughter of William Cecil, Lord Burleigh. See Notes and Quories. 1st. Series, xi. 477. **G.**

Till death, ye mortals cannot happy be,
What can I then but woe, and dangers see,
If in your liues I write ? now when ye rest,
I will insert your names among the blest :
And now, perhaps, my verses may increase
Your rising fame, though not your boundlesse
      peace :
Which if they euer could, may they make thine,
Great lady, further, if not clearer shine :
I could thy husband's highest styles relate,
Thy father's earldome, and that England's State
Was wholly manag'd by thy grandsire's brow :
But those that loue thee best, will best allow
That I omit to praise thy match and line,
And speake of things that were more truely thine :
Thou thought'st it base to build on poore remaines
Of noble bloud, which ranne in others' veines ;
As many doe, who beare no flowres, nor fruite,
But shew dead stocks, which haue beene of repute,
And liue by meere remembrance of a sound,
Which was long since by winds disperst and
      drown'd :
While that false worth, which they suppose they
      haue,
Is digg'd vp new from the corrupting graue :
For thou hadst liuing honours, not decay'd
With wearing Time, and needing not the ayd

M

Of heraulds; in the haruest of whose art
None but the vertuous iustly clayme a part:
Since they our parent's memories renew,
For imitation, not for idle view;
Yet what is all their skill, if we compare
Their paper works with those which liuely are,
In such as thou hast been? whose present lookes,
If many such were, would suppresse all bookes;
For their examples would alone suffice:
They that the countrey see, the map despise.
For thee a crowne of vertues we prepare,
The chiefe is wisdome—in thy sex most rare—
By which thou didst thy husband's state maintaine,
Which sure had falne without thee; and in vaine
Had aged Paulet, wealth and honours heap'd
Vpon his house, if strangers had them reapt.
In vaine to height, by safe still steps he climes,
And serues fiue princes in most diff'rent times.
In vaine is he a willow, not an oke,
Which winds might easly bend, yet neuer broke.
In vaine he breakes his sleepe, and is diseas'd,[1]
And grieues himself that others may be pleas'd:
In vaine he striues to beare an equall hand,
'Twixt Somerset and bold Northumberland:
And to his owne close ends directing all,

---

1 Dis-cased. Cf. our Phineas Fletcher, iii, 194.   G.

Will rise with both, but will with neither fall.
All this had been in vaine, vnlèsse he might
Haue left his heires cleare knowledge as their
    right.
But this no sonne infallibly can draw
From his descent, by Nature, or by Law :
That treasure which the soule with glory decks,
Respects not birth-right, nor the nobler sex :
For women oft haue men's defects suppli'd,
Whose office is to keepe what men prouide.
So hast thou done, and made thy name as great,
As his who first exalted Paulet's seate :
Neere dew, yet not too neere, the thunders blow,
Some stood 'twixt Iouc, and him, though most
    below.
O well waigh'd dignity, selected place,
Prouided for continuance of his race,
Not by astrologie, but prudence, farre
More pow'rfull then the force of any starre !
The dukes are gone, and now—though much be-
    neath—
His coronet is next th' imperiall wreath :
No richer signe his flowry garland drown's,
Which shines alone aboue the lesser crownes.
This thou inioyd'st, as sicke men tedious houres,
And thought'st of brighter pearles, and fairer
    flowres,

And higher crownes, which heau'n for thee
    reserues,
When this thy worldy pompe decayes and starues.
This sacred feruour in thy mind did glow :
And though supprest with outward state and
    show,
Yet at thy death those hind'ring clouds it clear'd,
And like the lost sunne to the world appear'd ;
Euen as a strong fire vnder ashes turn'd,
Which with more force long secretly hath burn'd,
Breaks forth to be the obiect of our sight,
Aimes at the orbe, and ioynes his flame with light.

VPON HIS NOBLE FRIEND, SIR WILLIAM SKIPWITH.[1]

O frame a man, who in those gifts excels,
    Which makes the country happy where
      hee dwells,
We first conceiue, what names his line adorne ;
It kindles vertue to be nobly borne.

---

1 He was the oldest son of Henry Skipwith, by Jane,
his wife, daughter of John Hall of Grantham, Esquire, sur-
veyor of the works of Calais, and sister to Arthur Hall, an
early translator of Homer. He married a daughter of Roger

This picture of true gentry must be grac'd,
With glitt'ring iewels round about him plac'd;
A comely body and a beauteous mind;
A heart to loue, a hand to giue inclin'd;
A house as free and open as the ayre;
A tongue which ioyes in language sweet and faire;
Yet can, when need requires, with courage bold,
To publike eares his neighbour's griefes vnfold.
All these we neuer more shall find in one,
And yet all these are clos'd within this stone.

Cave of Stamford, a relative of Lord Burghley, by whom
he had a numerous issue, who married prosperously. He
was one of the three friends to whom John Fletcher dedicated 'The Faithfull Shepherdess': and had himself a
poetic vein. Several of his poems are printed by Nichols
in his *Leicestershire*, Vol. ii., p. 367, and in the Lansdowne
MS., No. 207, is a translation by him of the Eighth Satire
of Juvenal, written at the request of his cousin, Gervas
Holles. Certain 'Lines' of his have been mistaken for
Shakespeare's. He died 3rd May, 1610. See Hunter's
New Illustrations of .... Shakespeare, Vol. I. 75,
Vol. II., 336—337, and Dyce's Beaumont and Fletcher,
Vol. I., xxxiii. *et alibi.* Sir John Beaumont's Lines are
said by Nichols to have been " engraven " on Sir William
Skipwith's tomb (Vol. III., pt. ii., p. 359). G.

AN EPITAPH VPON MY DEARE BROTHER,
FRANCIS BEAUMONT.[1]

N Death, thy murd'rer, this reuenge I take :
I slight his terror, and iust question
make,
Which of vs two the best precedence haue,
Mine to this wretched world, thine to the graue :
Thou shouldst haue followed me, but death to[2]
blame,
Miscounted yeeres, and measur'd age by fame.
So dearely hast thou bought thy precious lines,
Their praise grew swiftly ; so thy life declines :
Thy Muse, the hearer's queene, the reader's loue :
All eares, all hearts—but Death's—could please
and moue.

---

1 The renowned associate of John Fletcher. Probably
his earliest published verses were the few but weighty
lines prefixed to his elder brother's 'Metamorphosis
of Tabacco ' (1602)—given in their place, onward. He
died in 1616. See our Memorial-Introduction for more. G.

2 Misprinted ' too.'   G.

OF MY DEARE SONNE, GERUASE BEAUMONT.

AN I, who haue for others oft compil'd
The songs of Death, forget my sweetest
child,
Which like a flower crusht, with a blast is dead,
And ere full time hangs downe his smiling head,
Expecting with cleare hope to liue anew,
Among the angels fed with heau'nly dew?
We haue this signe of ioy, that many dayes,
While on the earth his struggling spirit stayes,
The name of Iesus in his mouth containes,
His onely food, his sleepe, his ease from paines.
O may that sound be rooted in my mind,
Of which in him such strong effect I find.
Deare Lord, receiue my sonne, whose winning
loue
To me was like a friendship, farre aboue
The course of nature, or his tender age,
Whose lookes could all my bitter griefes asswage;
Let his pure soule ordain'd seu'n yeeres to be
In that fraile body, which was part of me,
Remain my pledge in heau'n, as sent to shew,
How to this port at eu'ry step I goe.

TEARES FOR THE DEATH OF THE TRULY HONOURABLE, THE LORD CHANDOS.[1]

ET him whose lines a priuate losse deplore,
Call them to weepe, that neuer wept
before;
My griefe is more audacious : giue me one
Who eu'ry day hath heard a dying grone.
The subiect of my verses may suffice
To draw new teares from dry and weary eyes.
We dare not loue a man, nor pleasure take
In others' worth for noble Chandos' sake :
And when we seeke the best with reason's light,
We feare to wish him longer in our sight.
Time had increast his vertue and our woe,
For sorrow gathers weight by comming slow :
Should him the God of life, to life restore
Againe, we lose him, and lament the more.
If mortals could a thousand liues renew,
They were but shades of death which must insue.
Our gracious God hath fitter bounds assign'd,
And earthly paines to one short life confin'd ;
Yet when His hand hath quencht the vitall flame,
It leaues some cinders of immortall fame.
At these we blow, and—like Prometheus—striue

---

1 Gray Brugges, Lord Chandos : died in July, 1621. G.

By such weake sparkes, to make dead clay aliue :
Breath flyes to ayre, the body falls to ground,
And nothing dwels with vs but mournfull sound.
O, might his honor'd name liue in my song,
Reflected as with ecchoes shrill and strong!
But when my lines of glorious obiects treate,
They should rise high, because the worke is great.
No quill can paint this lord, vnlesse it haue
Some tincture from his actions free and braue :
Yet from this height I must descend againe,
And—like the calme sea—lay my verses plaine,
When I describe the smoothnesse of his mind,
Where reason's chaines rebellious passions bind :
My poem must in harmony excell,
His sweet behauiour and discourse to tell ;
It should be deepe and full of many arts,
To teach his wisdome, and his happy parts.
But since I want these graces, and despaire
To make my picture—like the patterne—faire ;
These hasty strokes, vnperfect draughts shall stand,
Expecting life from some more skilfull hand.

VPON THE UNTIMELY DEATH OF THE HONOURABLE, HOPEFULL YOUNG GENTLEMAN, EDWARD STAFFORD, SONNE AND HEIRE TO THE LORD STAFFORD.[1]

EAD is the hope of Stafford, in whose line
So many dukes, and carles, and barons
    shine :
And from this Edward's death his kin[d]red drawes
More griefe, then mighty Edward's fall could
    cause :
For to this house his vertue promist more
Then all those great ones that had gone before.
No lofty titles can securely frame
The happinesse and glory of a name :
Bright honours at the point of noone decay,
And feele a sad declining like the day.
But he that from the race of kings is borne,
And can their mem'ries with his worth adorne,
Is farre more blest, then those of whom he springs ;
He from aboue, the soule of goodnesse brings,
T' inspire the body of his noble birth ;
This makes it moue, before but liuelesse earth.
Of such I write, who show'd he would haue been

---

1 Of the house of Buckingham.   See next Lines. G.

Complete in action; but we lost him greene.
We onely saw him crown'd with flowres of hope :
O that the fruits had giu'n me larger scope !
And yet the bloomes which on his herse we strow,
Surpasse the cherries, and the grapes that grow
In others' gardens.   Here fresh roses lie,
Whose ruddy blushes modest thoughts descry,
In flowre-de-luces dide with azure hue,
His constant loue to heau'nly things we view :
The spotlesse lillies shew his pure intent,
The flaming marigold his zeale present,
The purple violets his noble minde,
Degen'rate neuer from his princely kind ;
And last of all the hyacinths we throw,
In which are writ the letters of our woe.

TO THE MEMORY OF EDWARD, LORD STAFFORD.[1]

S over-rich men find it harder farre
T'employ what they possess, then poore
men are :
Such is the state of those who write of thee ;

---

1 This is the father of the youth of the preceding
Lines. He died in 1625. The present Lines appeared

While in that larger field displaid they see
All objects which may help invention in,
They know not where to end, where to begin.
And as into this labyrinth they fall,
Loath to omit the least praise, lose them all.
Then whilst some stile thee with the glorious name
Of lineall heire to mighty Buckingham,
And tells[1] the greatnesse of thy line, that springs
From such as could raise up, and throw down
        kings,
Ile not looke back ; but with the Indians runne
To meete and court thee as my rising sunne.

---

originally in a volume now rarely to be met with viz:
"Honour and Vertue triumphing over the Grave. Exem-
plified in a faire devout Life and Death, adorned with the
surviving perfections of Edward, Lord Stafford, lately
deceased; the last Baron of that illustrious Family :
which honour in him ended with as great lustre as the
Sunne sets within a serene Skye.............By Anth :
Stafford, his most humble Kinsman." (1640 4o.) There
are a great number of Elegics and Verses : and this by
our Sir John Beaumont is the first. It must have been
over-looked by his son in preparing the volume of 1629.
By 1640 the male representatives of the Family were
extinct. Henry, 5th Lord Stafford, died in 1637, under
age, leaving Mary, his only sister his heir. Hence
Anthony Stafford's title-page. G.

    1 Misprinted, tels. G.

My offrings to thy mem'ry shall be seene,
In telling what thou wast, or wouldst haue beene.
Why say I wouldst? when the most jealous eye
Could find no want, though in thine infancy,
Which some say promist much; this I disdaine,
For where the gifts are, promises are vaine;
Since in this noble youth, who did not see
The old man's wisdome, young man's industrie?
An humble maiesty, that could tell how
To scorne a league with pride; yet make it bow.
Whose courage was not in extreames like ours,
With ebs and flowes, causd by the passions' powers:
But was a constant ever grafted loue
To blessed goodnesse, and the Powers aboue.
Who though he joyed in this fraile mortall life,
As one whose soule had felt no ingor'd strife:
Nor labour'd with impatient hast like some
To breake their prison ere the freedome come.
Yet when the euer seeing Power had found
So faire a flowre planted in barren ground;
Whose glorious beauties which that frame inspir'd
Were envyed more then followed or admir'd:
Resolv'd to take what he had onely lent,
As giving him reward, us punishment;
Then death was welcome, and he so resign'd
—Not feeling griefe to leaue, nor feare to find—
That such his parting was as might be said

Whilst he staid here, he liv'd not, but obey'd
That happy call, which all cleare soules expect,
Whose doubtfull states are chang'd to be elect.
Let then such friends as mourne such sad decay
Of his great house—in him the onely stay—
Lift up their wondring eyes and for him looke
In angels' quires, not in a herald's Booke.
Yet though the roote be taken hence to plant,
Where heavenly moisture it can never want ;
There yet remaines a branch shall ever shine
Engrafted in the noble Howards line.

TO THE MEMORY OF THE LEARNED AND RELIGIOUS, FERDINANDO PUL-TON, ESQUIRE.[1]

S at a ioyfull marriage, or the birth
Of some long wishèd child ; or when the earth
Yeelds plenteous fruit, and makes the ploughman
sing :
Such is the sound, and subject of my string :

---

1 By the kindness of a collateral descendant of this
lamented friend of our Poet's—Henry N. Poulton, Esq.,
St. Peter's, Jersey—I have been favoured with an elabor-
ate pedigree of the Family, showing marriages and inter-

Ripe age, full vertue need no fun'rall song,
Here mournfull tunes would Grace and Nature
    wrong.

---

marriages, from John Poulton of Desborough (Richard II.
to Henry IV.) to Martin Poulton with Giles Poulton,
youngest son, married to Alice, daughter and co-heir of
Thomas More, of Bourton, co. Bucks. of the family of Sir
Thomas More, and onward marriage-relationships to
the Penns of the illustrious family of the Founder of
Pensylvania.   It were out of place to use these rich and
laborious genealogical details here.   But I note that our
Ferdinando Poulton, Esq, of Bourton, co. Bucks, was a
barrister of Lincoln's Inn, and author of several legal
works.   He is generally described as of Brasenose College,
Oxford : but this is an error, inasmuch as he completed
his educational studies at Christ's College, Cambridge—
though later in life he entered at Oxford, probably because
of its nearness to Bourton, where he lived.   Among the
Wood MSS. in the Bodleian is the following :

Densbroug. in Com. N'hapt.   In yᵉ chancel of the
Church there on a flat stone :

Hic jacet sepultus Ferdinandus Poulton
de Borton in parochia et comitatu Buckingham natus in hac villa vir omni virtutis
et doctrinarum genere quondam illustrissimus
necnon sedulus scriptor et propagator legum
hujus regni.   Obiit 20 die. Januarii An.
dom : 1617 ætatis 82.

Curiously enough, in the Parish Register he is stated to
have been buried 6th January, 1617.   For all these data

Why should vaine sorrow follow him with teares,
Who shakes off burdens of declining yeeres ?
Whose thread exceeds the vsuall bounds of life,
And feeles no stroke of any fatall knife ?
The Destinies enioyne their wheeles to run,
Vntill the length of his whole course be spun.
No enuious cloud obscures his struggling light,
Which sets contented at the point of night :
Yet this large time no greater profit brings,
Then eu'ry little moment whence it springs,
Vnlesse imploy'd in workes deseruing praise ;
Most weare out many yeeres, and liue few dayes.
Time flowes from instants, and of these each one
Should be esteem'd, as if it were alone :
The shortest space, which we so lightly prize
When it is comming, and before our eyes :
Let it but slide into th' eternall maine,
No realmes, no world can purchase it againe :
Remembrance onely makes the footsteps last,
When winged Time, which fixt the prints, is past.
This he well knowing, all occasions tries,
T' enrich his owne, and others' learnèd eyes.
This noble end, not hope of gaine did draw

I owe thanks to the above Mr. Poulton. They correct
blunders of Lipscombe's ' Buckinghamshire ' and of ' Col-
lectanea Topographica et Genealogica ' and other works.
G.

His minde to trauaile in the knotty Law :
That was to him by serious labour made
A science, which to many is a trade;
Who purchase lands, build houses by their tongue,
And study right, that they may practise wrong.
His bookes were his rich purchases : his fees
That praise which Fame to painefull works[1] decrees :
His mem'ry hath a surer ground then theirs,
Who trust in stately tombes, or wealthy heires.

TO THE IMMORTAL MEMORY OF THE FAIREST AND MOST VERTUOUS LADY, THE LADY CLIFTON.[2]

ER tongue hath ceast to speake, which
      might make dumbe :
All tongues might stay, all pens, all
      hands benum :
Yet I must write : O that it might haue beene

---

1 Painstaking. G.

2 Lady Penelope Clifton, was the daughter of Robert
Rich, earl of Warwick, and wife of Sir Gervase Clifton,
Bart. The dramatist Francis Beaumont also wrote an
'Elegy' on her, and Drayton another. She died 26th of
October, 1613. Sir Gervase, the " sad husband" had (only)
six wives after Lady Penelope. G.

N

While she had liu'd, and had my verses seene,
Before sad cries deaf'd my vntunèd eares,
When verses flow'd more easily then teares.
Ah why neglected I to write her prayse,
And paint her vertues in those happy dayes!
Then my now trembling hand and dazled eye,
Had seldome fail'd, hauing the patterne by ;
Or had it err'd, or made some strokes amisse,
—For who can pourtray Vertue as it is ?—
Art might with Nature haue maintain'd her strife,
By curious lines to imitate true life.
But now those pictures want their liuely grace,
As after death none can well draw the face :
We let our friends passe idly, like our time,
Till they be gone, and then we see our crime,
And think what worth in them might haue beene
        known,
What duties done, and what affection showne :
Vntimely knowledge, which so deare doth cost,
And then beginnes when the thing knowne is lost ;
Yet this cold loue, this enuie, this neglect,
Proclaimes vs modest, while our due respect
To goodnesse, is restrain'd by seruile feare,
Lest to the world it flatt'ry should appeare:
As if the present houres deseru'd no prayse :
But age is past, whose knowledge onely stayes
On that weake prop which memory sustaines,

Should be the proper subiect of our straines :
Or as if foolish men asham'd to sing
Of violets and roses in the Spring,
Should tarry till the flow'rs were blowne away,
And till the Muses' life and heate decay ;
Then is the fury slak'd, the vigour fled,
As here in mine, since it with her was dead :
Which still may sparkle, but shall flame no more,
Because no time shall her to vs restore :
Yet may these sparks, thus kindled with her fame,
Shine brighter and liue longer then some flame.
Here expectation vrgeth me to tell
Her high perfections, which the world knew well.
But they are farre beyond my skill t'vnfold :
They were poore vertues if they might be told.
But thou, who faine would'st take a gen'rall view
Of timely fruites which in this garden grew,
On all the vertues in men's actions looke,
Or reade their names writ in some morall booke ;
And summe the number which thou there shalt
    find :
So many liu'd, and triumph'd in her minde.
Nor dwelt these Graces in a house obscure,
But in a palace faire, which might allure
The wretch who no respect to Vertue bore,
To loue it for the garments which it wore.
So that in her the body and the soule

Contended, which should most adorn the whole.
O happy soule for such a body meete,
How are the firme chaines of that vnion sweete,
Disseur'd in the twinkling of an eye !
And we amaz'd dare aske no reason why,
But silent think, that God is pleas'd to show,
That He hath workes whose end we cannot know
Let vs then ccase to make a vaine request,
To learn why die the fairest, why the best ;
For all these things, which mortals hold most
    deare,
Most slipp'ry are, and yeeld lesse ioy then feare ;
And being lifted high by men's desire,
Are more perspicuous markes for heau'nly fire ;
And are laid prostrate with the first assault,
Because, our loue makes their desert their fault.
Thou Iustice, vs to some amends should mooue
For this our fruitlesse, nay our hurtfull loue ;
We in their honour, piles of stone erect
With their deare names, and worthy prayses deckt :
But since those faile, their glories we rehearse,
In better marble, euerlasting verse :
By which we gather from consuming houres,
Some parts of them, though Time the rest
    deuoures ;
Then if the Muses can forbid to die,
As we their priests suppose, why may not I ?

Although the least and hoarsest in the quire,
Cleare beames of blessed immortality inspire
To keepe thy blest remembrance euer young,
Still to be freshly in all ages sung :
Or if my worke in this vnable be,
Yet shall it euer liue, vpheld by thee :
For thou shalt liue, though poems should decay,
Since parents teach their sonnes, thy prayse to say ;
And to posterity from hand to hand
Conuay it with their blessing and their land.
Thy quiet rest from death, this good deriues
In stead of one, it giues thee many liues :
While these lines last, thy shadow dwelleth here,
Thy fame, it selfe extendeth eu'rywhere ;
In Heau'n our hopes haue plac'd thy better part :
Thine image liues, in thy sad husband's heart :
Who as when he enioy'd thee, he was chiefe
In loue and comfort, so is he now in griefe.

VPON THE DEATH OF THE MOST NOBLE LORD, HENRY, EARLE OF SOUTH-AMPTON, 1624.[1]

HEN now the life of great Southampton
    ends,
His fainting seruants, and astonisht
    friends
Stand like so many weeping marble stones,
No passage left to vtter sighes, or grones :
And must I first dissolue the bonds of griefe,
And straine forth words, to giue the rest reliefe ?
I will be bold my trembling voyce to trie,
That his deare name may not in silence die.
The world must pardon if my song bee weake,

---

1 Henry Wriothesley, Earl of Southampton and
Baron of Tichfield: born 6th Oct. 1573, succeeded his
father, the second Earl, in 1581. In 1585 he became a
Student of St. John's College, Cambridge, and in four
years passed M.A. He married Elizabeth, daughter of
John Vernon, Esq. He died 10th November, 1624, leav-
ing two sons and three daughters, the second of the five
being the celebrated Thomas, earl of Southampton, and
Lord High Treasurer, and—supremost honour—father of
Lady Rachel Russell. See Bell's annotated edition of
Shakespeare's 'Poems' (1855, pp. 36-37—this reference
recalling the enigmatical dedication of 'Venus and
Adonis' and 'Rape of Lucrece.' G.

In such a case it is enough to speake :
My verses are not for the present age :
For what man liues or breathes on England's stage,
That knew not braue Southampton, in whose sight
Most plac'd their day, and in his absence night ?
I striue, that vnborne children may conceiue,
Of what a iewell angry Fates bereaue
This mournefull kingdome, and when heauy woes
Oppresse their hearts, thinke our's as great as those :
In what estate shall I him first expresse,
In youth, or age, in ioy, or in distresse ?
When he was young, no ornament of youth
Was wanting in him, acting that in truth
Which Cyrus did in shadow, and to men
Appear'd like Peleus' sonne, from Chiron's den :
While through this iland Fame his praise reports,
As best in martiall deedes, and courtly sports :
When riper age with wingèd feete repaires,
Graue care adornes his head with siluer haires ;
His valiant feruour was not then decaide,
But ioyn'd with counsell, as a further aide.
Behold his constant and vndaunted eye,
In greatest danger ; when condemn'd to dye,
He scornes th'insulting aduersarie's breath,
And will admit no feare, though neere to Death :
But when our gracious soueraigne had regain'd
  This light, with clouds obscur'd, in walls detain'd :

And by his fauour plac'd this starre on high,
Fixt in the garter, England's azure skie ;
He pride—which dimms such change—as much
    did hate,
As base dejection in his former state :
When he was call'd to sit, by Ioue's command,
Among the demigods, that rule this Land,
No pow'r, no strong perswasion could him draw
From that which he conceiu'd as right and law.
When shall we in this realme a father finde
So truly sweet, or husband halfe so kinde ?
Thus he enioyde the best contents of life,
Obedient children, and a louing wife.
These were his parts in Peace ; but O how farre
This noble soule excell'd it selfe in Warre :
He was directed by a nat'rall vaine,[1]
True honour by this painefull[2] way to gaine.
Let Ireland witnesse, where he first appeares,
And to the sight his warlike ensignes beares.
And thou O Belgia, wert in hope to see
The trophees of his conquests wrought in thee,
But Death, who durst not meet him in the field,
In priuate by close trech'ry made him yeeld.
I keepe that glory last, which is the best;
The loue of learning, which he oft exprest

---

1 Vein. G.   2 Painstaking. G.

By conuersation, and respect to those
Who had a name in artes, in verse or prose :
Shall euer I forget with what delight.
He on my simple lines would cast his sight ?
His onely mem'ry my poore worke adornes,
He is a father to my crowne of thornes :
Now since his death how can I euer looke,
Without some teares, vpon that orphan booke ?
Ye sacred Muses, if ye will admit
My name into the roll, which ye haue writ
Of all your seruants, to my thoughts display
Some rich conceipt, some vnfrequented way,
Which may hereafter to the world commend
A picture fit for this my noble friend :
For this is nothing, all these rimes I scorne ;
Let pens be broken, and the paper torne :
And with his last breath let my musick cease,
Vnlesse my lowly poem could increase
In true description of immortall things,
And rays'd aboue the earth with nimble wings,
Fly like an eagle from his fun'rall fire,
Admir'd by all, as all did him admire.

AN EPITAPH VPON THAT HOPEFULL YOUNG GENTLEMAN, THE LORD WRIOTHESLEY.[1]

ERE lies a souldier, who in youth desir'd
His valiant father's noble steps to tread
And swiftly from his friends and Countrey
    fled,
While to the height of glory he aspir'd.

The cruell Fates with bitter enuy fir'd,
    To see Warre's prudence in so young a head,
    Sent from their dusky caues to strike him dead,
A strong disease in peacefull robes attir'd.

This Murd'rer kills him with a silent dart,
    And hauing drawne it bloody from the sonne,
Throwes it againe into the father's heart,
    And to his lady boasts what he hath done.

What helpe can men against pale Death prouide,
When twice within few dayes Southampton dide?

---

1 James, lord Wriothesley, eldest son of the earl of Southampton, died in the Netherlands a few days before his father. G.

OF THE DEATH OF THE MOST NOBLE THE LORD MARQUESSE HAMILTON.[1]

ANOTHER noble gone ! what art thou Death
That puts a stoppe to eache heroic breath ?
Art thou an enemie to all that's great ?
Doe godlike actions still provoke thy hate ?
Must the best blood then of the sister Land
Still feel the uengeance of thy tyrant hand ?
I bid thee stoppe in this thy bold careere,
We haue a soueraigne of that Land now here ;
Who reigns so noble in his People's loue,
He still mvst waite before he goes aboue.
A loyal subiect bids you to forbear,
Go where you will or chuse, you come not there.
I'll say no more, it goes to eu'ry heart
When even kings are forc'd from friends to part.

---

1 James, second Marquis of Hamilton, was born in
1589 ; succeeded his father 1604, and was created a peer of
England by the titles of Baron of Ennerdale in Cumber-
land and Earl of Cambridge, by patent dated 16th June,
1619. He died at Whitehall 2nd March, 1624-25 in the
36th year of his age.   G.

VPON A FUNERALLE.

O their long home the greatest Princes goe
　　In hearses drest with faire escutcheons
　　　round.
The blazonnes of an antient race, renown'd
　For deeds of valour; and in costly show
The traine moves forward in procession slowe
　　Towards some hallow'd Fane; no common
　　　ground,
　　But the archd uavlt and tombe with scvlpture
　　　crownd
Receive the corse, with honours laid belowe.
Alas! whate'er their wealthe, their witt, their
　　worthe,
Such is the end of all the sonnes of Earthe.[1]

---

1 The preceding and present piece are what occupy
pp. 181—182 (i. e. the cancelled leaf) in the Grenville
copy in the British Museum. I give them here, but there
is a difficulty in accepting them as what was really suppressed. See our Memorial-Introduction for details. G.

TO THE AUTHOUR.[1]

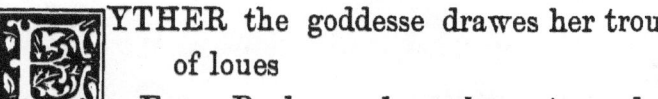

EYTHER the goddesse drawes her troupe
  of loues
 From Paphos, where she erst was held
  diuine,
And doth vnyoke her tender-neckèd doues,
Placing her seat in this small papry shrine ;
Or the sweet Graces through the Idalian groue,
Led the blest Author in their dauncèd rings ;
Or wanton Nymphs in watry bowres haue woue,
With fine Mylesian threds, the verse he sings ;
Or curious Pallas once againe doth striue,
With proud Arachne for illustrious glory,
And once againe doth loues of gods reuiue,
Spinning in silken twists a lasting story :
 If none of these, then Venus chose his sight,
 To leade the steps of her blind sonne aright.

I. B.

---

1 From "Salmacis and Hermaphroditvs" (1602). See
our Memorial-Introduction on the authorship of this
volume, and our edition of Joseph Fletcher's Poems,
pp. 230 G.

TO MY MOST ESTEEMED FRIEND
MAISTER THOMAS COLLINS.[1]

ROM Newport's bloudy battell—sung by
    thee—
    With Yaxley's death — the flow'r of
    Chivalry—
And from thy well-pen'd Publican, to bee
Transported thus to fields of Arcady,
Shewes that thy Muse is apt for all assayes,
And thou a man that meriteth renowne.
Divine, poeticall, and past'rall layes,
Do all concurre thy browes with bayes to crowne
Collins, live ever, in thy lines live ever,
Live ever honord by the trumpe of Fame :
And let all those that in those Arts endeavour,
In their praise-worthy works, still praise thy name :
Who—on all subjects—doth so sweetly sing,
Envie her selfe to touch thee hath no sting.

Io. B.

---

1 From " The Teares of Love : or Cupid's Progress.
Together with the Complaint of the sorrowfull Shepherdesse, fayre (but unfortunate) Candida, deploring the
death of her deare-lov'd Coravin, a late living (and an
ever to be lamented) Shepheard. For a (passionate) pastorall Elegie. Composed by Thomas Collins, &c. (1615
4o)." Collins was author of 'The Penitent Publican ', &c.

TO THE TRANSLATOUR. [1]

WHAT shal I first commend ? your happy choice
    Of this most vsefull poet ? or your skill,
To make the eccho equall with the voice,
And trace the lines drawne by the Author's quill ?
The Latine writers by vnlearnèd hands,
In forraine robes vnwillingly are drest,
But thus inuited into other Lands,
Are glad to change their tongue at such request.
The good, which in our minds their labours breed,
Layes open to their Fame a larger way.
These strangers England with rich plentie feed,
Which with our Countrey's freedome we repay :
    When sitting in a pure language like a throne,
    They proue as great with vs, as with their owne.

(1610 4o)—as alluded to by our Poet. I owe thanks to S. Christie Miller, Esq., of Britwell, for transcript of above. G.

1 From "Odes of Horace, the best of Lyrick Poets : Contayning much morallity and swetnesse. Selected and Translated by Sr. T[homas] H[awkins], 1625. Imprinted at London by A: M: for Will: Lee, and are to be sold at his shoppe in Fleet : street, at the signe of the Golden Bucke" (p. 5th from title-page): Above is usually ascribed— even in Wood's Athenæ by Dr. Bliss, as before— to the son of our Sir John Beaumont. The mistake originated from the rare first edition, *supra*, not having been known. G.

Translations.

Translations.

IVVENAL. SAT. 10.

N all the countries, which from Gades ex-
    tend
  To Ganges, where the Morning's beames
    ascend,
Few men the clouds of errour can remooue,
And know what ill t' auoide, what good to loue :
For what doe we by reason seeke or leaue,
Or what canst thou so happily conceiue,
But straight thou wilt thine enterprise repent,
And blame thy wish, when thou behold'st th'
    euent ?
The easie gods cause houses to decay,
By granting that for which the owners pray ;
In Peace or Warre we aske for hurtfull things,
The copious flood of speech to many brings
Vntimely death ; another rashly dyes,
While he vpon his wondrous strength relyes :
But most by heapes of money chokèd are,
Which they haue gather'd with too earnest care,

Till others they in wealth as much excell,
As British whales aboue the dolphins swell :
In bloody times by Neroe's fierce commands,
The armèd troope about Longinus stands ;
Rich Senecae's large gardens circling round,
And Lateranus' palace much renown'd.
The greedy tyrant's souldier seldome comes,
To ransack beggers in the vpper roomes.
If siluer vessels, though but few thou bear'st,
Thou in the night the sword and trunchion fear'st ;
And at the shadow of each reed wilt quake,
When by the moone light thou perceiu'st it shake :
But he that trauailes empty, feeles no griefe,
And boldly sings in presence of the thiefe :
The first desires, and those which best we know
In all our temples, are that wealth may grow,
That riches may increase, and that our chest
In publike banke may farre exceed the rest.
But men in earthen vessels neuer drinke
Dyre poysons : then thy selfe in danger thinke,
When cups beset with pearles thy hand doth hold,
And precious wine burnes bright in ample gold :
Do'st thou not now perceiue sufficient cause,
To giue those two wise men descru'd applause,
Who when abroad they from their thresholds stept,
The one did alwaies laugh, the other wept ?
But all are apt to laugh in euery place,

And censvre actions with a wrinkled face ;
It is more maruell how the other's eyes
Could moysture find his weeping to suffice.
Democritus did euer shake his spleen
With laughter's force : yet had there neuer been
Within his natiue soyle such garments braue,
And such vaine signes of honour as we haue.
What if he saw the pretor standing out
From lofty chariots in the thronging rout,
Clad in a coate with noble palme-trees wrought,
A signe of triumph, from Ioue's temple brought,
And deckt with an imbrodred purple gowne,
Like hangings from his shoulders trailing downe :
No necke can lift the crowne which then he weares,
For it a publike seruant sweating beares :
And lest the consul should exceed in pride,
A slaue with him in the same coach doth ride.
The bird which on the iu'ry scepter stands,
The cornets, and the long officious bands
Of those that walk before to grace the sight,
The troope of seruile Romans cloth'd in white,
 Which all the way vpon thy horse attends,
Who[m] thy goodcheare and purse haue made thy
        friends ;
To him each thing he meets occasion mooues
Of earnest laughter, and his wisdome prooues,
That worthy men, who great examples giue,

In barb'rous countries and thicke ayre may liue :
He laught at common people's cares and feares,
Oft at their ioyes, and sometimes at their teares ;
He in contempt to threatning Fortune throwes
A halter, and his scornefull finger showes.
  We rub the knees of gods with waxe, to gaine
From them such things as hurtfull are, or vaine ;
Pow'r subiect to fierce spite, casts many downe,
Whom their large stiles, and famous titles drowne.
The statues fall, and through the streets are roll'd :
The wheeles, which did the chariot's weight vp-
    hold,
Are knockt in pieces with the hatchet's stroke ;
The harmelesse horses legs are also broke :
The fires make hissing sovnds, the bellowes blow,
That head dissolu'd, must in the furnace glow,
Which all with honours like the gods did grace.
The great Seianus crackes, and of that face,
Which once the second in the world was nam'd,
Are basons, frying-pans, and dishes fram'd :
Place bayes at home, to Ioue's chiefe temple walke,
And leade with thee a great oxe, white as chalke.
Behold Seianus drawne vpon a hooke,
All men reioyce, what lips had he, what looke ?
Trust me—saith one—I neuer could abide
This fellow ; yet none askes for what he dy'd :
None knowes who was the man that him accus'd ;

What proofes were brought, what testimony vs'd ;
A large epistle fraught with words' great store,
From Capreæ comes: 'tis well, I seeke no more,
The wau'ring people follow Fortune still,
And hate those whom the State intends to kill.
Had Nurtia fauor'd this her Tuscan child,
Had he the aged carelesse prince beguild ;
The same base tongues would in that very houre
Haue rays'd Seianus to Augustus pow'r.
It is long since that we forbidden are,
To sell our voyces free from publike care :
The people which gaue pow'r in Warre and Peace,
Now from those troubles is content to cease,
And eu'ry wish for these two ends bestowes,
For bread in plenty, and Circensian showes.
I heare that many are condemn'd to dye ;
No doubt the flame is great, and swelleth high.
Brutidius looking pale, did meet me neere
To Mars, his altar, therefore much I feare,
Lest vanquisht Aiax find out some pretence,
To punish those that faild in his defence :
Let vs run headlong, trampling Cesar's foe,
While on the banke he lies, our fury show :
Let all our seruants see, and witnesse beare,
How forward we against the traytors were,
Lest any should deny, and to the law,
His fearefull master by the necke should draw.

These were the speeches of Seianus then,
The secret murmures of the basest men.
Would'st thou be flatter'd and ador'd by such
As bow'd to him? Would'st thou possesse as much?
Would'st thou giue ciuill dignities to these?
Would'st thou appoint the[m] gen'rals who thee
    please?
Be tutor to the prince, who on the rock
Of Capreæ sits with his Chaldean flock :
Thou surely seek'st it as a great reward,
T' enioy high places in the field or guard.
This thou defend'st, for those that haue no will,
To make men die, would haue the power to kill :
Yet what such fame or fortune can be found,
But still the woes aboue the ioyes abound?
Had'st thou then rather chuse the rich attire
Of this great lord, now drawne through common
    mire,
Or beare some office in the wretched State
Of Gabij and Fidenæ, and relate
The lawes of measures in a ragged gowne,
And breake small vessels in an empty towne ;
By this time I perceiue thou hast confest,
That proud Seianus could not wish the best :
He that for too much wealth and honour cares,
The heapèd lofts of raysed towres prepares,
Whence from the top his fall declines more steepe,

And headlong ruiue drawes him to the deepe.
This done, rich Crassus and the Pompeys threw,
And him who[m] Romane freedome could subdue,
Because to height by cunning they aspire,
And enuious gods giue way to their desire.
Few tyrants can to Pluto's Court descend,
Without fierce slaughter and a bloody end.

Demosthenes and Tullie's fame and speech,
Each one that studies Rhet'rike, will beseech
At Pallas hands, and during all the dayes
Of her Quinquatria for this only prayes,
Though worshipping her picture basely wrought,
Such as with brazen money he hath bought,
While in a little chest his papers lie,
Which one poore seruant carries waiting nigh :
Yet both these orators whom he admires,
Dy'd for that eloquence which he desires :
What did them both to sad destruction bring,
But wit which flow'd from an abundant spring ?
The wit of Tully caus'd his head and hand
To be cut off, and in the Court to stand.
The pulpits[1] are not moistned with the flood
Of any meane vnlearnèd pleader's blood.
When Tully wrote ; O Rome most blest by fate,
New-borne when I enioy'd the Consul's state :

---

1 See foot-note onward. G.

If he his prose had like his verses shap'd,
He Antonie's sharpe swords might haue escap'd.
Let critikes here their sharpe derision spend,
Yet those harsh poems rather I commend,
Then thee, diuine Philippicke, which in place
Art next the first, but hast the highest grace :
He also with a cruell death expir'd,
Whose flowing torrent Athens so admir'd,
Who rul'd th' vnconstant people when he list,
As if he held their bridles in his fist.
Ah wretched man, begotten with the hate
Of all the gods, and by sinister Fate,
Whom his poore father, bleare-ey'd with the soote
Of sparkes which from the burning ir'n did shoote,
From coales, tongs, anuile, and the cutler's tooles,
And durty forge, sent to the Rhet'ricke Schooles.

   The spoyles of Warre, some rusty corslet plac'd
Of maymèd trophees, cheekes of helmes defac'd ;
Defectiue chariots, conquer'd nauies decks,
And captiues, who themselues with sorrow vexe ;
—Their faces on triumphant arches wrought—
Are things aboue the bliss of mortall thought :
For these incitements to this fruitlesse end,
The Romane, Greeke, and barbr'ous captaines tend.
This caus'd their danger and their willing paine,
So much their thirst is greater for the gaine
Of fame then vertue : for what man regards

Bare vertue, if we take away rewards ?
In ages past the glory of a few,
Their Countrey rashly to destruction drew,
Desiring prayse and titles full of pride,
Inscrib'd on graue-stones which their ashes hide,
Which perish by the sauage fig-tree's strength :
For tombes themselues must haue their fate at
 length.
Let Annibal be ponder'd in thy mind ;
In him thou shalt that waight and value find,
Which fits a great commander. This is he,
Whose spirit could not comprehended be
In Africk, reaching from th' Atlantick streames,
To Nilus heated with the sunny beames ;
And southward stretcht as farre as Ethiope feeds
Huge elephants, like those which India breeds :
He conquers Spaine, which cannot him inclose
With Pyrenæan hills, the Alpes and snowes,
Which Nature armes against him, he derides,
And rockes made soft with vinegar diuides.
He Italy attaines, yet striues to runne
On further : Nothing yet saith he, is done,
Till Punicke souldiers shall Rome's gates deface,
And in her noblest streets mine ensignes place.
How would this one-ey'd generale appeare
With that Gentulian beast which did him beare,
If they were set in picture ? What became

Of all his bold attempts? O deare-bought fame,
He vanquisht, into exile head-long flies,
Where—all men wondring—he in humble wise,
Must at the palace doore attendance make,
Till the Bythinian tyrant please to wake.
No warlike weapons end that restlesse life,
Which in the world caus'd such confusèd strife.
His king reuengeth all the Romans dead
At Cannæ, and the blood which he had shed.
Foole, passe the sharpe Alpes, that thy glorie's
    dreame
May schoole-boyes please, and be their publike
    theame.
One world contents not Alexander's mind,
He thinkes himselfe in narrow bounds confin'd:
It seemes as strait as any little ile,
Or desart rocke to him, whom lawes exile:
But when he comes into the towne, whose walls
Were made of clay, his whole ambition falls
Into a graue: death onely can declare
How base the bodies of all mortals are.
The lying Greekes perswade vs not to doubt,
That Persian nauies sailèd round about
The mountaine Athos, seuer'd from the maine:
Such stuffe their fabulous reports containe:
They tell vs what a passage framèd was
Of ships, that wheeles on solid seas might passe:

That deepest riuers sailèd we must thinke,
Whose floods the Medians at one meale could drink :
And must beleeue such other wond'rous things,
Which Sostratus relates with moyst'ned wings.
But that great king of whom these tales they
  frame,
Tell me how backe from Salamis he came :
That barb'rous prince who vs'd to whip the winds,
Not suff'ring strokes when Aeolus them binds,
He who proud Neptune in his fetters chain'd,
And thought his rage by mildnesse much restrain'd,
Because he did not brand him for his slaue ;
Which of the gods would such a master haue ?
But how return'd he with one slender bote,
Which through the bloody waues did slowly flote,
Oft stay'd with heapes of carkases : these paines
He as the fruits of long-wisht glory gaines.
 Giue length of life, O Ioue, giue many yeeres,
Thou prayst with vpright count'nance, pale with
  feares
Not to be heard ; yet long old age complaines
Of great continuall griefes which it containes :
As first a foule and a deformèd face
Vnlike it selfe, a rugged hide in place
Of softer skin, loose cheekes, and wrinkles made,
As large as those which in the wooddy shade
Of spacious Tabraca, the mother ape

Deepe furrow'd in her agèd chaps doth scrape.
Great diff'rence is in persons that be young,
Some are more beautifull, and some more strong
Then others : but in each old man we see
The same aspect ; his trembling limbes agree
With shaking voyce, and thou may'st adde to those
A bald head, and a childish dropping nose.
The wretched man when to this state he comes,
Must breake his hard bread with vnarmèd gummes
So lothsome, that his children and his wife
Grow weary of him, he of his owne life ;
And Cossus hardly can his fight sustaine,
Though wont to flatter dying men for gaine.
Now his benummèd palate cannot taste
His meate or drinke ; the pleasures now are past
Of sensuall lust ; yet he in buried fires
Retaines vnable and vnfit desires.
What ioy can musicke to his hearing bring,
Though best musicians, yea, Seleucus sing,
Who purchase golden raiments by their voyce :
In theaters he needs not make his choice
Of place to sit, since that his deaf'ned eare
Can scarce the cornets and the trumpets heare :
His boy must cry aloud to let him know
Who comes to see him, how the time doth goe :
A feuer onely heates his wasted blood
In cu'ry part assaulted with a flood

Of all diseases : if their names thou aske,
Thou mayst as well appoint me for a taske,
To tell what close adulterers Hippia loues;
How many sick-men Themison remoues
Out of this world within one Autumne's date :
How many poore confederates of our State,
Haue been by griping Basilus distrest ;
How many orphanes Irus hath opprest ;
To what possessions he is now preferr'd,
Who in my youth scorn'd not to cut my beard :
Some feeble are in shoulders, loynes, or thighes,
Another is depriu'd of both his eyes,
And enuies those as happy that haue one.
This man too weake to take his meate alone,
With his pale lips must feede at others' hands,
While he according to his custome stands
With gaping iawes like to the swallowe's brood,
To whom their hungry mother carries food
In her full mouth : yet worse in him we find
Then these defects in limbes, a doting mind ;
He cannot his owne seruants names recite,
Nor know his friend with whom he supt last night ;
Not those he got and bred : with cruell spots
Out of his Will his doubtlesse heires he blots,
And all his goods to Phiale bequeathes :
So sweet to him a common strumpet breathes.
But if his senses should not thus be spent,

His children's fun'ralls he must oft lament,
He his dear wiue's and brother's death bemones,
And sees the vrnes full of his sister's bones.
Those that liue long endure this lingring paine,
That oft they find new causes to complaine,
While they mishaps in their own house behold,
In woes and mournefull garments growing old.
The Pylian king, as Homer's verses show,
In length of life came nearest to the crow :
Thou think'st him blest whom death so long for-
     beares,
Who on his right hand now accounts his yeeres
By hundreds with an ancient num'rall signe,
And hath the fortune oft to drinke new wine.'
But now obserue how much he blames the law
Of Fates, because too large a thread they draw :
When to Antilochus' last rites he came,
And saw his beard blaze in the fun'rall flame,
Then with demands to those that present are,
He thus his gre'uous mis'ry doth declare :
Why should I last thus long, what hainous crime
Hath made me worthy of such spatious time ?
Like voyces Peleus vs'd, when he bewail'd
Achilles, whom vntimely death assail'd :
And sad Laertes, who had cause to weepe
For his Vlisses swimming on the deepe.
When Troy was safe, then Priam might haue gone

With stately exequies[1] and solemne mone,
T'accompany Assaracus, his ghost,
His fun'rall herse, enricht with princely cost,
Which Hector with his other brothers beares,
Amidst the flood of Ilian women's teares.
When first Cassandra practis'd to lament,
And faire Polyxena with garments rent :
If he had dy'd ere Paris plac'd his sayles
In ventrous ships ; see what long age auailes :
This caus'd him to behold his ruin'd towne,
The swords and fiers which conquer'd Asia drowne ;
Then he, a trembling souldier, off doth cast
His diademe, takes armour ; but at last
Falls at Ioue's altar, like an oxe decai'd ;
Whose pittifull thinne necke is prostrate laid
To his hard master's knife, disdainèd now,
Because not fit to draw th' vngratefull plow :
Yet dy'd he humane death ; but his curst wife
Bark't like a dog, remaining still in life.
To our examples willingly I haste,
And therefore Mithridates haue orepast ;
And Crœsus whom iust Solon bids t'attend,
And not to iudge men happy till the end.
This is the cause that banisht Marius flies,
That he imprison'd is, and that he lies

---

1 Obsequies = Funeral rites.   G.

P

In close Minturnæ's fennes to hide his head,
And necre to conquer'd Carthage begs his bread.
Wise nature had not fram'd, nor Rome brought
    forth
A citizen more noble for his worth;
If hauing to the view his captiues led,
And all his warlike pompe, in glory spred;
Then his triumphant soule he forth had sent,
When from his Cimbrian chariot downe he went.
Campania did for Pompeye's good prouide
Strong feuers, which—if he had then espy'd
What would ensue—were much to be desir'd.
But many cities publike vowes conspir'd,
And this so happy sicknesse could deface,
Reseruing him to dye with more disgrace:
Rome's and his fortune onely sau'd his head,
To be cut off when ouercom'n he fled.
This paine the traytor Lentulus doth scape:
Cethegus not disfigur'd in his shape,
Enioying all his limbes vnmaimèd lyes,
And Catiline with his whole carkase dyes.

    The carefull mother, when she casts her eyes
On Venus' temple in soft lowly wise,
Demands the gift of beauty for her boyes,
But askes it for her girles with greater noyse;
At common formes her wish she neuer staies,
But for the height of delicacy prayes.

And why should'st thou reprooue this prudent
    choice?
Latona in fair Phœbe doth reioyce.
O but Lucretia's haplesse fate deterres,
That others wish not such a face as her's:
Virginia her sweet feature would forsake,
And Rutilae's crook'd backe would gladly take.
Where sonnes are beautifull, the parents' vext
With care and feare, are wretched and perplext.
So seldome an exact consent betweene
Well-fauour'd shapes and chastity is seene.
For should they be with holy manners taught
In homely houses, such as Sabines wrought:
Should bounteous Nature's lib'rall hand bestow
Chast dispositions, modest lookes, which glow
With sanguine blushes—what more happy thing
To boyes can fauourable Nature bring?
Whose inclinations farre more pow'rfull are,
Then many keepers and continuall care:—
Yet they are neuer suffer'd to possesse
The name of man; such foule corrupters presse,
And by the force of large expences trust,
To make their parents instruments of lust.
No tyrant in his cruell palace gelt
Deform'd youths; no noble child had felt
Fierce Neroe's rapes, if all wry-leg'd had beene
If in their necks foule swellings had been seene;

If windy tumours had their bellies rays'd ;
Or camels' bunches had their backs disprais'd :
Goe now with ioy thy young-man's forme affect,
Whom greater dangers and worse fates expect ;
Perhaps he shortly will the title beare
Of a profest adulterer, and will feare
To suffer iustly for his wicked fact,[1]
Such paines as angry husbands shall exact :
Nor can he happier be then Mars, his starre,
T' escape those snares which caught the god of
　　Warre.
Yet oft that griefe to sharper vengeance drawes,
Then is permitted by th' indulgent lawes ;
Some kill with swords, others with scourges cut,
And some th' offenders to foule torments put.
But thine Endymion happily will proue
Some matron's minion, who may merit louc ;
Yet when Seruilia him with money hires,
He must be her's against his owne desires :
Her richest ornaments she off will take,
And strip her selfe of iewcls for his sake.
What will not Hippia and Catulla giue
To those, that with them in adult'ry liue :
For wicked women in these base respects
Place all their manners, and their whole affects.

---

1 Act or deed, as before.　G.

But thou wilt say, can beauty hurt the chaste ?
Tell me what ioy Hippolitus did taste,
What good seuere Bellerophon receiu'd,
When to their pure intents they strictly cleau'd ?
Both Sthenobæa and the Cretan queene,
Asham'd of their repulse, stirr'd vp their teene :[1]
For then a woman breeds most fierce debate,
When shame adds piercing stings to cruell hate.
How would'st thou counsell him, whom th' emp'ror's
      wife
Resolues to marry in her husband's life :
The best and fairest of the lords must dye ;
His life is quencht by Messallinae's eye :
She in her nuptiall robes doth him expect,
And openly hath in her gardens deckt
A purple marriage bed, nor will refuse
To giue a dowre, and ancient rites to vse.
The cunning wizzard who must tell the doome
Of his successe, with notaries must come :
Thou think'st these things are hid from publike
      view,
And but committed to the trust of few.
Nay, she will haue her solemne wedding, drest
With shew of law : then teach him what is best,
He dies ere night vnlesse he will obay :

---

1 Vengeance. Cf. Our Joseph Fletcher, page 11. G.

Admit the crime, he gaines a little stay,
Till that which now the common people heares,
May come by rumour to the prince's eares :
For he is sure to be the last that knowes
The secret shame which in his household growes :
Thy selfe awhile to her desires apply,
And life for some few days so dearely buy.
What way soeuer he as best shall chuse,
That faire white necke he by the sword must luse.
   Shall men wish nothing ? wilt thou counsell take?
Permit the heau'nly powers the choyce to make,
What shall be most conuenient for our fates,
Or bring most profit to our doubtfull states :
The prudent gods can place their gifts aright,
And grant true goods in stead of vaine delight.
A man is neuer to himselfe so deare,
As vnto them when they his fortunes steare :
We carried with the fury of our minds,
And strong affection which our iudgement blinds,
Would husbands proue, and fathers, but they see
What our wisht children and our wiues will bee:
Yet that I may to thee some pray'rs allow,
When to the sacred temples thou do'st vow
Diuinest entrailes in white pockets found,
Pray for a sound mind in a body sound ;
Desire braue spirit, free from feare of death,
Which can esteeme the latest houre of breath,

Among the gifts of Nature which can beare
All sorrowes from desire and anger cleare,
And thinkes the paines of Hercules more blest,
Then wanton lust, the suppers and soft rest,
Wherein Sardanapalus ioy'd to liue.
I show thee what thou to thy selfe mayst giue ;
If thou the way to quiet life wilt treade,
No guide but Vertue can thee thither leade :
No pow'r diuine is euer absent there,
Where wisdome dwells, and equall rule doth beare.
But we, O Fortune, striue to make thee great,
Plac'd as a goddesse in a heau'nly seate.

A FUNERALL HYMNE OUT OF PRUDEN-
TIUS.

 GOD, the soules pure fi'ry spring.
Who diff'rent natures wouldst combine :
That man whom thou to life didst bring,
By weaknesse may to death decline,
By Thee they both are fram'd aright,
They by Thy hand vnited be ;
And while they ioyne with growing might,
Both flesh and spirit liue to Thee :
But when disunion them recals.
They bend their course to seu'rall ends,

Into dry earth the body falls,
The feruent soule to heau'n ascends :
For all created things at length,
By slow corruption growing old,
Must needs forsake compacted strength,
And disagreeing webs vnfold.
But thou, deare Lord, hast meanes prepar'd,
That death in Thine may neuer reigne,
And hast vndoubted waies declar'd,
How members lost may rise againe :
That while those gen'rous rayes are bound
In prison vnder fading things ;
That part may still be stronger found,
Which from aboue directly springs.
If man with baser thoughts possest,
His will in earthly mud shall drowne ;
The soules with such a weight opprest,
Is by the body carried downe :
But when she mindfull of her birth,
Her self from vgly spots debarres ;
She lifts her friendly house from earth,
And beares it with her to the starres.
See how the empty bodies lyes,
Where now no liuely soule remaines :
Yet when short time with swiftnesse flyes,
The height of senses it regaines.
Those ages shall be soon at hand,

When kindly heate the bones reniewes ;
And shall the former house command,
Where liuing blood it shall infuse.
Dull carkases to dust now worne,
Which long in graues corrupted lay,
Shall to the nimble ayre be borne,
Where soules before haue led the way.
Hence comes it, to adorne the graue,
With carefull labour men affect :
The limbes dissolu'd last honour haue,
And fun'rall rites with pompe are deckt :
The custome is to spread abroad
White linnens, grac'd with splendour pure,
Sabæan myrrh on bodies strow'd,
Preserues them from decay secure.
The hollow stones by caruers wrought,
Which in faire monuments are laid,
Declare that pledges thither brought,
Are not to death but sleepe conuay'd.
The pious Christians this ordaine,
Beleeuing with a prudent eye,
That those shall rise and liue againe,
Who now in freezing slumbers lye.
He that the dead—disperst in fields—
In pittie hides, with heapes of molds,
To his Almighty Sauiour yeelds,
A worke which he with ioy beholds.

The same law warnes vs all to grone,
Whom one seuere condition ties,
And in another's death to mone.
All fun'rals, as of our allies :
That reu'rend man in goodnesse bred,
Who blest Tobias did beget,
Preferr'd the buriall of the dead
Before his meate, though ready set ;
He, while the seruants waiting stand,
Forsakes the cups, the dishes leaues,
And digges a graue with speedy hand,
Which with the bones his teares receiues.
Rewards from heau'n this worke requite :
No slender price is here repaid,
God cleares the eyes that saw no light,
While fishes' gall on them is laid.
Then the Creator would descry,
How farre from reason they are led,
Who sharpe and bitter things apply,
To soules on which new life is spred.
He also taught that to no wight,
The heau'nly kingdome can be scene,
Till vext with wounds and darksome night,
He in the world's rough waues hath been.
The curse of death a blessing finds,
Because by this tormenting woe,
Steepe waies lye plaine to spotlesse minds,

Who to the starres by sorrowes goe.
The bodies which long perisht lay,
Returne to liue in better yeeres :
That vnion neuer shall decay,
Where after death new warmth appeares.
The face where now pale color dwels,
Whence foule infection shall arise,
The flowres in splendour then excels,
When blood the skinne with beauty dies.
No age by Time's imperious law,
With enuious prints the forehead dimmes :
No drought, no leanenesse then can draw
The moysture from the wither'd limmes.
Diseases which the body eate,
Infected with oppressing paines,
In midst of torments then shall sweate,
Imprison'd in a thousand chaines.
The conqu'ring flesh immortall growes,
Beholding from the skies aboue,
The endlesse groning of her foes,
For sorrowes which from them did moue.
Why are vndecent howlings mixt
By liuing men in such a case ?
Why are decrees so sweetly fixt,
Reprou'd with discontented face ?
Let all complaints and murmurs fai le ;
Ye tender mothers stay your teares,

Let none their children deare bewaile,
For life renew'd in death appears.
So buried seeds, though dry and dead,
Againe with smiling greennesse spring :
And from the hollow furrowes bred,
Attempt new eares of corne to bring.
Earth, take this man with kind embrace,
In thy soft bosome him conceiue :
For humane members here I place,
And gen'rous parts in trust I leaue.
This house, the soule her guest once felt,
Which from the Maker's mouth proceeds :
Here sometime feruent wisdome dwelt,
Which Christ the Prince of Wisedome breeds.
A cou'ring for this body make :
The Author neuer will forget
His workes ; nor will those lookes forsake,
In which He hath His picture set.
For when the course of time is past,
And all our hopes fulfill'd shall be,
Thou op'ning must restore at last
The limbes in shape which now we see.
Nor if long age with pow'rfull reigne,
Shall turne the bones to scatter'd dust,
And onely ashes shall retaine,
In compasse of a handfull thrust :
Nor if swift floods, or strong command

Of windes through empty ayre haue tost
The members with the flying sand ;
Yet man is neuer fully lost,
O God, while mortall bodies are
Recall'd by Thee, and form'd againe.
What happy seate wilt Thou prepare,
Where spotlesse soules may safe remaine ;
In Abraham's bosome they shall lie
Like Lazarus, whose flowry crowne
The rich man doth farre off espie,
While him sharpe fiery torments drowne.
Thy words, O Sauiour we respect,
Whose triumph driues black Death to losse,
When in Thy steps thou woulds't direct
The thiefe Thy fellow on the crosse.
The faithfull see a shining way,
Whose length to paradise extends,
This can them to those trees conuay,
Lost by the Serpent's cunning ends.
To Thee I pray most certaine Guide :
O let this soule which Thee obay'd,
In her faire birth-place pure abide,
From which she, banisht, long hath stray'd.
While we vpon the couer'd bones
Sweet violets and leaues will throw :
The title and the cold hard stones,
Shall with our liquid odours flow.

AN EPIGRAM CONCERNING MAN'S LIFE COMPOSED BY CRATES OR POSIDIPPUS.[1]

WHAT course of life should wretched mortals take ?
     In Courts, hard questions, large contentions make,
Care dwels in houses, labour in the field,
Tumultuous seas affrighting dangers yeeld,
In forraine Lands thou neuer canst be blest ;
If rich, thou art in feare ; if poore distrest.
In wedlock, frequent discontentments swell :
Vnmarried persons, as in desarts dwell.
How many troubles are with children borne !
Yet he that wants them, counts himselfe forlorne.
Young men are wanton, and of wisedome void :
Gray haires are cold, vnfit to be imploid.
Who would not one of these two offers choose :
Not to be borne, or breath with speede to loose ?

---

1 Bp. Henry King in his "Elegy occasioned by Sickness" alludes to and quotes from this Epigram as follows :

——" with that Greek Sage still make us cry
Not to be born, or being born, to dy."

Cf. last line of above. The Original is given from Brunck, (Gnomon Gr. P. p 196.) in HANNAH's edition of KING,

THE ANSWER OF METRODORUS.[1]

N eu'ry way of life, true pleasure flowes,
    Immortall fame, from publike action
      growes :
Within the doores is found appeasing rest ;
In fields, the gifts of Nature are exprest.
The sea brings gaine, the rich abroad prouide,
To blaze[2] their names, the poore their wants to hide :
All housholds best are gouern'd by a wife ;
His cares are light, who leades a single life.
Sweet children, are delights, which marriage blesse :
He that hath none, disturbs his thoughts the lessè.
Strong youth, can triumph in victorious deeds :

Notes p. 173. Bacon has the sentiment in his well-known grave and tender poem, after the same Epigram, thus :

" What then remains but that we still should cry
    For being born, and being born to die."

I may note that this Poem, bearing Bacon's name, is found appended to Sylvester's 'Panthea' (1630). See further in our edition of the Poems of Bacon, in first Series of 'Miscellanies' in our Worthies. G.

1 For an ample collection of similar passages to above and preceding, see Davis's notes to Cicero's Tusc. Disp. I. 48. Hannah, as before, p. 173. G.

2. Cf. our Phineas Fletcher, ii., 313 ; iii, 36 : iv., 42, 411. G.

Old age the soule, with pious motion feeds.
All states are good, and they are falsly led,
Who wish to be vnborne, or quickly dead.

HORAT. LIB. 2. SAT.

THIS was my wish : no ample space of
ground :
T' include my garden with a mod'rate
bound,
And neere my house a fountaine neuer dry,
A little wood, which might my wants supply ;
The gods haue made me blest with larger store :
It is sufficient, I desire no more.
O sonne of Maia, but this grant alone,
That quiet vse may make these gifts mine owne.
If I increase them by no lawlesse way,
Nor through my fault will cause them to decay.
If not to these fond hopes my thoughts decline,
O that this ioyning corner could be mine,
Which with disgrace deformes, and maimes my
field :
Or fortune would a pot of siluer yeeld,
—As vnto him who being hir'd to worke,
Discouer'd treasure, which in mold did lurke,
And bought the land which he before had till'd

Since friendly Hercules his bosome fill'd—
If I with thankfull minde these blessings take,
Disdaine not this petition which I make.
Let fat in all things, but my wit, be seene,
And be my safest guard as thou hast been.
When from the citty I my selfe remoue
Vp to the hills, as to a towre aboue,
I find no fitter labours, nor delights
Then Satyres, which my lowly Muse indites.
No foule ambition can me there expose
To danger, nor the leaden wind that blowes
From Southerne parts, nor Autumne's grieuous
    raine,
Whence bitter Libitina reapes her gaine.
O father of the morning's purple light!
Or if thou rather would'st be Ianus hight,
From whose diuine beginning, mortalls draw
The paines of life, according to the law,
Which is appointed by the gods decree,
Thou shalt the entrance of my verses be.
At Rome thou driu'st me, as a pledge to goe,
That none himselfe may more officious show.
Although the fury of the Northerne blast
Shall sweepe the earth; or Winter's force hath
    cast
The snowy day, into a narrow sphere,
I must proceed, and hauing spoken cleare

Q

And certaine truth, must wrestle in the throng,
Where by my haste, the slower suffer wrong,
And crie,   What ayles the mad man ? whither tend
His speedy steps ? while mine imperions frend
Intreates, and chafes, admitting no delay,
And I must beate all those, that stop my way.
The glad remembrance of Mecænas lends
A sweete content : but when my iourney bends,
To blacke Esquiliæ, there a hundred tides
Of strangers' causes presse my head and sides,
You must, before the second houre, appeare
In Court to morrow, and for Roscius sweare.
The scribes desire you would to them repaire,
About a publike, great, and new affaire,
Procure such fauour from Mecænas' hand,
As that his seale may on this paper stand.
I answer, I will trie : he vrgeth still,
I know you can performe it if you will :
Seu'n yeeres are fled, the eighth is almost gone,
Since first Mecænas tooke me for his owne,
That I with him might in his chariot sit,
And only then would to my trust commit
Such toyes[1] as these : what is the time of day ?
The Thracian is the Syrian's match in play.
Now carelesse men are nipt with morning cold :

---

1 Trifles.   G.

And words which open eares may safely hold.
In all this space for eur'y day and houre
I grew more subiect to pale Enuie's pow'r.
This sonne of Fortune to the stage resorts,
And with the fau'rite in the field disports:
Fame from the pulpits[1] runnes through eu'ry
    streete,
And I am strictly askt by all I meete:
Good Sir you needes must know, for you are neare
Vnto the gods—doe you no tidings heare
Concerning Dacian troubles? Nothing I.
You allwayes loue your friends with scoffes to try,
If I can tell, the gods my life confound.
But where will Cæsar giue his souldiers ground,
In Italie, or the Trinacrian Ile?
I sweare I know not: they admire[2] the while,
And thinke me full of silence, graue and deepe,
The onely man that should high secrets keepe;
For these respects—poore wretch—I lose the light,
And longing thus repine: when shall my sight

---

1 Cf. Nehemiah viii.. 4 : another of the few words over-
looked by Mr. W. A. Wright in his Bible Word-Book.
From the Latin *pulpitum*, as in Horace, Ep. 1, 19, 39 : A.
P. 174, 278 : Juvenal 3, 174; 7, 93 *et alibi* : but in
Juvenal above, and in Horace before, the word is rostra.
G.

   2 Wonder. G.

Againe bee happy in beholding thee
My countrey farme? or when shall I be free
To reade in bookes what ancient writers speake,
To rest in sleepe, which others may not breake,
To taste—in houres secure from courtly strife—
The soft obliuion of a carefull life?
O when shall beanes vpon my boord appeare,
Which wise Pythagoras esteem'd so deare?
Or when shall fatnesse of the lard anoint
The herbes, which for my table I appoint?
O suppers of the gods! O nights diuine!
When I before our Lar might feast with mine,
And feede my prating slaues with tasted meate,
As eu'ry one should haue desire to eate.
The frolike guest not bound with heauy lawes,
The liquor from vnequall measures drawes:
Some being strong, delight in larger draughts,
Some call for lesser cups to cleere their thoughts.
Of others house and lands no speaches grow,
Nor whether Lepos danceth well or no.
We talke of things which to our selues pertaine,
Which not to know would be a sinfull staine.
Are men by riches or by vertue blest?
Of friendship's ends is vse or right the best?
Of good what is the nature, what excells?
My neighbour Ceruius old wiues fables tells;
When any one Arellius' wealth admires,

And little knowes what troubles it requires,
He thus beginnes : ' Long since a countrey mouse
Receau'd into his low and homely house
A citty mouse, his friend and guest before ;
The host was sharpe and sparing of his store,
Yet much to hospitality inclin'd :
For such occasions could dilate his mind.
He chiches[1] giues, for Winter layd aside,
Nor are the long and slender otes deny'd :
Dry grapes he in his lib'rall mouth doth beare,
And bits of bacon which halfe eaten were :
With various meates to please the stranger's pride,
Whose dainty teeth through all the dishes slide.
The father of the family in straw
Lies stretcht along, disdaigning not to gnaw
Base corne or darnell, and reserues the best,
To make a perfect banquet for his guest.
To him at last the citizen thus spake :
My friend, I muse what pleasure thou canst take,
Or how thou canst endure to spend thy time
In shady groues, and vp steepe hills to clime.
In sauage forrrest build no more thy den :
Goe to the city, there to dwell with men.
Begin this happy iourney, trust to me,
I will thee guide, thou shalt my fellow be :

---

1 A dwarf-pea or vetch. G.

Since earthly things are ty'd to mortall liues,
And eu'ry great, and little creauture striues
In vaine the certaine stroke of death to flie,
Stay not till moments past thy ioyes denie.
Liue in rich plenty, and perpetuall sport,
Liue euer mindfull, that thine age is short.
The rauisht field-mouse holds these words so sweet,
That from his home he leapes with nimble feet.
They to the citie trauaile with delight,
And vnderneath the walles they creepe at night.
Now darknesse had possest heau'n's middle space,
When these two friends their weary steps did place
Within a wealthy palace, where was spred
A scarlet cou'ring on an iu'ry bed :
The basket—set farre off aside— contain'd
The meates, which after plenteous meales remain'd :
The citie mouse with courtly phrase intreates
His country friend to rest in purple scates ;
With ready care the master of the feast
Runnes vp and downe to see the store increast :
He all the duties of a seruant showes,
And tastes of eu'ry dish, that he bestowes.
The poore plaine mouse, exalted thus in state,
Glad of the change, his former life doth hate.
And striues in lookes and gesture to declare
With what contentment he receiues this fare.
But straight the sudden creaking of a doore

Shakes both these mice from beds into the floore.
They runne about the roome halfe dead with feare,
Through all the house the noise of dogs they heare.
The stranger now counts not the place so good,
He bids farewell, and saith, the silent wood
Shall me hereafter from these dangers saue,
Well pleas'd with simple vetches in my caue.'

HORAT. CARM. LIB. 3. OD. 29.

ECÆNAS,—sprung from Tuscan kings—
    for thee
      Milde wine in vessels neuer toucht, I
    keepe :
  Here roses, and sweete odours be,
    Whose dew thy haire shall steepe :
O stay not, let moyst Tibur be disdain'd,
And Æsulae's declining fields, and hills,
    Where once Telegonus remain'd,
      Whose hand his father kills ;
Forsake that height where lothsome plenty cloyes,
And towres, which to the lofty clouds aspire ;
    The smoke of Rome, her wealth and noyse
      Thou wilt not here admire.
In pleasing change, the rich man takes delight
And frugall meales in homely seates allowes,

Where hangings want, and purple bright
   He cleares his carefull browes.
Now Cepheus plainely shewes his hidden fire,
The Dog-starre now his furious heate displayes,
   The Lion spreads his raging ire,
     The Sunne brings parching dayes.
The Shepheard now his sickly flocke restores,
With shades, and riuers, and the thickets finds
   Of rough Siluanus; silent shores
     Are free from playing winds.
To keepe the State in order is thy care,
Sollicitous for Rome, thou fear'st the warres,
   Which barbrous easterne troopes prepare,
     And Tanais vs'd to iarres.
The wise Creator from our knowledge hides
The end of future times in darksome night;
   False thoughts of mortals He derides,
     When them vaine toyes affright.
With mindfull temper present houres compose,
The rest are like a riuer, which with ease,
   Sometimes within his channell flowes,
     Into Etrurian seas.
Oft stones, trees, flocks, and houses it deuoures,
With echoes from the hills, and neighb'ring woods,
   When some fierce deluge, rais'd by showres,
     Turnes quiet brookes to floods.
He master of himselfe, in mirth may liue,

Who saith, I rest well pleas'd with former dayes;
   Let God from heau'n to morrow giue
      Blacke clouds, or sunny rayes.
No force can make that voide, which once is past,
Those things are neuer alter'd, or vndone,
   Which from the instant rolling fast,
      With flying moments run.
Proud Fortune ioyfull sad affaires to finde,
Insulting in her sport, delights to change
   Vncertaine honours : quickly kinde,
      And straight againe as strange.
I prayse her stay, but if she stirre her wings,
Her gifts I leaue, and to my selfe retire,
   Wrapt in my vertue : honest things
      In want no dowre require.
When Lybian stormes, the mast in pieces shake,
I neuer God with pray'rs and vowes implore,
   Lest precious wares addition make
      To greedy Neptune's store.
Then I contented, with a little bote,
Am through Ægean waues, by winds conuay'd,
Where Pollux makes me safely flote,
      And Castor's friendly aide.

HORAT. EPOD. 2.

E happy is, who farre from busie sounds,
   —As ancient mortals dwelt—
With his owne oxen tills his father's
   grounds,
   And debts hath neuer felt.
No Warre disturbes his rest with fierce alarmes,
   Nor angry seas offend :
He shunnes the law, and those ambitious charmes,
   Which great men's doores attend.
The lofty poplers with delight he weds
   To vines that grow apace,
And with his hooke vnfruitfull branches shreds,
   More happy sprouts to place ;
Or else beholds, how lowing heards astray,
   In narrow valleys creepe ;
Or in cleane pots doth pleasant hony lay,
   Or sheares his feeble sheepe.
When Autumne from the ground his head vpreares,
   With timely apples chain'd,
How glad is he to pluck ingrafted peares,
   And grapes with purple stain'd !
Thus he Priapus, or Syluanus payes,
   Who keepes his limits free,
His weary limbes, in holding[1] grasse he layes,

---

1 = matted. G.

Or vnder some old tree :
Along the lofty bankes the waters slide,
   The birds in woods lament,
The springs with trickling streams the ayre diuide,
   Whence gentle sleepes are lent.
But when great Ioue, in Winter's dayes restores
   Vnpleasing showres and snowes,
With many dogs he drives the angry bores
   To snares which them oppose.
His slender nets dispos'd on little stakes,
   The greedy thrush preuent :
The fearefull hare, and forraine crane he takes,
   With this reward content.
Who will not in these ioyes forget the cares,
   Which oft in loue we meete :
But when a modest wife the trouble shares
   Of house and children sweete,
—Like Sabines, or the swift Apulian's wiues,
   Whose cheekes the sunbeames harme ;
When from old wood she sacred fire contriues,
   Her weary mate to warme,
When she with hurdles, her glad flockes confines,
   And their full vdders dries,
And from sweet vessels drawes the yearely wines,
   And meates vnbought supplies ;
No Lucrine oysters can my palate please,
   Those fishes I neglect,

Which tempests thundring on the easterne seas
   Into our waues direct.
No bird from Affrike sent, my taste allowes,
   Nor fowle which Asia breeds :
The oliue—gather'd from the fatty boughes—
   With more delight me feeds.
Sowre herbs, which loue the meades, or mallowes
     good,
   To ease the body, pain'd :
A lambe which sheds to Terminus her blood,
   Or kid from wolues regain'd.
What ioy is at these feasts, when well-fed flocks
   Themselues for home prepare !
Or when the weake necke of the weary oxe
   Drawes back th' inuerted share ?
When slaues—the swarmes that wealthy houses
     charge—
   Neere smiling Lar, sit downe :
This life when Alphius hath describ'd at large,
   Inclining to the clowne,
He at the Ides calles all that money in,
   Which he hath let for gaine :
But when the next month shall his course begin,
   He puts it out againe.

PER. SAT. 2.

ACRINUS, let this happy day be knowne
As white, and noted with a better stone,
Which to thine age doth sliding yeeres
    combine :
Before thy genius powre forth cups of wine,
Thy pray'rs expect no base and greedy end,
Which to the gods thou closely must commend :
Though most of those whom honours lift on high,
In all their off'rings silent incense frie,
All from the temple are not apt to take
Soft lowly sounds, and open vowes to make.
The gifts of minde, fame, faith he vtters cleare,
That strangers may farre off his wishes heare :
But this he mumbles vnderneath his tongue :
O that mine vnkle's death expected long,
Would bring a fun'rall which no cost shall lacke !
O that a pot of siluer once would cracke
Beneath my harrow, by Alcides sent !
Or that I could the orphan's hopes preuent,[1]
To whom I am next heire, and must succeed !
—Since swelling humours in his body breed,
Which threaten oft the shortnesse of his life—
How blest is Nerius, thrice to change his wife !

---

1 Anticipate = come before. G.

Those are the holy pray'rs for which thy head
—When first the morning hath her mantle spred—
Is dipt so many times in Tiber's streames,
Where running waters purge the nightly dreames.
I thus demand : in answer be not slow,
It is not much that I desire to know :
Of Ioue what think'st thou ? if thy iudgement can
Esteeme him iuster then a mortall man ?
Then Staius ? doubt'st thou which of these is best
To iudge aright the fatherlesse opprest?
The speech with which thine impious wishes dare
Prophane Ioue's cares, to Staius now declare :
O Ioue, O good Ioue, he will straight exclaime,
And shall not Ioue crie out on his owne name ?
For pardon can'st thou hope, because the oke
Is sooner by the sacred brimstone broke,
When thunder teares the ayre, then thou and
        thine,
Because thou ly'st not, as a dismall signe
In woods, while entrailes, and Ergennae's art,
Bid all from thy sad carkase to depart,
Will therefore Ioue his foolish beard extend,
For thee to pull ? what treasure can'st thou spend
To make the cares of gods by purchase thine ?
Can lights[1] and bowels bribe the pow'rs diuine ?

---

1 The original is ' *pulmone* et lactibus unctis.' I had

Some grandame, or religious aunt, whose ioy
Is from the cradle to take out the boy,
In lustral spittle her long finger dips,
And expiates his forehead and his lips.
Her cunning from bewitching eyes defends,
Then in her armes she dandles him, and sends
Her slender hope, which humble vowes propound
To Crassus house, or to Licinius' ground.
Let kings and queenes wish him their sonne in
    law;
Let all the wenches him in pieces draw;
May eu'ry stalke of grasse on which he goes,
Be soone transform'd into a fragrant rose.
No such request to nurses I allow,
Ioue—though she pray in white—refuse her vow:
Thou would'st firme sinewes haue, a body strong,
Which may in age continue able long,
But thy grosse meates, and ample dishes stay
The gods from granting this, and Ioue delay.
With hope to raise thy wealth, thou kill'st an oxe,
Inuoking Hermes : blesse my house and flockes.
How can it be—vaine foole—when in the fires
The melted fat of many steeres expires?
Yet still thou think'st to ouercome at last,

---

thought that 'lights'=lungs, was limited to Scotland as
applied to oxen and the like. G.

While many offrings in the flame are cast !
Now shall my fields be large, my sheepe increase;
Now it will come, now, now ; nor wilt thou cease,
Vntil deceiu'd, and in thy hopes deprest,
Thou sigh'st to see the bottom of thy chest :
When I to thee haue cups of siluer brought,
Or gifts in solid golden metall wrought :
The left side of thy brest will dropping, sweate,
And full of ioy thy trembling heart will beate.
Hence comes it, that with gold in triumph borne,
Thou do'st the faces of the gods adorne,
Among the brazen brethren they that send
Those dreames, where euill humours least extend,
The highest place in men's affections hold,
And for their care receiue a beard[1] of gold :
The glorious name of gold hath put away
The vse of Saturne's brasse, and Numac's clay.
This glitt'ring pride to richer substance turnes
The Tuscan earthen pots, and vestall vrnes.
O crooked soules, declining to the earth,
Whose empty thoughts forget their heau'nly birth :
What end, what profit haue we, when we striue
Our manners to the temples to deriue ?[2]
Can we suppose, that to the gods we bring
Some pleasing good for this corrupted spring ?

---

1 Cf the Commentators on the original, aurea barba. G.
2 Communicate. G.

This flesh, which Casia doth dissolue and spoyle,
And with that mixture taints the natiue oyle :
This boyles the fish with purple liquor full,
And staines the whitenesse of Calabrian wooll.
This from the shell scrapes out the pearle, and
    straines
From raw rude earth the feruent metal's veines
This sinnes, it sinnes,[1] yet makes some vse of vice :
But tell me, ye great Flamins, can the price
Raise gold to more account in holy things,
Then babies, which the maid to Venus brings ?
Nay rather let us yeeld the gods such gifts,
As great Messallae's off-spring neuer lifts,
In costly chargers strecht to ample space,
Because degen'rate from his noble race :
A soule where iust and pious thoughts are chain'd :
A mind, whose secret corners are vnstain'd :
A brest, in which all gen'rous vertues lie,
And paint it with a neuer-fading die.
Thus to the temples let me come with zeale,
The gods will heare me, though I offer meale.

---

1 The original is 'peccat et hæc, peccat: vitio tamen utitur' = The flesh too errs, it errs : but yet makes profit of its error.' G.

R

AVSON. IDYLL. 16.

A MAN, both good and wise, whose perfect
    mind
  Apollo cannot in a thousand find :
As his owne iudge, himselfe exactly knowes,
Secure what lords or vulgar brests suppose :
He, like the world an equall roundnesse beares,
On his smooth sides no outward spot appeares :
He thinkes, how Cancer's starre increaseth light ;
How Capricorne's cold tropicke lengthens night ;
And by iust scales will all his actions trie,
That nothing sinke too low, nor rise too high,
That corners may with euen parts incline,
And measures erre not with a faulty line,
That all within be solid, lest some blow
Should by the sound the empty vessel show ;
Ere he to gentle sleepe his eyes will lay,
His thoughts reuolue the actions of the day,[1]
What houres from me with dull neglect haue
    runne,
What was in time, or out of season done?
Why hath this worke, adorning beauty lackt,

---

1 The Sir Charles Bawdin of Chatterton
     " Summed the actions of the day
    Each night before he slept." G.

Or reason wanted in another fact ?[1]
What things haue I forgotten, why design'd
To seeke those ends, which better were declin'd ?
When to the needy wretch I gaue reliefe,
Why was my broken soule possest with griefe ?
In what haue my mistaking wishes err'd,
Why profit more then honesty preferr'd ?
Could my sharpe words another man incense,
Or were my bookes compos'd to breed offence ?
How comes it that corrupted nature drawes
My will from discipline's amending lawes?
Thus going slowly through his words and deeds,
He from one eu'ning to the next proceeds:
Peruerting crimes he checkes with angry frownes,
Straight leuell'd vertues he rewards with crownes.

CLAUDIAN'S EPIGRAM OF THE OLD MAN OF VERONA.[2]

THRICE happy he, whose age is spent vpon his owne,
    The same house sees him old, which him a child hath known ;

---

1 Deed, act. G.

2 Cf. THOMAS RANDOLPH's De Senec. Veron: ex Claudian (1640) and Cowley's, the latter eliciting the praise of Byron in his caustic " Age of Bronze " ix. G.

He leanes vpon his staffe in sand where once he
    crept,

His mem'ry, long descents of one poore cote hath
    kept ;

He through the various strife of fortune neuer past,

Nor as a wand'ring guest would forraine waters
    taste ;

He neuer fear'd the seas in trade, nor sound of
    warres,

Nor in hoarse courts of law, hath felt litigious iarres;

Vnskilfull in affaires, he knowes no city neare,

So freely he enioyes the sight of heau'n more cleare ;

The yeeres by seu'rall corne, not consuls he com-
    putes,

He notes the Spring by flowres, and Autumne by
    the fruits ;

One space put downe the sunne, and brings againe
    the rayes,

Thus by a certain orbe he measures out the dayes.

Remembring some great oke from small beginning
    spred,

He sees the wood grow old, which with himselfe
    was bred.

Verona next of townes as farre as India seemes,

And for the Ruddy Sea, Benacus he esteemes :

Yet still his armes are firme, his strength vntam'd
    and greene ;

The full third age hath him a lusty grandsire seene.
Let others trauaile farre, and hidden coasts display
This man hath more of life, and those haue more
of way.

Finis.

Metamorphosis

of

Tabacco.

Note.

The following is the original title-page:

THE

METAMOR-
PHOSIS OF

TABACCO.

Lusimus Octaui &c.
[An oval wood-cut of bi-forked
Parnassus, with a tobacco plant,
a sun-flower and a pansy, with
the conventional sun a-top.
The motto round it is 'Parnasso
et Apolline digna.]

AT LONDON

Imprinted for *Iohn Flasket*, and are to be sold at his
shop in Paules Church-yard at the signe
of the black Beare. 1602.

Collation—21 leaves, including the title-page. The only
known copy is in the British Museum, among the King's
books: 1077. h. 15. The title-page is somewhat soiled
and mended: bound in saffron morocco. Mr. Collier re-
printed it in his 'First Series' but I have been unable to
meet with it, though helped by himself. He kindly
favoured me with his own transcript: but I have collated
every line and word myself with the original exemplar,
correcting a very considerable aggregate of mistakes, and
adding notes as required. I notice reluctantly Mr.
Collier's mistakes: but it is necessary in respect of comparison between his reprint and my own—assuming that he

followed his faulty transcript. The motto in title-page is taken from the first line of Virgil's Culex :

"Lusimus, Octavi, gracili modulante Thalia "

—kindly pointed out to me by Mr. W. A. Wright of Cambridge. For the authorship of the ' Metamorphosis,' see our Memorial-Introduction. G.

Ad mare riuuli
TO MY LOVING
FRIEND, MASTER
MICHAEL DRAYTON.[1]

The tender labour of my wearie pen,
And doubtfull triall of my first-borne rimes,
Loaths to adorne the triumphs of those men,
Which hold the raines of fortunes, and the times :
Only to thee, which art with ioy possest
Of the faire hill, where troupes of Poets stand,
Where thou enthron'd with laurell garlands blest,
Maist lift me vp with thy propitious hand ;
  I send this poëme, which for nought doth care,
  But words for words, and loue for loue to share.

.................namq. tu solebas
  Meas esse aliquid putare nugas.[2]

---

1 Born 1563: died 1631.   See Memorial-Introduction
for Drayton's friendship with our Poet.   G.
2 From Catullus i, 3, 4.   G.

Preliminary Verses.

IN LAVDEM AUTHORIS.

RAUNT me smooth utt'rance Muses, to
  reherse
  The pleasing smoothnesse of thy worthy
  verse :
If there be words fram'd by admirèd wits
To sing thy praise, those words my verse befits ;
But such are scant, and there's not one remaines
Can giue thee due, none worth enough containes
To sing thy praise in an vp-raisèd straine,
And giue desert to thy admirèd paine.[1]
Feare not the censure of each babbling tongue,
They care not whom they pleasure, whom they
  wrong.
Respect it not if fooles thy Muse miscall,

---

1 Pains = painstaking, and so onward. G.

Thy paine, her worth, deserues applause of all :
In whose adoring if my pen offends,
My heart my pen's defaults will make amends.

Z. D¹.

SEE how the chattring throngs of Poets vaine
Besiege the paths unto the Muses' cell :
See how they pant, and beate with fruitlesse paine
The steepie traces to the learnèd well :
Securely thou their vaine assaults discount,
Thou, whom Apollo by the hand hath guided
A new-found passage to the hornèd mount,
And from the rout vnhallowed hath deuided,
  And taught thee raise thy soring Muse on wing,
  And thy triumphant name in learnèd eares to
    ring.
There didst thou gather on Parnassus clift
This precious herbe, Tabacco most diuine,
Then which nere Greece, nere Italy did lift
A flower more fragrant to the Muses' shrine :
A purer sacrifice did nere adorne

---

1 It was a common contemporary practice to reverse
initials: and probably this was one of the Zouch family,
who joined our Poet in his lamentations for Lord Stafford,
See pp 187—120, *ante*. G.

Apollo's altar, then this Indian fire ;
The pipe, thy head : the flame to make it burne,
The furie, which the Muses doe inspire.
　　O sacred smoke, that doth from hence arise,
　　The author's wingèd praise, which beates upon
　　　the skies.

W. B.[1]

When Helicon and Tempe doe adorne
With sugred gifts of diuine poetrie,
Let no detracting Zoilus him scorne,
Thinking thereby to cure his maladie ;
　　For he that once doth Homer's pen dispraise,
　　Cannot himselfe to Laureat's honour raise.
Then thou, that art the author of this booke,
Send forth that sacred fume from out thy braine,

---

1 Query—William Barkstead, author of " Mirrha, the
mother of Adonis : or Lustes Prodegies " (1607) and
" Hiren : or the Faire Greeke" (1611.)   He is probably
also the ' W. B.' of the Verses "in laudem Auctoris "
prefixed to " Salmasis and Hermaphroditus " (1602) of
Francis Beaumont, the Dramatist : but see our Memorial-
Introduction on the authorship of that volume.   G

That thereon well-disposèd wits may looke,
And say, Giue me Tabacco once againe;
   For Castile nere did such a pipe afford
   Of Trinidade, upon mine honest word.

H. H.[1]

Iff that the Bee, whose winter paines are rest
For gath'ring honey in the fruitfull Spring,
And making choise of eu'ry flowre the best,
That to her hiue she may the sweetnesse bring :
Doth to her selfe deserue so great a praise,
What may be his, whose whole yeares worst spent
    hower.
For recreation on some idle daies,
Hath suckt such hony from an Indian flower ?
What may be his whose yonger yeares are such ?
What may be his whose first fruits are so faire ?
What may be his, I cannot say too much,

---

1 A " Henry Harrington " wrote the " Charme." in
the 1640 edition of ' Salmasis and Hermaphroditus, " as
before: (Collier's Bibl : Account, i. 62-63) and also commendatory Verses prefixed with numerous others, to
Beaumont and Fletcher (Vol. i., pp. lvi-ii). Query—the
present Verses by him ? G.

Nay, what is his to giue I doe despaire :
As one too weake to giue them their desart,
Yet rather chuse my selfe to take a maime,
Then for to faile to shew a louing hart
Vnto my friend to recompence his paine.

I. A.[1]

WHAT my poore Muse can do, she vowes is thine :
Black set to white makes it farre cleerer shine.
This like a faithfull friend she first assaies
With her owne shame to purchase thee the praise :
And yet if enuie seeke thy worth to blot,
—As what deserts be they she staineth not—
Through truer zeale shee plaies this second part :
The spite, that's aimd at thee, comes through her
    hart.   N. P.

SOMETIMES all man, that hath usd soule and
    breath,
Must print his heele on the black way of Death :
But this small poeme, though the least of manie,

---

1 Query—John Andrew, author of " The Anatomie of
Basenesse " (1615) ?   G.

Shall liue like soules, though Nature's worst gifts
    die:
Till all the compounds weare their fierie sheete,
Not till all Death, shall this slight storie fleete.

                    M. G.[1]

TO THE WHITE READER.

TAKE up these lines Tabacco-like vnto thy braine,
And that diuinely toucht, puffe out the smoke
    againe.   B. H.[2]

My new-borne Muse assaies her tender wing,
And where she should crie is enforst to sing:
Her children prophesie thy pleasing rime
Shall neuer be a dish for hungrie Time:
Yet be regardlesse what those verses say,
Whose infant mother was but borne to day.

                    F. B.[3]

---

1 Query—Matthew Grove, author of "The most
famous Historie of Pelops and Hippodamia." (1587) ? G.

2 A 'B. H,' was author of "The Glasse of Man's
Folly." (1615). G.

3 Francis Beaumont, the Dramatist, younger brother

I DOE inuoke none but thy selfe to praise thee,
For there's no other Muse so high can raise thee.
Thou art my Muse, I can thy praises tell:
My Muse hath tasted of the Muses well.

F. R.

THE tender plant which goodly fruit hath bore,
Being growne, doth promise farre more beautious
    store :
Seeing thy youth's prime a worthie worke hath
    dight,
What shall thy riper Muse produce to light?
Tabacco's spring, transforming, soueraigntie[1]
Set'st forth with truth, fictions, Philosophie ;
Merits enroulment with Mæonian quill,
Thy wit, zeale, labours, and thy learned skill.
    Doctrina, ingenio, studijs, pietate, labore,
        Exurpera, polle, profice, cresce, vige.

I. P.

---

of our Poet.   See Memorial-Introduction and the pathetic
lines on his death, p. 182. **G.**
   1 Such is the pointing. **G.**

The Metamorphosis of Tabacco.

 SING the loues of the superiour powers
With the faire mother of all fragrant
flowers :
From which first loue a glorious simple springs,
Belou'd of heau'nly Gods, and earthly Kings.
Let others in their wanton verses chaunt
A beauteous face that doth the senses daunt,
And on their Muses' wings lift to the skie
The radiant beames of an inchaunting eye.
Me let the sound of great TABACCO' praise
A pitch aboue those loue-sicke Poets raise :
Let me adore with my thrice-happie pen
The sweete and sole delight of mortall men,
The cornu-copia of all earthly pleasure,
Where bank-rupt Nature hath consumed her
treasure ;
A worthie plant springing from Florae's hand,
The blessed offspring of an uncouth land.

Breath-giuing herbe, none other I inuoke
To helpe me paint the praise of sugred smoke :
Not that corrupted artificiall drug,
Which euery Gull as his owne soule doth hug,
And in the sweete composure of a docke,
Drinkes to his ladie's dog, and mistresse' smocke :
Whose best conceits are broacht of bastard fume,
Whose wittie salt depends on the salt rheume,
Which first, like vapours, doe ascend on high,
But quickly vanish ere they touch the skie;
Which, like to meteors, for a while amaze
The simple soules which wondring stand at gaze ;
But being knowne from whence they first were
    fir'd
Are counted base, and cease to be admir'd.
Auant, base Hypocrite ; I call not thee,
But thou great god of Indian melodie,
Which at the Caribes banquet gouern'st all,[1]
And gently rul'st the sturdiest Caniball ;
Which at their bloodie feasts dost crownèd sit,
And smok'st their barking iawes at eu'ry bit ;
Which lead'st the circle of a sauage round
With iarring songs, and homely musick's sound ;
Which to fond mirth their cruell minds dost frame,
And after with a pleasing sleepe dost tame ;

---

1 Caribes bo sauago peoplo of America. B.

By whom the Indian priests inspirèd bc,
When they presage in barbarous poetrie :
Infume my braine, make my soule's powers subtile,
Giue nimble cadence to my harsher stile ;
Inspire me with thy flame, which doth excell
The purest streams of the Castalian well,
That I on thy ascensiue wings may flie,
By thine ethereall vapours borne on high,
And with thy feathers added to my quill
May pitch thy[1] tents on the Parnassian hill.
Teach me what power thee on the earth did place,
What god was bounteous to the humane race,
On what occasion, and by whom it stood,
That the blest world received so great a good.

   Before the earth and heau'n were create,
When the rude chaos[2] lay disconsolate,
When this great All, and wondrous worke we see
Had neither forme, nor part, nor qualitie.
Blind Nature did her *atomi*[3] disperse
Ouer the large confusèd vniverse,
And heau'nly powers all out of order plac't
Were buried in the bowels of the Vast :

---

   1 Query—my ? G.

   2 This Chaos, ancients fame to be a disorde red masse,
out of which the world was made. B.

   3 Some Philosophers fained that the world was composed *ex atomis*, of little motes gathered together. B.

Then did these seedes, which yet vnpolish't were,
Wage warre against the seedes of single-beere[1]
And smothered in that topsi-turuie trance,
Nourisht some smacke of mirth and iouisance :[2]
But when this massie lumpe had chang'd her face,
And cu'ry thing possest his proper place,
Yet did this plant in darke obliuion lurke
Small trauaile could not bring forth such a worke.
—Like to Alcmenae's sonne, the god of might,
Whom to beget, Ioue made a treble night—
Till wise Prometheus, which compos'd a creature
Excelling all the world in forme and feature,
When he that rare immortall worke had done,
Stole fire from the bright chariot of the Sunne ;
Which farre-fetcht fire had seru'd him to no end,
But that the Earth her chiefest powers did lend :
For seeing how great Phœbus was beguil'd
To make a God of her beloued child,
And alwaies enuying at the gods aboue,
—As her Viperean brood of giants proue,[3]

---

1 Single-beere = weak beer : called in the "Ancient Chronicle of London" quoted by Thomas Wright *s. v.* 'sougyl beer'. G.

2 = joyfulness, jollity, as in Peele's 'Arraignment of Paris' : 'Such jouisance, such mirth and merriment.' (by Dyce p 354). G.

3 The rebellious giants were fained to haue Viperian or snakie feete. B.

And totall ruine of her stubborne race,

For whom in teares she washt her watrie face—[1]

She call'd her Herald-winds, and charg'd them all

That they a councell of her subiects call :

Out goes her Purseuent, the blustring gale,

And summons eu'ry hill and euery dale,

Curles eu'ry riuer with a sliding[2] touch

From Titan's rising to his Westerne couch,

And with the whissing trumpet it doth beare,

Commaunds each earthly subiect to appeare,

And on a high embassage doth repaire,

To Earth's three sisters, Water, Fire, and Aire :

—These foure are ioynt co-partners, and co-heires

Of all that lies below the starry spheres ;

Who for their kingdome's bounds haue beene at
    ods,

But now they, by the sentence of the gods,

And their dread vmpires, Hot, Drie, Moist, and
    Cold,

In common, and without diuision hold—

The day was comen, when on a stately pile

Four seates are plac't on the Americke Ile :

Where these great Princes and their portly traines

---

1 At the generall flood. B.

2 Cf. our Phineas Fletcher, Index of words *s.v.* G.

Made enterview on the Atlantick plaines. [1]
    After Pandora [2] had made euident
The cause of this so sudden Parlement,
Tearing her flowrie locks, and furrowed face,
She gan lament the poore Prometheus' case.
Stand out—quoth she—thou that are thus distrest;
Declare thy case, for here thou maist be blest.
Then stept out he as a condemnèd man
Clothèd in blacke, and thus his speech began.
Know, most dread Soueraignes of the lower globe,
I am a dead man, and this guiltie robe
Shewes that by colour of the gods contemn'd,
I to a vultur's mercie am condemn'd,
On Caucasus, amid the Scythian groue,
By the fear'd sentence of almightie Ioue;
There to be tide in euerlasting chaines,
Plung'd in the horrour of eternall paines :
Yet this torments me not, this must be borne,
—And patience comes perforce to men forlorne—
But that my worke, which I haue erst begun,—
For all my labour, should be left vndone ;
That's my vexation, that's my only griefe,
And only rests in you to giue reliefe :

---

1 Atalantis (the Island which Plato mẻ ntions) some
suppose to be America. B.
    2 The earth. B.

For Ioue enuies the beautie of the frame,
And seekes all meanes how to deface the same
Looking on me with a suspitious eye,
As a corriuall of his dignitie ;
When he may well remember—if he please—
How little I deserue such lookes as these;
When I, with counsell of an aged head,
Did stay his youthfull thoughts from Thetis' bed,
And told him there he should beget a sonne
Should him depose, as he before had done
His father Saturne : then he thankt me faire :
—But words are quickly turn'd to fleeting aire—
Now hates he me, and doth my worke detest,
Which must, unlesse you helpe, vnperfect rest;
For all my sharpe inuentions cannot find
How life vnto this trunke may be combin'd.
Here grandame Ops[1] her grieuèd head did shake,
And made the massie Earth's foundation quake :
Then gusht cleere fountaines from her hollow eyes,
—Floods from the Earth's strange motions often
      rise—
And at the last her lips did part in two,
—As after earthquakes they are wont to doe :—
Is't not enough—quoth she—that tyrant Ioue
Hath my sonne Saturne from his kingdome droue?

---

1 The earth. B.

And me, his mother, hath confin'd below,
Because I wept as partner of his woe?
Is't not enough my middle part doth frie,
While head and feete benumd with cold doth lie?
That alwaies halfe my realme the sunne doth lack,
And for his absence mourne in gloomie black?
Or that my louing subiects neuer see,
But halfe the heau'n, wheresoere they be?
Is not all this enough, and more then this
To be secluded from all heau'nly blisse?
Bound in a dungeon, vs'd as though I were
A beast ordain'd laborious waights to beare?
Each massie thing, and the world's waightiest
     part
Pressing vnto my center, to my hart,
Where he hath made huge caues, and darksome
     holes,
Places of torture for offending soules,
Whose howling yells, cries, curses, grones and
     teares
Are pois'ned obiects to mine eyes and cares:
And is not this enough, but must he still
Crosse the good purpose of my harmlesse will,
Hindring the proiect of our gen'rall care,
Our sonne: whose wishèd fruite we hope to share,
Nor shall too sweete an expectation mocke
Vs happie beldames of a blessed stocke:

Only it resteth that we now deuise
To seate our darling in the starrie skies ;
Which purpose that we to effect may bring,
A plant shall from my wrinkled forehead spring,
And eu'ry ladie shall that herbe endow
With the best gemmes that deck her glorious brow :
Which once inflam'd with the stolne heau'nly fire
Shall breath into this liuelesse corse inspire.
Scarse had she spoke, but by vnite consent
It was allowed by eu'ry element ;
Each mountaine nodded, and each riuer sleeke
Approv'd the sentence with a dimpled cheeke,
And eu'ry thing in dauncing measure sprung,
As erst they did when gentle Orpheus sung.
As when the actors of some enterlude
Which please the senses of the multitude,
Are backt by the spectators of the Play
With a wisht laughter, or a plaudite :
So with vnperfect voyces all the rout
Grace this opinion with a loftie shout.
—Like Bacchus' priests whom Strymon's banks
    rebound,
Whom the shrill ecchoes of fleete Hebrus sound[1]—
Till Fire, the eldest sister, vp did stand
—And silence made with her imperiall hand—

---

1 Strymon and Hebrus, rivers in Thracia. B.

Praising the proiect, swore to grace the same
With actiue powers of her eternall flame.
Aire likewise promist she would rarefie
The earthly drosse to simple puritie ;
And caus'd her skipping meteors to addresse
Their gifts of light, and iocund nimblenesse ;
Her cloudes from heau'nly flood-gates manuring[1]
The ground, where this expected herb should
     spring.
Water refus'd her vertues to inspire,
Least she should quench the hope of future fire ;
Yet did the seruants of her excellence
Offer each one their best parts' quintessence :
The icy waues were all with christall fraught ;
The Magellanick Sea her vnions[2] brought ;
Tagus with golden gifts doth proudly rise,
And doth the famous Indian rills despise ;
Eridanus his pearl'd electrum[3] gaue ;
Euripus the swift fluxure of his waue ;
From British Seas doth holesome corall come ;
The Danish gulfe doth send her succinum ;[4]
And each thus hoped embryon dignifies

---

1 Cf. our Ph. Fletcher ; Index of Words, *s. v.*　G.

2 Onions.　G.

3 Amber.　Cf. our Giles Fletcher p 167.　G.

4 Another name for amber, the usual one being elec-
rum, as above.　G.

With offring of a seu'rall sacrifice.
The Earth her selfe at last did procreate
This herbe, composèd in despite of Fate,
And chargèd eu'ry countrie, and each hill
A speciall power into this leafe distill,
Which thus adorn'd, by holy fire inflam'd,
Sweete life and breath within the carkasse fram'd;
And had not Tellus temper'd too much mud,
Too much terrene corruption in the bud,
The man that tasted it should neuer die,
But stand in records of eternitie :
And as the ashes of the phœnix burn'd,
Into another liuing bird are turn'd,
So should the man that takes this sacred fume,
Another life within himselfe resume :
So Iolaus[1] when his first was done,
His second life was of Tabacco spunne.
Some say for this, Ioue vexèd at the heart,
Did hide it long from the world's better part :
Hence came, that former ages neuer knew
The goods that by this seeming weede accrue.
Till as the Graces trauaill'd through the Earth,
Giuing to men their gifts of heau'nly mirth,
At last when they into Americk came,

---

1 Iolaus was the only man that euer had two liues.   B.

Drawne by the strange delights, and countrie's
     fame,
They in the palace of great Mutezume[1]
Were entertain'd with this celestiall fume ;
When they forgetting all their wonted pleasure
Imbrac'd with ioy this truest Indian treasure,
And there remaining did no more respect
Our petie world, with nought but trifles deckt.
So the faire Graces, which were wont to sport
Amid our louing feasts, and sweete resort ;
Were now secluded from our lucklesse eyes,
And in their place did braules and quarrels rise ;
All friendship banisht from false Europe's sight,
Where flattring lurkt in stead of deare delight,
Till we, poore soules, in many troubles tost,
Seeking the Graces which we erst had lost,
When we had often sought them farre and neere,
After great paine[2] and trauaile found them there.

    Others doe tell a long and serious tale
Of a faire nymph that sported in the vale,
Where Cipo with his siluer streames doth goe
Along the valleys of Wingandekoe :[3]

---

1 Mutezume, was king of the West Indies, when
Cortez first arrived there. B. [Montezuma ? G.]

2 = painstaking : hence the old words, a *painfull*
preacher. G.

3 Wingandekoe is a countrey in the North part of
America, called by the Queene, Virginia. B.

—Which now a farre more glorious name doth
    beare
Since a more beauteous nymph was worshipt
    there—
There in a greene bowre did this maiden dwell,
Where pretie waues of a delicious well
Leapt at her sight, and with a faint rebound
Bubbled sweete musicke with a daintie sound.
—This fountaine as a nymph did whilom range,
Till by her prayers the gods her forme did change,
When Cipo sought her chastitie's abuse,
As Alpheus did to virgin Arethuse—
There dwelt this nymph, which with her feature
    daunted
The soueraigne gods, and mortall men inchaunted.
So full she was of most delightfull grace,
That by the modell of her beautious face
Ioue was about to build the heau'n anew,
And change the azure to a ruddie hew,
And pull the starrie lights from out the skies,
Leauing but two in likenes of her eyes:
But when the Fates so great a change forbade,
In imitation of her red he made
A ruddie night before a ioyfull day,
And by her white he fram'd the milk-white way:
Her golden threeds were so inchaunting faire,
Men scorn'd the sunne, to gaze upon her haire;

Phœbus asham'd of this, immur'd his beames
Within the cincture of the Ocean streames:
Whereat Ioue angrie, sent swift Mercurie,
Who to the palace of the Sunne did hie.
Now the Sunne's court was glorious to behold,
Supported with strong pillers of bright gold,
The top of iu'ry was, the doores of plate,
Where Vulcan did so liuely imitate
The heau'n, the earth, the sea, the ayre, the flame,
That heau'n and earth, and sea enui'd the frame.
Thither came Hermes, and with lowring cheare[1]
Cited the Sunne in person to appeare
Before the gods, to tell his cause of stay,
Why he so long did dallie with the Sea.
Phœbus obey'd, and when the gods were met,
And eu'ry one in wonted order set,
A way was made by the fierce gods of Warre,
And Pluto brought the pris'ner to the barre.
Whom Suada[2], Ioue's sollicitour, accus'd,

---

1 Countenance. Mr. Thomas Wright *s.v.* did not seem to know of an example. G.

2 In Verses by T. Benlowes M.A., prefixed to ' Theophila ' we read:

  " Here heav'n-born Suadas, star-like, gild each dresse
  Of the bride-soul espous'd to Happinesse:
  Here Pictio performes poetick art;
  As all in all, and all in every part."

That he his light and vertue had abus'd ;
That whereas he had sworne by fearèd Styx,
When Ioue the seale did to his patent fixe,
That he would neuer in one place be found,
But restlesse runne about the massie round :
This solemn oth he had not duly kept,
But in the strumpet Thetis' lap had slept.
Here Ioue did Suade's accusation breake,
And beckning, gaue Apollo leaue to speake.
You gods—quoth he—that here as Iudges sit,
I seeke not to defend my cause by wit ;
My chiefest plea is speechlesse eloquence,
Grounded vpon my spotlesse innocence :
Yet if I pleas'd to winne eternall glorie,
By the sweet cadence of mine oratorie,
I could reuiue the dead, and heale the sick
By fluence of celestiall Rhetorick :
The pleasant musick of the heau'nly spheres
Should pleade my cause to your attentiue eares.
But with plaine terms shall[1] my iust act be tride

I add the remaining lines of the stanza for its allusive hit
to Cartwright's posthumous volume, with its astounding
collection of ' commendations ' :

"For all these dy'd not with fam'd Cartwright, though
A score of poets joyn'd to have it so." G.

1 ' I ' inserted here by misprint. G.

T

—Who laies on colours doth the substance hide—
I doe not make a night as long as three
To dallie with my loue in iollitie,
—And yet I might as well such dalliance proue,
As Ioue at Thebes for his Alcmenae's loue—
Nor my bright face in liquid teares doe steepe,
Though my sonne's fall haue giu'n me cause to
  weep ;
But on the Earth there is a greater light,
Which with her raies doth equall day and night.
Once from my couch I was about to rise,
But straight this brighter lampe strooke blind mine
  eyes :
My sister Luna, when the night drew nie,
Hath been as loth to shew her light as I :
Nor can our splendent glorious lampes compare
With her two lamps that farre more glorious are :
And my Aurora hides her face away
Sleeping with her Tithonus all the day,
And when she once beheld this radiant face
Hath euer since blusht at her owne disgrace :
The sphæres of planets with a sudden chaunge
Make her the center of their circled raunge,
And all the heau'nly orbes doe disagree
What part should oft'st in her horizon bee ;
And mortall men colour and light despise,
Esteeming her the obiect of the eyes ;

While she—as women be—proud of her honour,
Makes the night day, that men may gaze vpon
  her :
Ioue hearing this, dismist the Court in hast,
And in a sillie[1] shepheard's weedes[2] debas't
Shrouded with clowdes, downe from the heau'n
  did slide
And piping sate vpon a mountaine's side :
—Which Ocean's rolling current ouer-peares,
Descending from a faire Pastorae's teares,
Who now a marble stone, yet weepeth still
To see her louer chang'ed to a hill,
Whom iealous Phœbus did by force remoue
Brooking no riuall in his feruent loue,
Framing high pines of his inticing locks,
Changing his teeth to adamantine[3] rocks—
Thither from heau'n great Ioue did hie apace,
And sate on the transform'ed shepheard's face.
So sweetly sounded his melodious notes,
That sheepe and shepheards in their homely cotes
Daunc't to his layes, and following the sound
Did climbe the steepe hill with a solemne round.[4]

---

1 = Harmless. G.   2 Dress or garb. G.

3 Cf. our Ph. Fletcher: Index of Words, *s.v.* : printed
with a capital here. G.

4 A kind of dance, described in Sir John Davies'
"Orchestra." G.

Among those flocks the beautious nymph did pace,
Whose snowy neck vied beauties with her face ;
—Nor would it in so sweete a combat yeeld
Had not her ample forehead wonne the field—
And on that pole doth stand the orbe of loue,
Where Cupid in eccentrick rounds doth moue ;
And now from her faire eyes his shafts doth dart,
Then from her lips, and straight from euery part:
Sweet roseall lips, doores of those sacred places,
The gorgeous temples of the glorious Graces ;
Which gates of rubie, when they op'ned were,
A shrine of pearle and christall did appeare,
From whence delicious oracles were spoken,
Which pleasing wonders did to all betoken :
Nor is the murmure of Cecropian bees,
Nor songs of birds vpon the ayric trees,
Nor the swift riuer falling downe the steepe,
Lulling poore shepheards with a carelesse sleepe,
—Where Nature with her melodie amazeth
The sillie flocke that on the greene bankes grazeth—
Equiulent[1] with that celestiall sound,
From whence, they say, Musicke receau'd her
　　　ground.
And first from her did Linus learne to sing,
And with the sweete touch of a pleasing string

---

1 A noticeable use of the now familiar word.　G.

Did imitate the playing of the ayre
With golden wires of her disheueled haire.
Her countenance was so angelike bright,
That the pure starres were blinded at her sight,
And euer since their lights so dazled were,
That they were forc't to twinkle in their sphere.
Her hands were framèd like a prettie gin
Ordaind to catch and hold all pleasure in :
And eu'ry part a feruent loue did teach,
Yet she her selfe aboue Loue's wanton reach :
A coronet she wore all whilome wonne
Striuing for beautie with the radiant sunne,
Which mightie Phœbus caus'd the houres to make
With cunning labour for Leucothoe'e sake :
This curious worke with Indian pearles was grac't,
Wherein the loues of gods and men were plac't :
There Neptune in a pretious margarite[1]
Did woe and winne the beautious Amphitrite:
There Iphis[2] did in humble sort obey
The cruell frownes of Anaxcarete ;
And princes loues in art's affections clad
Excell'd the passions they by nature had.
Thus deckt by Art and Nature did she come,
Whose features strook the seeming shepheard
dumbe,

---

1 Pearl. G. 2 Hercules. B.

Nor could his wau'ring thoughts themselues con-
　　taine,
But now left off, and straightway pip'd againe.
Sometimes his notes he with shrill tunes did raise
To chaunt aloud the skipping roundelaies ;
And then againe his lowly voyce did fall
To sing a pleasant homely pastorall :
And eu'ry song to the nymph's honour was
Like shepheard's musicke to a countrey lasse,
Lik'ning her eyes unto the glimsing light,
That guides poore heardsmen to their home at
　　night ;
Her haire vnto the golden flowres that grow
Along the fragrant bank of siluer Po :
Her lips to waxe by curious workmanship
Form'd as a patterne to each other lip :
Thus sung he till the blacke and shadie Night
With vgly forme did feare away the light,
And Hesperus, [1] that stands as euening scout,
Began to leade the starrie ring about :
—Which durst not in her spangled suite appeare,
As long as mightie Titan's light was neere,
By reason of some euerlasting iarres
That did arise 'twixt Phœbus and the starres—
Then all the shepheards, wearie of the sunne,

---

1 The euening starre.   B.

And glad that the laborious day was done,
Began to driue their tender flocks away ;
But Ioue did force this sillie[1] maide to stay,
Telling her stories how the force of loue
Had bow'd the hearts of gods that dwelt aboue ;
How Ioue orecome by this celestiall power,
Deceiu'd poore Danaë in a golden shower ;
How with laments and teares Apollo rued
Faire Daphne's change, when he so fast pursued.
Hereat she blusht and to depart she stroue ;
But all in vaine against the force of Ioue.
This saw the Night, and glad she was to see
So fit reuenge for the great inuirie
Whereat Ioue wrong'd her at Alcides' birth.
Making her watch three daies vpon the earth :
Therefore in hast the darke malicious Night
To iealous Iuno doth relate this sight :
Iuno enrag'd, with threatning speeches storm'd,
Which Ioue perceiuing by a vaine embrace
The infant herbe with heau'nly powers did grace,
And on the Night he did inflict this paine,
That while the pleasant Summer. did remaine,
The lucklesse Night should haue but small com-
    mand,
But in the frostie Winter longest stand.

---

1 Simple, innocent.   G.

Yet could not Ioue forget his former loue,
But ioyning earthly powers, and powers aboue,
Therewith he did adorne this glorious bud
And fram'd it as a micro-cosme of good :
Making the ground where this sweet plant did
　　spring,
To be a cordiall 'gainst each noysome thing,
Endu'd with force all euils to asswage.
And now began the famous Golden Age :
No publike bond of law, no priuate oth
Was needfull to the simple faith and troth :
Each had a censure in his owne consent,
Without the feare of death or punishment.
Nor did the busie client feare his cause,
Nor in strong brasse did they engraue the lawes ;
Nor did the doubtfull parties faintly tremble
While the brib'd Iudge did dreadful looks dissemble :
Then safe from harme the vaunting pine did stand,
And had no triall of the shipwright's hand,
But stood vpon the hill where first it grew
Nor yet was forc'd another world to view :
Nor vnto greedie merchants yet were knowne
The shores of any land beyond their owne :
Eu'ry defencelesse citie then was sure,
Nor could deepe ditches make it more secure.
The harmlesse thoughts of that blest age did beare
No warlike trumpets, cornet, sword or speare ;

No furious souldier needed to defend
The carelesse folke which quiet liues did spend ;
Nor did ambitious captaines know the way
To passe the cliffie shores of their owne sea :
The earth yet free from any forcd abuse
Brought forth all things fit for each creature's vse,
Without the helpe of any humane care,
Vntoucht by harrow, and vncut by share ;
And mortall men vpon those meates did feede
Which of themselues did from the Earth proceede.
The mountaine strawberie and bitter sloe,
And mulberies, which on rough boughs doe grow,
And homely akornes, which did whilome fall
From the high trees, which Ioue his owne doth call :
The pleasant yeare was an eternall Spring,
Where Westerne winds continuall flowres did bring.
The fertile Earth vnmanur'd and vntil'd,
The bounteous gift of plenteous corne did yeeld :
Now[1] did the field renew'd each seuerall yeere
Make windy sounds with many a waightie eare.
Brookes did with milke, and pleasant nectar goe,
And yellow hony from the trees did flow :
Al good without constraint, heau'n, sea, men,
    ground,
No gold, no ship, no law, no plough, no bound,
Till Proserpine by this abusèd flame

---

1 Misprinted, nor.   G.

—Striuing to purchase an immortall name—
Reueng'd with raging fire her ancient spite
On Tellus and the scornefull Amphitrite;[1]
—Which oft had mockt her mansion place of Hell,
And call'd it darksome hole and duskie cell—
Therefore the Furies she in hast commands
To burne the fruitfull Earth with fierie brands,
And when their hands such instruments did want,
She made them torches of the sacred plant ;
By which she fir'd the world, and that once done,
About the Earth in raging sort they runne,
And euer since they by these flames did cause
Famine, dissention, plagues, and breach of lawes.
—Yet was the hellish queene with feare distract,
Least Ioue should know and punish the foule fact :
Therefore she hir'd the poets long agone,
To cast the fault upon poore Phaeton.—
Now when this honour'd herb was once abus'd,
All paines, all plagues were on the world infus'd,
And then the wicked Iron Age began ;
Shame, truth and faith from earthly mansions ran,
And in their place came fraud and clokèd vice,
Treason and force, and impious auarice.
The mariner whom hope of lucre blinds
Hasts to the sea, vnexpert in the winds,

1 The goddesse of the sea. B.

And trees that long had stood on mountaines high,
As ships vpon the vncouth waues doe lie :
The merchant then the boistrous sea did plow,
Spite of the frowne of Neptune's angrie brow ;
Nor could the horrour of one iourneye's paine
Feare greedie thoughts from ventring so againe.
Neptune then grieuèd with the wounds and dints
Which in his face this curious worke emprints :
—And mou'd with Cybel's[1] outcries, which did
      frowne
To see her hils defac'd and pines puld downe,
And Nature's plaints, whose lawes it had beguil'd—
Made the sea stormie, which before was mild :
Since which the ribs of broken ships doe show
What hurts and dangers by this engine grow ;
Which makes each fertile countrie want the more
By seeming steward of each countrie's store.
Now did the warie reaper with long bounds
Deuide to portions the vnited grounds,
Which erst were common to each mortall wight
As is the liquid ayre or pleasant light :
Nor did they onely take the needfull corne,
And daily food which from the Earth was borne,
But to the bowels of their mother sought,
And cursèd riches from the center brought,

---

1 The Goddesse to whom the pine is dedicated. B.

And neere vnto the Stygian waues did hide.
First then began the phrases, mine and thine :
Pure water turn'd to artificiall wine :
Which the wise Earth had couer'd vnespide,
Pleasure vnknowne, and more then simple mirth
Start vp with gold from out the mangled Earth.
The bounds, then contracts at a racking price,
And from those bounds spring boundlesse auarice :[1]
Then hurtfull steele the workman's hand did feele
And gold, more hurtfull then the hurtfull steele.
And when both these were comen to perfect
    growth,
From thence came Warre, that fights with help of
    both :
Then did the souldier, which in battell stands
Shake glittring weapons with his bloodie hands :
All liu'd by wrong : each friend did [daily] feare,
And brethren seldome linkt in friendship were.
The husband seekes the death of his owne wife,
And she againe grieves at her husband's life.
The angrie stepdames, fearefull poysons make,
Which their new husband's [ailing] child may take ;
And the sonne, wearie of his father's stay,
Longs for his death before his fatall day ;
White Pietie's dispersèd reliques lie
Conquer'd, and spoil'd of earthly dignitie.

---

1 Qu : = bonds ?   G.

And then Astræa,[1] last of heau'nly powers
Forsooke the Earth reeking with bloodie showers.
Yet was not Vice ascended to the height :
Yet might our pond'rous soules endure the weight
Of our corrupted flesh : yet might we say
The growth of Sinne's perfection wants a day ;
Till the fierce giants of Viperean birth
Made loftie Heau'n no more secure then Earth,
Seeking Ioue's kingdome by presumptuous Warres,
Building high mountaines to the trembling starres.
But Ioue the hils did from Olympus tosse,
And cast great Pelion from the top of Osse :[2]
And when the furious giants thus were kild
By the great weight which their own hands did
            build,
The Earth gaue life vnto her children's blood,
And fram'd them liuing bodies of her mud ;
And—least no signe should of his stocke remaine—
She chang'd them to the formes of men againe,
Who, not degen'rate from their bloodie birth,
Defi'd the heauen, and defild the Earth.
Then first ambitious mortals gan to rise,
And with vaine pride did the great gods despise :

---

1 Justice. B.
2 Cf. our Ph. Fletcher, Vol. ii., pp. 185—6, note 6. G.

Still warr'd they with the gods, still had the
  worst,
And when their hands could do no more, they
  curst.
Nor could the flood that inward spot deface;
Still it continued in the humane race,
Creeping vnseene, subiecting eu'ry part,
Till it possest our chiefest towne, our hart ;
Which thus infected did a battell wage
'Gainst the remainders of the Golden Age.
Then cursed Ate[1] first began her raigne,
And plac't her throne vpon the fluent maine,
Joying to see the billowes in their pride
Tosse totterd ships with perill on each side ;
Yet sorie Neptune should so largely sup,
And glad againe, when ought he vomits vp.
By her hath eu'ry thing corrupted beene
From the Earth's center to the heau'nly queene ;
—Which stands aboue the reach of earthly feares,
The lowest of the pure celestiall spheres.—
The fertile Earth corrupted by these seedes
Brought forth vnwholesome plants and fruitlesse
  weeds :
The Water, not content with her owne bounds,
Vsurpt vpon the neere adiacent grounds :

---

1 Goddesse of wrath and despite. B.

The Ayre infected did infect the breath,
From whence arose the instruments of death :
The Fire so hid her selfe, that none could see
Where her abode or proper place should bee :
Then sicknesse came on the infected Earth ;
Some fell in youth, some perisht in their birth ;
And whereas mortals neuer died before,
Till spent with age their lights could burne no more,
Now fathers' eyes were made a watrie sourse
To wash their sonnes' graues in prepost'rous[1]
    course.
And had not the immortall gods at last,
Pitying the sorrowes sillie men had past,
Cherisht poore soules with their eternall loue,
And sent Apollo Pœan from aboue
To crosse the purpose that the hag intended,
Long since her malice all the world had ended :
Yet could not carefull Phœbus quite deface
The venome Ate on the Earth did place,
Till Aesculapius, great Apolloe's sonne :
—Envying the glorie, shepheard Pan had wonne,
When of his loue transform'd he did inuent
The pleasure of a musicke instrument—
Descri'd this herbe to our new Golden Age,
And did deuise a pipe, which should asswage
The wounds which sorrow in our hearts did fixe

---

1 Inverted. G.

More then the sound of flutes, and fiddle-sticks :
And by the˜force thereof—as Poets faine—
Brought torne Hippolytus to life againe,
And watchmen set, and them Phisitians call'd :
Men, whom the Muses had before enstall'd,
Whose carefull soules were by this potion fir'd
And by the power of this sweete herb inspir'd ;
Which by the vertue of their sacred hands
Deliuer'd men from death and sicknes' bands.
　Others affirme the gods were ignorant
Of the confection of so sweet a plant ;
For had they knowne this smoke's delicious smack
The vault of heau'n ere this time had been black,
And by the operation of this fume
Been purg'd for euer of her clowdie rheume.
Daintie ambrosia with a loth'd disdaine
Had been made meate for each milk-pottage braine :
Ioue's Ganymede had neuer smelt of drinke
The heau'nly Mazers[1] flowing ore the brinke,
Nor fixen[2] Iuno euer broke his head
For spilling nectar on the gorgeous bed :
Gods would haue reuel'd at their feasts of **mirth**
With the pure distillation of the Earth :
The marrow of the world, starre of the West,

1 Cf. Job xxxviii., 32. G.
2 Vixen. G.

The pearle, whereby this lower orbe is blest,
The ioy of mortals, vmpire of all strife,
Delight of nature, Mithridate of life,
The daintiest dish of a delicious feast,
By taking which man differs from a beast.
Thrice happie Isles, which steale the world's
    delight,
And doe produce so rich a Margarite !
Had but the old heroick spirits knowne
The newes, which Fame vnto our eares hath blowne,
Colchis, and the remote Hesperides
Had not been sought for halfe so much as these ;
Nor had the fluent wits of ancient Greece
Prais'd the rich apples, or the Golden Fleece ;
Nor had Apolloe's garland been of bayes,
Nor Homer writ of sweete Nepenthe's[2] praise :
Nor had Anacreon with a sugred glose
Extold the vertues of the fragrant rose ;
Nor needed Hermes with his fluent tongue
Haue ioin'd in one a rude vnciuill throng,
And by perswasions made that companie
An order'd politike societie,
When this dumbe oratour would more perswade

---

1 Vixen. G.

2 Nepenthes signifieth a drink to take away sorrow or
care. B.

    U

Then all the speeches Mercurie had made ;
Nor honour'd Ceres been create diuine,
And worshipt so at curious Eleusine,
Whom blinder ages did so much adorne
For the inuention of the vse of corne :
Nor Saturne's feast had been the ioyfull day
Wherein the Romans washt their cares away :
But in the honour of great Trinidade
A new Tobacconalia had been made :
Had watrie Neptune knowne the force of this,
He had preuail'd, and Athens had been his ;
His gift the oliue would as farre exceed
As Pallas' gift excell'd his trampling steed :
Immortall Chiron, had he knowne this leafe
—Hurt by an arrow from Alcides' sheafe—
Had neuer wisht the troden mortall way,
But might haue well been cur'd, and liu'd for aye.
Had foule Thersites, with his spitefull hart,
Crook'd in each inward, and each outward part
By this elixir been but once refin'd,
He would haue chang'd his bodie, and his mind :
Or had the bees that Platoe's lips did grace
Suckt hony from this sweete Tabacco-place,
He had surpast, and stain'd himself as farre
As others by his stile obscurèd are.
With this had Circe in her pleasant caue
Temper'd the potion she Vlysses gaue,

He neuer would haue wisht, that his blest eyes
Might once behold his countrie's smoke arise.
Had ancient Heralds knowne this sacred plant,
Of which their lucklesse age was ignorant,
When they did giue the world's most worthie
  things
As glorious ensignes to victorious kings :
Tabacco had been richer armorie
Then Lions, Crosses, or spread Eaglets be :
Did the French Druids[1] liue, and were obey'd,
Nicot—that first this herbe to France convey'd—
Should be the god of pleasures and delights,
Worshipt with pompe on Bacchanalian nights,
And in his praise the barb'rous priests would sing
Vntunèd numbers in a iarring string,
Caruing harsh rimes on eu'ry knottie tree,
More crookt and rugged then the booke could bee,
Sounding in eu'ry homely verse they frame
The treble accent of god Nicot's name.
Had the sage Chaldees which did name the stars,
And were the first, and best Astronomers,
Seene the great wonders which our eyes haue seene,
This plant had then a constellation beene.[2]

---

1 The Druids were priests, much reuerenced among the
sauage Britaines and Frenchmen. B.

2 Cf. our Sir John Davies Vol. I pp 336—339 and
461 for curious Lines on Tobacco. G.

Nor had the honour'd Ramme begun the yeare
Nor the high Northerne pole adorn'd the Beare,
Nor Ioue disgrac'd, nor with his minions fild
Th' engrauen vault, which first his hands did
     build.
Our herbe had been a planet, and indu'd
With light aboue the greatest magnitude :
And when this starre had stood in good aspect,
With happie planets of the best effect,
He, whom the proud world then to light should
     bring
Had been a Poet, or at least a King :
Saturne had neuer brag'd his chariot went
The next vnto the azure firmament,
Nor had the sunne in his maiestick pride
Been thron'd with equall planets on each side,
Nor for high births had the Astrologer
Markt the coniunction of great Iupiter.
Were my quaint polisht tongue my soule's best
     hopes,
And grac't with figures, colours, schemes and tropes,
This herbe would [far] surpasse in excellence
The great'st hyperboles of eloquence.
Yet this sweete simple of misordred vse
Death or some dang'rous sicknesse may induce ;
Should we not for our sustentation eate,
Because a surfet comes from too much meate ?

Should we not thirst, with mod'rate drinke represse,
Because a dropsie springs from such excesse?
Should we not take some holesome exercise,
To chafe our vaines and stretch our arteries,
Because abus'd in a laborious kind,
It hurts the bodie and amates[1] the mind?
So our faire plant, that doth so needfull stand
As heau'n, or fire, or aire, or sea, or land,
As moone, or starres, that rule the gloomie night,
Or Tullie's friendship, or the sunnie light:
Her sacred vertue in her selfe enroules,
And leaues the euil in vain-glorious soules:
And yet who dyes cloid with celestiall breath,
Shall dye with ioy a Diagorian death[2]
All goods, all pleasures it in one doth linke,
'Tis phisick, clothing, musick, meate and drinke.
It makes the hungry soules forget their wants,
And nimbly daunce like skipping Corybants.[3]
By force of this, Timon that odious beast,
Would haue turn'd iester at each solemne feast,
And by one draught of this Americk grape
Haue been Laberius' or Sarmentus' ape:

---

1 Daunts, dismays: here = weakens (?) G.
2 Diagoras died for ioy. B.
3 Cybel's priests that daunced much in their sacrifice. B.

Nor would the Cynick[1] in his hourely tunne
Haue askt the shining of the gen'rall sunne:
But had he then this herbe's great vertues knowne,
He would haue beg'd it of the Macedone.[2]
The Faunes and Satyres, which doe lightly praunce
The beasts that after Orpheus' musick daunce,
At sight of this would haue forgot the sound,
The ecchoes would no more the voice rebound,
Orpheus himselfe would haue forsook his lute,
And altogether stood amaz'd and mute.
The lumpish Stoicks, which did thus decree
A mortall man might without passion bee,
Had they once cast their carelesse eyes on this,
Would soone haue shown what humane nature is.
The Epicureans, whose chiefe good was plac't
In earthly pleasures' vaine voluptuous tast,
Had our Tabacco in their daies been found
Had built their frame on a more likely ground.
Pyrrho, that held all by opinion stood,
Would haue affirm'd this were by nature good.
The rude Laconians, with Lycurgus' care
Barr'd from the traffick of exotick ware,
Had Malea[3] been with such a treasure fraught
Would haue esteem'd their strictest acts at nought,

---

1 Diogenes. B. 2 Alexander. B.
3 A Hauen nere Sparta among the Lacædemonians. B.

And with a slight pretence or fainèd cause,
Haue crackt the credit of their cobweb lawes.
When eloquent Hegesias caus'd men die
With disputation of liue's miserie,
Had this life-giuing pleasant potion then
Been once imparted to those desp'rate men,
It would haue sooner forcèd them to liue,
Then the commaunds great Ptolmie could giue.
Had Phœbus, Hyacinth, or faire Narcissus,
Venus, Adonis, or sweete Cyparissus
By the propitious gods haue turn'd to this,
Happie had been their Metamorphosis :
Yet it may be, to this they were not turn'd
Because their louers grieu'd to see them burn'd.
This is the Opium which the Turks doe take,
When they their hearts would light and iocund
          make,
By this Medea did her drinke compose,
Which Aeson did from aged bonds vnlose.
You finde not a diuiner herbe then this
In all Albertus de miraculis,
Or the huge Herbals which vaine fooles obey,
In Porta,[1] Fuschsius,[2] and great Dodoney :[3]

---

1 I. Baptista Porta wrote Phytognomonica.   Neapol.
1588.   He lived circ. 1545—1615.   G.

2 Leonhard Fuschius, professor of Anatomy at Tubin-
gen : born 1501, died 1566.   Wrote De Historia Stirpium

In it phisitians haue no skill at all,
It is an essence metaphysicall,
Nor is a thing so exquisite, so pure
Compos'd of only common temp'rature,
Nor can the Scepticks[1] or Empiricks see
This herb's great vertue, nature, and degree.
Who takes this med'cine need not greatly care
Who Galenists, who Paracelsians are :
Nor need he seeke their Rosaries, their Summues,
Their Secrets, their Dispensatoriums ;
Nor fill his pocket with their costly bils,
Nor stuffe his maw with their vnsau'ry pils ;
Nor make huge pitfals in his tender vaines,
With thousand other more then hellish paines,
But by this herbe's celestiall qualitie
May keepe his health in mirth and iollitie.
It is the fountaine whence all pleasure springs,

Commentarii : Basil.   1542.   The well-known garden-
plant, the 'Fuschia' is named after him.   G.

    3 Dodoney, is Rembertus Dodonæus—1518—1585—of
Mechlin : physician to the Emperor Maximilian II, and
professor of medicine at Leyden.   His 'Herbal' was
translated into English by Henry Lyte, and went through
several editions.   The dedication to Queen Elizabeth is
dated 1578.   G.

    Scepticks are those Phisitians which deale by
searching into nature, but Empiricks by experience.

A potion for imperial crownèd kings :
He that is master of so rich a store
May laugh at Crœsus, and esteeme him poore,
And with his smokie scepter in his fist
Securely flout the toyling Alchymist,
Who daily labours with a vaine expence
In distillations of the quint-essence,
Not knowing that this golden herbe alone
Is the philosopher's admirèd stone.
It is your gallant's med'cine singular,
As possets to the wearied ploughmen are :
Alcinous'[1] trees nor the Isles Fortunate
Cannot afford so sweet a delicate :
Teucer had purg'd his cares with wine,
Had he but dream't of physick so divine ;
Nor Bacchus had been patron of delight,
Nor gouern'd with his princely might,
Nor conquer'd all the nations of the Earth,
Because he tam'd their sauage minds with mirth :
Nor had Mercuriall[2] or herbe Gentiane
The glorious names of gods or princes tune :
Moly, of which the prince of Poet's[3] wrote

---

1 The king of the Phæacians, whose orchard Homer
describes. B.

2 Mercurial or Mercuria ; Gentiane of Gentius, king
of Illyricum. B.

3 Homer. B.

Spaine's Triacle,[1] or the strongest antidote,[2]
Is not so good against the magicke spell,
Nor deadly poyson from th' heart t' expell
As our more glorious plant, which had it beene
In ancient times, and famous ages seene,
The fruitfull Oliue, and sweet-smelling Bayes,
Had neuer been the signes of peace and praise:
Long since the blessed Thistle and Herbe-grace
Had lost their names, and been accounted base,
Had great Tabacco pleas'd to shew her powers,
As now she doth in this blest age of ours.
Blest age, wherein the Indian sunne had shin'd,
Whereby all Arts, all tongues haue been refin'd:
Learning, long buried in the darke abysme
Of dunsticall[3] and monkish barbarisme,
When once the herbe by carefull paines was found,
Sprung vp like Cadmus' followers from the ground,
Which Muses visitation bindeth vs
More to great Cortes, and Vespucius,[4]
Then to our wittie More's[5] immortall name,

---

1 Treacle.　G.

2 Antidote is a remedie against poyson.　B.

3 Stupid—albeit the commentators only, not Duns Scotus himself, justify the word.　G.

4 Cortez and Vespucius were two that helpt especially to the true knowledge of America.　B.

5 Sir Thomas More.　For his Epigram on Tabacco

To Valla, or the learnèd Rott' rodame[1]
And our poore tongue, which long had barren laine,
Wanting the fall of sweete Parnassian raine,
Was lightned by this planet's radiant beames,
Which, rising from the Westerne ocean streames,
Melting the drie cloudes to celestiall showres,
And on our heads those heau'nly fountaines powres.
Had the Castalian Muses knowne the place
Which this Ambrosia did with honour grace,
They would have left Parnassus long agoe,
And chang'd their Phocis for Wingandekoe ;
Yet it may be, the people voide of sense
With sauage rites and manners fear'd them thence ;
But our more glorious Nymph, our moderne Muse
Which life and light doth to the North infuse,
Which doth with ioynt and mutuall honour grace
Her place with learning, learning with her place,
In whose respect the Muses barb'rous are,
The Graces rude, nor is the phoenix rare ;
Which Faire exceedes her predecessours facts,
Nor, are her wondrous acts, now wondrous acts ;
Which by her wisdome, and her princely powers
Defends the walles of Albion's cliffie towres,

---

from his 'Lucubrationes' (1563) see our Sir John Davies,
Vol. I., p. 336. G.
 1 Erasmus. G.

Hath vncontrol'd stretcht out her mightie hand
Ouer Virginia and the New-found-land,
And spread the colours of our English Rose
In the far countries where Tabacco growes,
And tam'd the sauage nations of the West,
Which of this iewell were in vaine possest.
Nor is it maruaile that this pretious gem
Is thus beset with beasts, and kept by them,
When it is likely that Almightie Ioue
By such fierce keepers to obscure it stroue,
Bearing against it an immortall hate,
As the gainsayer of eternall fate :
Beside a thousand dangers circle round
Whatcuer good within this world is found,
Least mortals should no worke, nor trade professe,
But spend their daies in lust and idlenesse :
And least their fickle thoughts should soone dis-
     daine
The things they get but with a little paine :
Therefore best fruites are couer'd with hard shels,
The sweetest water is in deepest wels,
And Indian ants as big as mastiues hold
A place more fertile of desirèd gold.
Sicile the garner of the Earth, her pride,
Hath Scylla and Charybdis on each side.
And in times past had a plague worse then these,

Of the fierce Cyclops and Loestrygones,[1]
The horride Dragon, which did neuer sleepe,
The Orchard of the golden fruite did keepe;
And in the countries which be hot and drie
The dreadfull beasts about the fountaines lie,
And Gotthish Spaniards haue the royaltie
Where glorious gold, and rich Tabacco be:
A nation worse than the Loestrygones,
And farre more sauage then the Sauages.
Yet doth not this diuine Tabacco soile,
Which shines like a bright diamond in a foile,
And doth as farre excell the golden graines,
As gold the brasse, or siluer, pewter staines:
Although the Chymists say, our mother beares
Gold in her wombe so many thousand yeares,
Ere she can perfect what she hath begunne,
And bring to full growth that terrestiall sunne;
And though the Thebian lyrick[2] crown'd with
        bayes
Begins his Odes with that sweet mettal's praise,
Yet coounteruailes it not this herb's desart,
But only shares a younger brother's part;
For this our praisèd plant on high doth sore,   ˄
Aboue the baser drosse of earthly ore,

---

1 Fierce people dwelling neare Sicelie, of whom Homer
speakes. B.
2 Pindarus. B.

Like the braue spirit and ambitious mind,
Whose eaglet's eyes the sunnebeames cannot blind;
Nor can the clog of pouerty depresse
Such soules in base and natiue lowlinesse,
But proudly scorning to behold the Earth,
They leape at crownes, and reach aboue their birth:
Despisèd mud sinkes to the center straight,
But worthie things will striue to get on height:
So our sweete herbe all earthly drosse doth hate,
Though in the Earth both nourisht, and create,
And as the nature is of smoke, and fire,
Leaues this low orbe, and labours to aspire
Wrapt in the cincture of her smokie shroudes,
Mixing her vapours with the ayrie cloudes;
And from these fumes, ascending to the skies,
Some say the dewes and gentle showres arise,
And from the fire thereof the Cyclops strooue
To frame the mightie thunderbolts of Ioue.
This is a sauour which the gods doth please,
If they doe feed on smoke—as Lucian sayes—
Therefore the cause that the bright sunne doth rest
At the low point of the declining West,
When his oft-wearied horses breathlesse pant,
Is to refresh himselfe with this sweet plant,
Which wanton Thetis from the West doth bring
To ioy her loue after his toilesome ring:
For 'tis a cordiall for an inward smart,

As is Dictamnum[1] to the wounded hart :
It is the sponge that wipes out all our woe ;
'Tis like the thorne that doth on Pelion grow,
With which who ere his frostie limbes anoints
Shall feele no cold in his benummèd ioints ;
'Tis like the riuer, which who ere doth tast
Forgets his present griefes and sorrowes past :
Musick, which causeth vexèd thoughts retire,
And for a while cease their tormenting fire ;
Musick, the prize, which when the eares haue stole
They doe convey it to th' attentiue soule ;
Musick, which forceth beasts to stand at gaze,
And doth the rude and senselesse soules amaze,
Compar'd to this is like delicious strings,
Which sound but harshly while Apollo sings.
The braine with this infum'd all quarrell ends
Tullie and Clodius will be faithfull friends,
And like another Crassus,[2] one carouse
Will linke againe Pompey and Cæsar's house,
And quickly stint the inhumane designes
Of furious Guelphes and warlike Gibellines.[3]

---

1 The plant dittany, which grew in great abundance
on Mount Dicte and Mount Ida. (Virgil, Aeneid 12.
412 : Cicero, Nat. Deorum, 2. 50, 126) G.

2 Crassus was the onely bond (while he liued) of
Cæsar and Pompeye's friendship. B.

3 Guelphes and Gibellines were a mightie faction in
Italie. B.

The man that shall this smoke magick proue,
Shall need no philters[1] to obtain his loue,
But shall be deckt with farre more pleasing grace
Then ere was Nireus or Narcissus face.
Here could I tell you how vpon the seas
Some men haue fasted with it fortie daies :
How those, to whom Plinie no mouthes did giue[2]
Doe onely on diuine Tabacco liue :
How Andron, which did passe the Lybian sands
Vnto the place where Hammon's Temple stands,
And neuer dranke, nor was he euer dry,
Supprest the heate of raging thirst thereby :
How a dull Cynick, by the force of it
Hath got a pleasing gesture and good wit :
How sparing Demea[3] whom the Comick chaung'd
By this was from his former selfe estraung'd :
How many cowards, base and recreant
By one pipe's draught were turnèd valiant,
And after in an artificiall mist
Haue ouerthrowne their foes before they wist :
How one that dreamt of a Tabacca roll,
Though sick before, was straight made perfect
　　whole.

---

1 Philters be charmes to obtaine loue.　B.
2 Astomi.　See our Sibbes, *s.v.*　G.
3 One of the characters in the Adelphi of Terence. G.

Peace, pratling Muse, offend sage eares no more,
Die in the seas which canst not get the shore,
And sinke, as ouerwhelm'd with too much matter,
Least telling, all the world should thinke thee
    flatter.
Doe not, like curious Plinie,[1] seeke to know
Whence the Earth's smoke and secret flames do
    grow,
Least this immortall fire, and sacred fume
Like to Vesuuius doe thy powers consume ;
But clok'd with vapours of a duskie hue,
Bid both the world and thy sweet herb, Adue.
Ἱέμενος καὶ καπνὸν ἀποθρώκοντα νοῆσαι.[2] . . . .

---

   1 Plinie was burnt searching to know from whence
the fire of the hill Vesuuius did rise.   B
   2 Homer: Od. i, 58.   G.

The literature of Tobacco is much more extensive and singular than is generally known. It is a wonder that a TIMBS has not been found to make it the object of a book. Having a spare corner here, I add an Epigram from JOHN HEATH's " Two Centuries of Epigrammes " (1610) :

TOBACCO.

We buy the driest wood that we can finde,
And willingly would leave the smoke behind :
But in Tobacco, a thwart course we take,
Buying the hearb onely for the smoke's sake.

[2nd Cent., Ep. 92.]   G.

Appendix.

Poems

BY

Sir John Beaumont, Bart.,

SON OF SIR JOHN BEAUMONT, BART.

Note.

Agreeably to our Memorial-Introduction and foot-
notes (pp. 4, 12, &c.) I give as an Appendix, two additional
poems by the son and heir of our Worthy—relatively
rather than intrinsically, of value. The first poem, in
memory of Ben Jonson is of the more interest from Jonson's striking Lines prefixed to the volume of 1629 (See
pp 15-16 *ante*): and the second reminds us that it appeared
in the same volume with Milton's ' Lycidas.' G.

Appendix.

Poems of Sir John Beaumont, Bart.,

SON OF

SIR JOHN BEAUMONT, BART.

I. TO THE MEMORY OF HIM WHO CAN NEVER BE FORGOTTEN, MASTER BENIAMIN IOHNSON.[1]

AD this bin for some meaner poet's hearse,
 I might have then observ'd the lawes of verse :
But here they faile, nor can I hope t'expresse
In numbers, what the world grants numberlesse ;
Such are the truths, we ought to speake of thee,
Thou great refiner of our Poesie ;

---

1 From 'Jonsonus Virbius' 1638 : pages 11—13. G.

Who turn'st to gold that which before was lead,
Then with that pure elixar rais'd the dead.
Nine sisters who—for all the poets lyes—
Had bin deem'd mortall, did not JOHNSON rise
And with celestiall sparkes—not stolne—revive
Those who could erst keep wingèd Fame alive:
T'was he that found—plac't—in the seat of wit,
Dull grinning Ignorance, and banish't it;
He on the prostituted stage appeares
To make men heare, not by their eyes, but eares;
Who painted Vertues, that each one might know,
And point the man, that did such treasure owe:
So that who could in JOHNSON's lines be high,
Needed not honours, or a ribbon buy:
But Vice he onely shew'd us in a glasse,
Which by reflection of those rayes that passe,
Retaines the figure lively, set before,
And that withdrawne, reflects at us no more;
So, he observed the like decorum, when
He whipt the vices, and yet spar'd the men;
When heretofore, the Vice's onely note,
And signe from Vertue was his party-coate,
When devils were the last men on the stage,
And pray'd for plenty and the present age;
Nor was our English language, onely bound
To thanke him for the Latin Horace found

—Who so inspir'd Rome, with his lyricke song,—
Translated in the Macaronicke toung,
Cloth'd in such raggs as one might safely vow,
That his Mœcenas would not owne him now;
On him he tooke this pitty, as to cloth
In words, and such expression, as for both,
Ther's none but judgeth the exchange will come
To twenty more, then when he sold at Rome.
Since then, he made our language pure and good,
And to us speake, but what we understood;
We owe this praise to him, that should we joyne
To pay him, he were paid but with the coyne
Himselfe hath minted; which we know by this
That no words passe for currant now, but his;
And though he in a blinder age could change
Faults to perfections, yet 'twas far more strange
To see—how ever times, and fashions frame—
His wit and language still remaine the same
In all men's mouths; grave preachers did it use
As golden pills, by which they might infuse
Their heavenly phisicke; ministers of State
Their grave dispatches in his language wrate;
Ladies made curt'sies in them, Courtiers, legs,
Physicians bills; perhaps some Pedant begs
He may not use it, for he heares 'tis such,
As in few words, a man may utter much.

Could I have spoken in his language too,
I had not said so much, as now I doe,
To whose cleare memory, I this tribute send
Who dead's my wonder, living was my friend.

IOHN BEAUMONT,

BARONET.

II. FROM "OBSEQUIES TO THE MEM-ORIE OF MR. EDWARD KING: ANNO DOM. 1638." [pp 4—8.]

HEN first this news, rough as the sea
From whence it came, began to be
Sigh'd out by Fame, and generall tears.
Drown'd him again, my stupid fears
Would not awake; but fostering still
The calm opinions of my will,
I said, the sea, though with disdain,
It proudly fomes, does still remain
A slave to Him, Who never wrought
This piece so fair, to wash it out.
I check't that Fame, and told her how
I knew her trade, and her; nay though
Her honest tongue had given before
A faithfull echo, yet his store
Of grand deserts, which did prepare

For Envie's tooth such dainty fare,
Would tempt her now to fain his fate
And then her lie for truth relate.

But when mature relation grew
Too strong for doubts, and still the new
Spake in the same disasterous grone
With all the old; my hopes alone
Could not sustain the double shock
Of these reports and of the rock:
And when the truth, the first—alas!—
That e're to me deformèd was,
Escap'd the sea, and ougly-fair
Did shine in our belovèd aire;
At length too soon my losse I found,
Him and my hopes together drown'd,
Oh! why was he—be quiet tears!—
Complete in all things, but in yeares?
Why did his proper goodnesse grace
The generous lustre of his race?
Why were his budding times so swell'd
With many fruites which parallel'd
Their mutuall beauteous selves alone,
In Vertue's best reflection?
As when th' Hesperian living gold
With priviledg'd power itself did mould
Into the apples, whose divine
And wealthy beames could onely shine

With equall splendour in the graces
Of their brethren's answering faces.
Why did his youth it self allot
To purchase that it needed not ?
Why did Perfection seek for parts ?
Why did his nature grace the Arts ?
Why strove he both the worlds to know,
Yet alwayes scorn'd the world below ?
Why did his brain a centre be
To Learning's circularitie,
Which, though the vastest arts did fill
Would like a point seem little still ?

Why did Discretion's constant hand
Direct both his ? why did he stand
Fixt in himself, and those intents
Deliberate Reason's help presents ?
Why did his well immuréd mind
Such strength in resolution find,
That still his pure and loyall heart
Did in its panting bear no part
Of trembling fear; but having wrought
Eternall peace with every thought,
Could with the shipwracke-losse abide
The splitting of the world beside ?
The universall axle so
Still boldly stands, and lets not go
The hold it fastens on the pole,

Though all the heavens about it roll,
   Why would his true discerning eye
His neighbour's excellencies spie,
And love those shadows his own worth
Had upon others darted forth ?
Whom he with double love intends
First to make good, and then his friends.
Why did he with his hony bring,
The med'cine of a faithtull sting,
And to his friend when need did move
Would cease his praise but not his love ?
Why made his life confession,
That he more mothers had then one ?
Why did his duty tread their way
His generall Parent to obey,
Whil'st in a meet and cheerful fear,
His whole subjection he did square
With those pure rules, whose load so light
Confesse a mother did them write ?
Why did his whole self now begin
With vertuous violence to win
Admiring eyes ? Why pleasèd he
All but his own sweet modestie ?
Why gave his noble worth such ground
Whereon our proudest hopes might found
Their choicest promises ; and he
Be Expectation's treasurie ?

O why was Justice made so blind ?
O why was heaven it self so kind,
And rocks so fierce ? O why were we
Thus partly blest ? O why was he ?
    Whil'st thus the senselesse murmure broke
From grieving lips, which would have spoke
Some longer grones, a sudden noise
Surpriz'd my soul ; which by that voice
Hath learn'd to quiet her self, and all
Her questions into question call.
She saw his soul too mighty grow,
To be imprison'd thus below .
And his intelligence fitted here,
As if intended for a sphere.
His spirits which meekly soar'd so high,
Grew good betimes, betimes to die.
And when in heaven there did befall
Some speciall businesse which did call
For present counsel, he with speed
Was sent for up. When heaven has need,
Let our relenting wills give way,
And teach our comfort thus to say ;
    Our Earth hath bred celestiall flowers :
    What heaven did covet, once was ours.

J. BEAUMONT.

Errata-Note.

——

On re-reading the completed sheets I am thankful to find little beyond punctuation-slips. The printing of the original text is extremely faulty, and the 'escapes' noted below, are nearly all inadvertent reproductions. The Reader will please correct the following before perusal :

Page 43, foot-note 4. By oversight, reference to the "Welcum to Bernard Stewart" and 'Elegy' of the famous Scottish poet, William Dunbar, was omitted here. See his 'Poems' by David Laing Esq., LL.D., [2 vols. 8vo. 1834: and supplement 1865]—where interesting details concerning this "Flour of Chivalry" are given, including a quotation from "Bosworth-Field :" Vol. I. p 129—134, and relative "Notes," pp 311—315.

Page 59, line 6th, a period not comma, after Queene.

Page 62, line 2nd, a comma after yeeld.

Page 142, line 21st, place — after containes, and remove from commencement of next line.

Page 170, line 15th, read 'Will *make*' not '*take*'.

Page 176 title of poem : as noted in Contents, insert 'Lady' before Marquesse.

Page 189 line 10th, read league.

Page 242, line 10th, a period after sides.

Page 245, line 14th, comma after family.

Page 260, line 12th, spell certaine.

Page 268, foot-note, read 190 for 120.

Page 270, line 11th, place comma not period after hower.

Page 281, line 2nd, place comma after same.

Page 312, foot-note 2, spell translated.

and perhaps some other mis-pointings : on all which,

actual and possible, I add from a " Brief Chronology:
1600 to 1660 " (anonymous) this ' *Candido Lectori* ':

Mend—friendly Reader—what escapes amiss,
And then it matters not whose fault it is:
For all men sinne, since Adam first transgrest,
The printer sinnes, I sinne, much like the rest:
  Yet here our comfort is, though both offend,
  We to our faults can quickly put an

End.